The Family

By
Doris P. Burke

Doris P. Burke

ISBN 1-56315-130-8

Trade Paperback
© Copyright 1999 Doris P. Burke
All rights reserved
First Printing—2000
Library of Congress #98-88554

Request for information should be addressed to:

SterlingHouse Publisher, Inc.
The Sterling Building
440 Friday Road
Pittsburgh, PA 15209
www.sterlinghousepublisher.com

Cover design: Michelle Vennare - SterlingHouse Publisher
Typesetting: Steve Buckley
Original photos provided by Doris Burke

All rights reserved. No part of this publication may be reproduced, stored in a retrieval system, or transmittedin any form or by any means—electronic, mechanical, photocopy, recording or any other, except for brief quotations in printed reviews —without prior permission of the publisher.

This is a work of Fiction. Names, characters, places, and incidents either are the product of the author's imagination or are used fictitiously. Any resemblance to actual events or persons, living or dead is entirely coincidental.

Printed in Canada

*Oh, to be young again,
with
dreams and visions,
and
dancing feet,
and
laughter
that
cleansed
the
very soul.
Let our thoughts
stray often,
to
those
memorable
days
and
nights,
let them linger
there
to bring a smile,
as
a gift,
a souvenir,
of the
good times,
and
in
our hearts
and
minds,
we will
be young again.*

This book is dedicated to
my granddaughters.
Especially to Dodi, whose
courage inspires us all.
And, to my Darby,
who will climb all her mountains.
And, to my Lacey, who has kept me
young at heart.
And, to my Libby, who truly has
dreams and visions and dancing feet.
And without whose encouragement,
this story would never have been written.

Doris P. Burke

Chapter One

Lula Fischer was happy. She had gotten herself the man she loved and that made her feel very content. She felt all warm inside as she peered at herself in the round vanity mirror. She smiled at her reflection, turning her head this way and that, liking the way her long hair moved from side to side, liking the way it fell back to the tight curls her mother had so patiently wrapped in rags the night before. She would wear her best Sunday dress, the one with the pink lace collar and tiny pink flowers embroidered on the bodice. She did so want to look pretty for her new husband to be.

She stood up to check her body in the mirror. With her bloomers on, she appeared quite plump in the belly and hips. If she could have grown another three inches, it wouldn't have shown, but she had this short body and that was it. Oh, well, she thought, Bill must like my body. She giggled, thinking how flushed his face had gotten the first time she had taken her clothes off in the hay mow that warm day in early summer when she had become a real woman. It had hurt at first, but after a few times, he told her she was doing real good. She sighed with happiness. She was marrying Bill Judd today. She patted her stomach. So, she was having his baby in five months. Bill wanted to marry her, he told her, just last night. A week ago, when she finally told Bill she thought she was "that way", he hadn't been very nice. His normal sun-tanned face had gotten a whitish tinge to it and he had muttered, "It ain't mine!" He'd even slapped her face in his anger, but she didn't care. Her pa had told his pa the next day and Bill showed up at her house that night with his hair all slicked down and his hat in his hand. Lula still smiled at herself in the mirror, as she thought about Bill. She didn't know what had happened after her Pa had slammed out of the house, after her ma had told him about her and Bill. She had heard him yell, "I'll kill that goddamn Judd kid!" She knew her pa wouldn't have killed Bill. He might have knocked him down. She really didn't know what had happened. Now, she was here getting ready for the wedding. It will be just swell, she told herself. Then, she spoke softly out loud, "I love my Bill. I'll be the best wife anybody ever saw. Maybe I'm only 15, but I'm a woman." She said this proudly, putting her new bonnet on over her tight curls and tying a perfect bow under her determined chin.

Ella Fischer had finally confronted her youngest daughter Lula,

The Family

asking her why she was so pale and had no appetite. Lula had cried the minute her ma asked, and she had whispered, "I haven't had my monthly thing, Ma." Ella had been angry and devastated all at the same time, especially when she got Lula to the details of what she had been doing with the Judd boy. Worst of all was the realization it was one of the Judd clan who had violated her daughter. She had wanted more for Lula. She was good in school, she could have been a teacher. They had planned for her to be. Ella had held back the tears when she had to tell her husband about what had happened to their daughter. "She doesn't need to marry the boy," she had pleaded when she saw the black look come over her husband's face. "We'll raise the child. Anything would be better than being tied up with the Judds. A heathen family, never stepping foot in church. That father, a holy terror, drinking, carousing, letting those boys run like a pack of wolves, not believing in schooling and the mother slinking around, scared of them all." Ella had hoped her husband would agree with her, but no, he had smashed his hat on his head and yelled, "That boy will marry Lula or I'll string him up in the hay mow where he had so much fun!" That was it. So be it. Ella knew she would have to pray the Lord would take care of Lula. Bill Judd got to the wedding at the Fischer home held up on each side by his two brothers, Jake and Junior. His face was the color of the white shirt he wore. He reeked of the home brew he had slopped down to give him courage. Old Bill Judd was on his best behavior, telling the Fischers he was sure proud to welcome that sweet little Lula into their family. His wife kept staring at her husband, wondering who this nice man was, while she rubbed her arm where he had squeezed it hard, telling her not to say a bad word about him or the boys to the new in-laws or he'd break her neck.

The wedding went well. Lula gazed at Bill with adoring eyes. Bill stared right straight at the ceiling. His head hurt, his belly was gurgling and he wished he had never been born. His brothers headed for the barn after the ceremony and proceeded to get rowdy on the rye whisky they had sneaked from their pa's hiding place in the milk house. They tried to get every girl invited to come to the barn, but the girls were wary of the Judd boys. Ella served a meal of fried chicken and home-smoked ham with all the fixin's. The wedding cake was beautifully decorated and a sight to behold. When the preacher said, "Bless this food," Ella whispered, "And please, God, take care of Lula." Bill managed to sneak to the barn without Lula or her ma seeing him and he swilled down the rye whiskey like he was dying of thirst. He then staggered back to the house, found

Doris P. Burke

Lula talking to the preacher, belched up some whiskey onto the preacher's shoes and then grabbed Lula, throwing her over his shoulder like a sack of flour. He shouted, "Time to go, Little Lula!" Ella had a fainting spell and had to be stretched out on the davenport. Old Bill rounded up his liquored-up boys, grabbed his wife by her sore arm and headed out of there. Lula's pa said many bad words about his new son-in-law, while he fanned his semi-conscious wife.

The Family
Chapter Two

Lula and Bill settled into their new life on the Judd farm. This is where they would live. Bill would help his pa and brothers work the fertile 500 acres and Lula would help Ma Judd cook, clean and wash clothes and be a farmer's wife. Lula thought she was in heaven the first couple of months. She liked cooking the meals for Bill and the other men. She scrubbed the floors all through the old farmhouse, finding layers of dirt embedded into the wood floors. She guessed Ma Judd had never noticed or cared that it was there. Lula's belly was getting heavier every day and every evening she felt a tiredness she had never felt before. She was excited one day to find an old sewing machine in the attic when she carried up wooden boxes that had been laying around the kitchen. She finally convinced Bill to carry the machine to their bedroom. She sewed colorful curtains from flour sacks and it pleased her so much to see them hanging on their bedroom windows so crisp and fresh looking. She didn't understand Bill not liking them: instead he snorted, "Don't need fancy things."

Time was getting close for the baby to be coming. Her ma had told her probably early spring. She decided to fix the wicker basket she would use to put the baby in. She made a pillowcase and packed it full of chicken feathers, making sure they were stuffed tight and not leaving softness for the baby to sink into. It made a nice cushion for the basket. She was getting excited about the baby and she would lie awake at night thinking of a name. Bill didn't seem to want to talk about the baby: When she mentioned the word, his face got kinda flushed and she felt sorry for him because he was so nervous about being a father. The brothers were getting on her nerves something fierce the closer her due date came. They were all grown men, but she thought they acted like little boys. They talked and argued among themselves at mealtime, boasting who could beat up whom and comparing the amount of alcohol they could consume. Old Man Judd was just as bad, she figured, always bragging about his great farm, his great bunch of boys and how they could single-handedly crush anybody in the county. He would sit at the kitchen table after supper and twirl his disgusting long mustache, which always showed signs of food stuck to the mass of unkempt hair. He always seem to be watching Lula's every move and he made her nervous.

Doris P. Burke

Ma Judd spent most of her time sitting in the dining room staring out the window. She helped Lula very little, just placing the dishes on the table at mealtime. Lula didn't understand what was the matter with her and when she asked Bill, he would just shrug his shoulders. Lots of nights in bed Lula would cover her ears with her pillow so she couldn't hear the swearing and abuse the old man gave his wife. If Bill heard he never said anything. Lula was glad Bill wasn't like his pa. She had noticed a change in him as the baby's time drew near. Their lovemaking had become difficult: Most of the time he would grumble when he laid a hand on her huge stomach and then he'd turn over and go to sleep. He spent more time in the barn with his brothers. She could hear them when she walked to the chicken coop to throw peelings and gather eggs. They were always telling tall tales and laughing. On Saturday nights, Bill would go off to town with his brothers and when he came home many hours later, she could smell the whiskey on his breath. She felt sad more than happy these days and so very tired. But she knew Bill would be back to his old self after the baby came. Ella Fischer thought of Lula and worried about her all the time. She very seldom saw her daughter. The farm work kept her and Sam busy with just the two of them to do everything. Sam often hired neighbor boys to help during the harvest season, but he never bothered to ask any of the Judd clan because his wife was so set against the idea. Bill would show up once in a while but he never brought Lula with him. This angered Ella and she would rave to her husband about the Judds keeping her daughter a prisoner in that heathen home. And so, on a brisk, snowy day in February, knowing Lula's baby would be coming soon. Ella suggested to her husband they drive over to the Judds to see if Lula was being treated all right. He finally agreed, grumbling a bit about the work he'd have to put off, but he harnessed the two roans and hooked them up to the cutter and patiently waited for Ella. She had baked two apple pies, knowing they were Lula's favorite. She carefully wrapped each in a clean dishtowel and set them in a large basket, ready for the six-mile trip to the Judd's. The horses stood quietly, except for a snort from their cold noses, as Ella walked through the cold, crunchy snow to the cutter. She and Sam rode silently, neither seeming to notice the loveliness of the countryside that was enveloped in frozen beauty. She again pray to God that Lula was all right.

Lula was feeding the chickens that morning when her pa and ma pulled into the driveway of the Judd farm. She peeked from the coop doorway when she heard the horses whinny and her pa's voice bringing them to a stop. She couldn't believe the lump that came to

The Family

her throat at the sight of her ma. She had a terrible realization that she might cry uncontrollably if she let herself. She must not, or her folks would think she wasn't happy here with Bill. No, she had to be strong and act like a woman, a mother to be. She coughed hard and the lump felt smaller in her throat. She wished she could hide her hands because they were so chapped from washing the never-ending work clothes the men wore and the piles of dishes that were always in the sink. Her hair, she knew, was stringy and her house dress was so tight her stomach protruded like she was carrying a watermelon in front of her. She stuck her hands in the pockets of the old, raggedy wool coat she had thrown on when she had hurried to feed the clucking chickens. Ella and Sam were a bit chilled when they reached the Judd farm and Ella clapped her gloved hands together, hoping to send some warmth to her stiff fingers. She gasped and put her hand over her heart when she saw Lula's white face peeking from the door of the chicken coop. She whispered, "Sam, they've put her in the chicken coop!" He scoffed, "My God woman, straighten up. She's probably been feeding the damn chickens. Get out and greet your daughter." Ella stepped carefully from the cutter as her daughter moved slowly toward her. She hadn't seen Lula for four months and she hoped her face didn't show the shock she felt. Lula's beautiful blond hair, always in curls before, looked as if it hadn't been brushed or cared for in weeks and her short body was enormous. She waddled as she walked. "Oh, my poor girl," Ella thought.

    Lula gave a smile to her ma and raised her hand in greeting to her pa. When she got close to the cutter, she yelled, "The men aren't here right now, Pa. Put the horses in the barn and come to the house when you're done. I'll fix some hot coffee." She hugged her ma as best she could, her belly pressing against the warmth of Ella's body. It felt so good feeling the love from her mother's arms around her. They walked to the house, Ella carrying the pies and telling Lula she had baked them just for her. She had never been in the Judd home, never wanted to be. She felt like a hypocrite now as she entered the kitchen. She noticed the breakfast dishes cluttering the sink and the table that needed wiping off. Lula hurried to the sink to pump water in the blackened coffeepot. She kept up a steady stream of chatter, telling her ma how glad she was they had come to visit and she was sorry her kitchen wasn't clean. All the time, she was trying to keep her hands moving fast so her ma didn't see the chapped redness. Ella stood holding the basket of pies, still trying to keep her composure, as she watched and listened to her daughter. "Where is Mrs. Judd?" she asked with a frown, reaching for the

Doris P. Burke

dishcloth to wipe the table before she put her clean basket on it. "Ma, she's not well. She's been sickly for a while," Lula answered, stoking the stove so the coffee would start to perk. "Sit down, Ma, I'll get the coffee cups. You must be chilled to the bone." Ella wondered if there were more cups in the cupboard, they all seemed to be in the sink. "Pour some water in the dishpan," she told Lula, "I'll have these dishes done in a jiffy."

Lula did as her ma told her and for the first time in a very long time a comfortable feeling came over her. Lula had been ashamed to have her ma see the messy kitchen. She remembered how clean and spotless their kitchen had been at home when she lived there. She wanted to be like her ma, a great cook and immaculate housekeeper. She really didn't feel ashamed anymore. It was as if her ma was supposed to be helping her. After all, that's what mothers do when they are needed. Her pa came through the door just as her ma finished the pile of dishes. She had already put most of them in the cupboard. Lula loved her pa's kind, wrinkled face. He had always been such a caring man and a good father. She couldn't help but remember how mad he had been at Bill. Now, he asked, "Where's all the menfolk?" "In the back forty, pa, fixing fences. You know they have that little old cabin back there and they go in there when they get cold. I sent some sandwiches with them, so they won't be back until chore time," Lula said. He shook his head, "Yep, it keeps a fella busy, this here farmin'," He shoved a chair back and slouched in it, then lifted the cup of coffee to his mouth, hoping the hot liquid would take the chill from his body. Lula knew her pa wouldn't have much to say, he would sit and listen while her ma did all the talking. "Have you been doing all the work around here, Lula?" her ma asked. "What seems to be ailing Mrs. Judd?" Ella knew the woman had always been different; all the neighbors knew that. Lula answered quickly, "I don't know, Ma. She sits there in the dining room and stares out the window. When I ask her something, she shakes her head. I wanted Bill to ask his pa to take her to see Doc Hanson, but Bill said it weren't none of our business." Lula hoped her ma didn't ask too many questions about things she didn't have the answers to.

Ella could have screamed right then because she knew Lula had been doing for six men , too much for a young girl, let alone a pregnant one. She had seen Lula's hands, as hard as her daughter had tried to hide them. She felt so sorry for her daughter. She hated Bill more than ever for letting his wife be used like a slave. Lula winced when she saw the look of contempt come to her ma's face. She spoke quickly, "Come up to the bedroom, Ma, and see the

The Family

basket I've fixed for the baby. I've made some nighties and diapers in the evenings." They passed the dining room and Ella saw for herself Mrs. Judd rocking back and forth in her chair, wearing a wrinkled robe; her gray hair laying in every direction, giving the appearance of not having been combed for a good long time. Her hands were clutched together and she seemed unaware of anyone around. After Lula showed her ma her new curtains and the baby things, her ma sat stiffly on the bed and began to talk. "They have to get some help in here, dear. The baby should be coming in a week or so. Have you seen the doctor?" Lula had been dreading this. She knew her ma would be probing. "Collette is coming; she is a midwife, you know," Lula said. "Bill says I don't need a doctor. His ma had a midwife for all the boys." "Yes, I know," Ella replied, "and so did I. But now we have a doctor in town. You need a doctor, Lula. The baby is big. Look at you. You can hardly walk, let alone be going all the work around here. Come home with your pa and me until the baby comes." Ella stood up and walked to the window. She could see the chicken coop and the barn and the clothesline, where overalls hung stiff as a board.

"Bill." Ella spoke his name as best she could, hoping the hatred didn't come out in her voice. "He and his pa can hire a girl to come in here, being as Mrs. Judd can't seem to move." Ella felt so exasperated she thought she would explode. Her poor baby being used like this, doing all the work with no one to help her and certainly no one to care how much she had to do. She turned to look at her daughter standing who, red hands clasped together, her head hanging, was trying not to cry. She wanted her home where she could take care of her. Brush her hair again and cook for her. She was just a baby herself. God, how she hated Bill Judd, even if it wasn't the Christian way to be. Lula knew this was coming, she knew her ma. She studied her now, a tall woman, taller than her pa by three inches. She was raw-boned and lean. Her face showed gentleness at times, but more often it had a haughty appearance, with lips pursed, defying anyone to challenge her. Only her pa could ever put her ma in her place, with a frown or a sharp word. She was used to taking over, doing everything right and perfect. Her home ran like a well-oiled sewing machine. Lula had never seen her pa with a hole in his pants, his socks or his long underwear. Her ma's fruit cellar was like a well-stocked grocery store, neat and dust-free. The cans of peaches, pears, applesauce and berries were on oilcloth-covered shelves, as were the varieties of vegetables and canned meats. There was a sign before you entered the cellar, telling you which shelf held what you were looking for. The icebox

Doris P. Burke

was clean and organized, the sweet butter covered with a cloth so as not to pick up any odor. The drip pan was always emptied on time and never ran over. And there was always the right amount of ice in the icehouse to last through the summer months.

The cupboards in the kitchens also had oilcloth-covered shelves and were dusted regularly. She had not one crack in plate or cup. That would be unacceptable. Her china closet was filled with fine porcelain handed down from her mother and grandmother. They looked as if they had been purchased yesterday. Lula's ma had always entertained her church ladies often, inviting them for quilting bees and bazaar meetings. When Lula was small she used to smile, seeing some of the busybodies parading through the house looking desperately for a cobweb or dust ball. Not ever finding one, they would tighten their lips and act as if they hadn't been snooping. Lula had come late in her folk's lives and she heard her ma tell her lady friends many times how she thanked God for giving them Lula for company in their later years. Now Lula had shamed them. She realized they had wanted her to be like her sister Eleanor, who lived in Michigan now and had married a church-going man who lived by the Good Book, or her brother Wesley, who had become a clergyman, having his own church in the next county. He had married a girl from his ministry and they had three perfect children. Lula knew she was the only imperfect thing in her ma's life. She was thinking all these things as her ma talked. She bit her lip, she wouldn't cry; she couldn't in front of her ma. She lifted her head and spoke, "It will be all right, ma. I have to stay here. This is my place, here with Bill."

Ella saw the same determined look in her daughter's eyes she had seen on her wedding day. It was no use. Ella knew she would stay here in this godforsaken house and be a slave to a bunch of howling men, who didn't have the brains or understanding to see what was happening to her darling Lula. The conversation was over. She went ahead of Lula to the stairway, the tears welling up in her eyes making it hard for her to see the way down the steps. She passed Mrs. Judd and hurried to the kitchen, telling her husband they had better be leaving. She couldn't stay here another minute and witness any more of this. If Bill showed up or any of his half-baked brothers, she knew she would scream at the sight of them. Lula followed slowly behind her ma, holding tight to the railing of the stairs. The weight of the baby was getting hard for her to carry. She watched her ma put her coat on and wrap her neck with a heavy knitted scarf, then pull the matching hat over her smooth, perfect hair. Her pa hugged her and said goodbye. Her ma waved a hand,

The Family

apparently having said all that she was going to say. Luia stood at the window and watched as the cutter left, moving quietly through the drift. Soon it was out of sight. It would have been nice to go home and be pampered, but she couldn't. Now she felt the tears coming that she had held back so long and the sobs rocked her misshapen body.

Doris P. Burke

Chapter Three

That evening, Bill listened to Lula tell of her folk's visit. She stood at the sink sloshing a sticky pan up and down in the warm, sudsy water. He didn't know it but her back hurt, her legs felt heavy and she was having pulling pains down low in her stomach. He peered at her; he did feel sorry for her, she looked like a bloated frog. God, how he wished she would have gone home with her pa and ma. Then he wouldn't have to look at her. He didn't know how he had let himself into this mess. He was only twenty-one. He had a lot of howlin' to do yet. His brothers bothered him all the time, telling him he should have kept his pants buttoned up. If the old man hadn't threatened him, telling him he had to marry Lula, he never would have. She was a nice girl, but he could have had lotsa girls; didn't care if they were nice or not. He wasn't ready for this. Damn the old man for putting the pressure on him. And ma, sitting there rockin' all the time, 'bout drove him nuts. He slapped his hand down on the table hard and yelled, "For Christ's sake, Lula, go to bed. You look like hell!"

Her shoulders shook and he knew she was going to cry. He didn't need that either. He grabbed his hat, shoved it on his head and went out the door. He needed a drink. Lula managed to finish the dishes, dripping a few tears into the dishpan. It hurt her feelings to have Bill yell at her like that. She knew she looked terrible. Her stomach felt so heavy and she put her hands on it, feeling the baby move every which way. She should go to bed; she'd feel better if she would lie down. Her legs hurt extremely bad and she limped a bit trying to get to the stairway. She stood with her hand on the railing and peeked into the living room. Ma Judd had left her chair in the dining room. Must have gone to bed, Lula figured. The old man, she noticed, lay on his back on the davenport, his mouth wide open, snoring. His mustache wriggling every time he blew out a breath. She realized how much Bill resembled his pa: the same dark hair and long, rugged face. She hoped the baby looked like Bill; she liked dark hair. Every step she took going up the steps made her aware of how bad her back felt and the little pains in the front were starting to get more severe. She wondered if this was the false-alarm pain she had heard about or was it the real thing? Lying on the bed didn't help. She was starting to feel pain everywhere. She wished her ma was still here; she would know what was hap-

The Family

pening. She sat up in the bed, feeling a sharp pain start around her middle. It brought the sweat to her forehead. Suddenly she felt very scared. "I'll have to call Ma Judd," she gasped. "She'll have to get Bill." The old man slept so sound downstairs, she didn't think he could hear her yell.

It had started to get dark outside. She had lit the lamp when she came in the room. It gave a minimum amount of light in the small room. She could barely see the basket, which sat in the corner she had gotten ready for the baby, but she could make out something different about it. She pushed herself up as best she could, the pain bothering her so much it made her catch her breath. She had made several flannel blankets to be used over the baby. They weren't there. The basket was empty, even the cushion was gone. A pain hit her hard and she moaned. She had to call Ma Judd. As her feet touched the floor, she heard a movement by the door. She cried out, "I'm so glad it's you, Ma Judd, will you help me? I think the baby is coming! Will you go to the barn and get Bill?" Lula could see the outline of Mrs. Judd's body in the doorway. She wore a long, flannel nightgown, her gray hair sticking up in bunches on her head. She moved toward the bed, her hands behind her back. "Did you hear me, Ma Judd? Help me. I think the baby is coming. Will you go to the barn and get Bill?" Lula asked again. Lula was on the verge of hysteria. Didn't the woman understand she was in terrible pain? Ma Judd had come close enough through the shadows that Lula could see her face. There was a weird smile there and her eyes were frightening, staring without movement at Lula. "No more babies," Ma Judd mumbled. God almighty, she's gone crazy, Lula thought. I've got to get out of this room. Her heart was beating fast and the pains were more extreme. She had to move, but she couldn't. Ma Judd blocked her way, standing close now, still with her hands behind her. Lula screamed as Ma Judd brought them in view: In one hand, she held a large hammer. She raised it above her head and repeated, "No more babies." Lula screamed as loud as she could, just as the Old Man Judd grabbed his wife from behind, throwing the hammer across the room. Bill appeared in the doorway as Lula screamed again, this time from the god-awful pain running through her body.

The old man gave orders to Bill as he carried his wife from the room: "Send Junior on the horse over to Doc Hanson's and bring him back. Tell Jake to take the cutter and pick up Collette. Your little woman is having trouble, gonna have a big youngun', I think." Bill stumbled down the steps to do as he was told. Then he heard the old man yell, "And then, you get your ass up here and sit with

Doris P. Burke

your wife until they get here." An hour later, the Doc was there, Collette was there and Lula was in unbelievable pain. Bill had let her hang on his hand; she had just about broken his fingers. He rubbed them as he paced the kitchen. This was the worst night of his life, he figured. His pa had told him what had happened up there in the bedroom, said his ma was "teched" in the head. He wanted Doc Hanson to take a look at her after the baby got there. The old man didn't want him telling the boys about what had happened with their Ma, didn't want them blabbin' about it. Poor ma. He guessed she couldn't take the work no more. He had to admit, he and the boys had been a handful and his pa sure wasn't nice to her anymore. He covered his ears: He could still here Lula yellin' up there. The doc had said the baby was big for her. God, what a helluva night, he thought. He needed a slug of booze, but the old man had told him to stay sober. Told him he was gonna be a pa, had to act like a pa. Ha, he thought, never kept him from taking a swig. He suddenly realized it had gotten quiet. He ran to the stairway. Yep, it was quiet. Then, he heard a noise like a lamb bleating and it got louder. Christ, the baby was here! He let out a relieved sigh. He hurried to the wood heater in the living room and threw some chunks in the opening, then slammed the door with a bang. Gotta keep it warm around here, he decided, babies gotta be warm. He heard somebody coming down the stairs.

Old Doc Hansen appeared, pushing his hair back, acting like it had been quite a chore up there. He did have a little crooked smile for Bill as he said, "You got a big youngun Bill, biggest one I've seen in a coon's age. A big, big boy!" He walked toward the kitchen, talking over his shoulder to Bill, "Get me some soap and a towel. Gotta wash up, and then you can go up and see that whopping big kid." Bill hesitated at the stairway, thinking, Jesus, I've got a boy. He wondered if Lula was disappointed, she was kinda partial to having a girl, so many damn men around here. He didn't feel any disappointment, his own baby boy. Things were gonna be all right now. Lula would feel better and except for ma and her troubles, he was feeling a helluva lot better. Lula was laying on the bed covered with a sheet when Bill got to the room. Collette was straightening things up, opening drawers, looking for something. Lula was as white as the sheet that covered her. Beside her was a wrapped bundle. Bill moved slowly, very hesitant and kinda scared. Lula spoke in a weak voice, " Bill, come see your son." And so, on February 5, 1900, Lloyd Ambrose Judd was born, weighing in at 13 pounds, 6 ounces. It was the same year Brooklyn won the National League Baseball Championship and the American League was formed by

The Family

six cities and a new ruling made home plate a five-sided object. The next year another baby was born to Bill and Lula. He was named Ralph Wesley Judd and, according to Doc Hanson's medical records, he was the biggest baby delivered in the state, weighing in barenaked at an unbelievable 15 pounds.

Doris P. Burke

Chapter Four

Old Man Judd had his wife committed to an institution after Lloyd was born. Doc Hanson had said, "That way, she won't be harming Lula or the baby. Something had snapped in her mind. Nobody knows what she's thinking." Lula was still doing all the work. And with two youunguns to take care of, it had gotten to be too much of a burden. Bill finally decided, after watching her face get more and more pale, she needed help. He told his pa he wanted his two little men to have good upbringin' and they needed their ma with them more often. After being told this, the old man drove into town early one morning and appeared back at the farm in the afternoon with a silly grin on his face. Seated beside him in the buggy was a so-called lady who, with her bag and baggage, gave every indication of moving in. Lula stared out the window as they drove up.

"Good grief," she muttered in amazement. "The old man has brought a hussy out here!" She covered her mouth and as shocked as she felt, she still wanted to laugh as she watched the old man help his flamboyant passenger from the buggy. Lula noticed the tight waistline on the jacket she wore, it billowed over the extremely tight skirt. The outfit showed her matronly figure in all its glory. She wore a fashionable hat, with yards of veiling. Lula glanced down at her own flour sack house dress, which was quite different from what this lady wore. The old man introduced the two women, saying, "This is Abigale Hauser. She's come to help with the work around here." Lula could tell the old man was nervous, because she couldn't look at her when he said this. "He jittered around like a rooster in a hen house," she told Bill later. After the brothers met the so-called hired woman, they immediately called her "the old man's tits." Lula found the only thing Abigale did well was dust the furniture. She did this wearing a ruffled organdy apron over her taffeta dress and using a pink dust mop she insisted the old man buy because it was so pretty. She couldn't cook, she couldn't wash dishes because she might break her fingernails. She surely didn't want Lloyd and Ralph, the little men, underfoot. She made that plain by frowning at them if they dared get near her. Lula knew what she did do well. They all did, hearing the giggling and other noises coming from the old man's room at night. Lula hoped her ma didn't come to visit. She knew Ella would have a fainting spell

The Family

if she saw Abigale and heard of the goings-on.

Life was never the same after Abigale showed up. Bill's brothers resented her taking the old man's attention away from them. He didn't drink with them or take part in their bragging conversations in the barn. They started spending more and more time in town. Even Bill couldn't stand the sight of Abigale, telling Lula, "Big Tits will be the ruination of the old man, you watch and see." The little men were five and six when Lula gave birth to a little girl with green eyes, whom she named Olive Marie, after a great aunt on the Fischer side of the family. She was called Little Lady by her pa and was the apple of his eye. The work was always there for Lula, with the new baby and all. The old man and Abigale were gadding now, going to nearby Perrysburg and spending their time in saloons and at cockfights. The little men were with their uncles often and liking it. They learned how to cuss, how to spit and most of all, how to play baseball. Even in the winter months, Bill's brothers laid out a small diamond on the floor of the hay barn to teach the little men the basics of ball playing. They got a big kick out of seeing Lloyd and Ralph pounding the ball back and forth. They were growing tall. Lloyd resembled the Judds, thin and dark skinned. Ralph was blonde and stocky, taking after the Fischers. There wasn't much Bill's brothers wouldn't do for the little men. They got them a dog to romp with and they taught the boys to saddle a horse, promising them a horse of their own when they grew old enough to mount it. To the little men, their uncles were the best. It all came to an end with a bang one pretty summer night, when Junior, the eldest brother, came home limping fast and started packing his satchel. The other brothers were in town, except Jake. He was having his fun in the barn, swigging some whiskey and exchanging yarns with a neighbor.

Lula had just put the baby to bed and had sent the little men up to their room to get their pajamas on. She was busy in the kitchen when Junior came hurrying by her, out of breath and headed for the stairway. She heard him throwing things in the room above her. He showed back up in a jiffy, still limping bad. He carried two satchels. His face had a panicked look as he said, "Me and Jake are leavin', Lula. Say goodbye to the little men for us!" He limped to the door, opened it fast and was gone. She ran to the window and saw him waving his arms and talking to Jake. Then the two of them struck up a running pace across the cornfield. Next, she heard horses coming down the road. It was Bill and the other two brothers, a buggy right behind them. The man driving the buggy was whipping the horses. It was Jim Hicks, a neighbor. "Mercy God! There's

Doris P. Burke

trouble," she whispered, hoping Bill wasn't in on it. The man in the buggy jumped out as they all stopped. She saw a rifle in his hand. She held her breath, scared it was Bill he was after. She opened the window wider so she could hear them better. "He ain't here," Bill was saying, backing toward the barn, pulling his horse with him. The other brothers were doing the same thing. Little did Lula know that Bill and the others had met Hicks on the road coming from town. He was hell-bent for their place, murder in his eyes, telling them, "I'm gonna kill that goddamned sneakin' brother of yours. I saw 'em jump from the window. Gotta shot off at 'em, but I missed. Sneakin' with my woman when I'm not home. Why, the dirty bastard, I'll shoot his balls off!" The brothers had ridden fast, hoping to get home and hide Junior before Hicks got there, not knowing that Junior and Jake had already left. Hicks kept raving and swinging the rifle from one brother to another.

"Don't get in my way, boys. Ain't your fault you got a weasel for a brother." Lula had heard enough and she yelled through the window, "If you're lookin' for Junior or Jake, Mr. Hicks, they're gone." Hicks whirled around when he heard her voice. "Where'd they go, missus?" he yelled back at her. "Don't know, she answered, "Didn't say, left through the wheat field." "Is that the truth, missus?" he asked, disappointment in his voice. "So help me God," she answered. She hoped she wouldn't be struck down by the Lord. He looked toward the wheat field, not knowing they had left in the opposite direction. "They on foot?" he asked, his voice quieter. She didn't want to lie, but she had liked the oldest brothers. They had been good to her boys. She answered, "No, they were on their horses." Hick's rifle came down by his side and he snarled, "Dirty rotten snake. I'll find him one of these days and you boys will be a-goin' to his funeral." he left, still shaking his fist and raving. What Jim Hicks didn't know was why Junior took Jake with him: It was because when he wasn't visiting Mrs. Hicks, Jake was.

The Family

Chapter Five

The two brothers were gone and the old man threw a fit for a week after he heard what had happened. He had just the three boys left now. Work had been easy with all of them doing it. The Judd farm was the most prosperous in the county. They didn't need nothin' from nobody, the old man had often bragged. Now, there was more to do for the three left behind. Besides, he would have to start doing something again. He had enjoyed the freedom with Abigale. They had good times and he didn't want to lose her. The boys would have to work harder, he decided. They were young, work was good for them. He started telling this to Bill one morning as Abigale flounced around the kitchen in her wraparound with the fur down the front. She batted her eyes at old Bill and he spent his time watching the opening to her wraparound, hoping to sneak a peek of that nice white skin under there.

"You see, Bill my boy, your old man is getting on in years, gotta slow down. You're the next oldest after Junior and Jake. Now that the cowards have snuck off, I'd like you to take over. Keep your brothers in line. You boys are all healthy and the best workers around. Yep, my sons are the best." He took a gulp of coffee, his eyes still on Abigale. Bill was getting a little fed up with his pa's attitude. He had been for a while. Now, seeing the idiotic grin on his pa's face as he ogled Abigale, he was beginning to think this was no place for him and his family. Abigale was a pain in the ass, strutting around like a whore in front of the little men and now he had his sweet Little Lady. They didn't need this, he decided. Ella Fischer was hearing of the goings-on over at the Judds. The entire church congregation was whispering about the sinful woman living there and what Junior Judd had done. This was most unacceptable and Ella knew her daughter and family had to get themselves away from that house of sin. It was no place for her grandchildren to be raised. It pained her to have her bazaar ladies whispering behind their handkerchiefs then stopping when she entered the room. Oh, the shame of it all, she thought one evening as she sat knitting while her husband puffed on his pipe. "The nerve of that old man flaunting that hussy," she said, giving a yank to the string of yarn, showing her frustration. "I tell you Sam, Lula and her family have to get themselves out of there."

Sam was tired. He'd been putting up hay all day with the help

Doris P. Burke

of some neighbor boys. He just wanted to sit in his old leather chair, smoke his pipe and maybe snooze a bit before supper. He knew all about what went on over at the Judds. When he was down at the barber shop, he and the fellows there had a darn good laugh about Junior Judd. He wanted to laugh right now, thinking about Junior jumping out that upstairs window. It had been a helluva drop to the ground. Somebody had seen Junior and Jake running to catch a freight train that would take them away out of the county. All the barber shop bunch agreed with Sam that Old Man Hicks had been asking for trouble when he married a woman half his age. And, as far as old Bill Judd was concerned, he wasn't any different now than when he and Sam were young pups together. Always a woman chaser. As far as being an honest man, he was. Never shirked on work when he was raising those youngun's, and he always paid his debts. Braggin'? Sure, he was guilty of that, and boozin' too. Sam was thinking all this as Ella continued to talk. God, he'd have to shut her up. "Listen, Ella, it ain't none of our business, but I did hear they're hiring over in Rochester, Michigan," he said. "Jess Franks has some kinfolks over there. They said the woolen mill and knitting mill are hiring and the railroad is looking for crews. Maybe I'll make a trip over to Bill and Lula's and mention it." With that, he figured the conversation had ended. He closed his eyes. She was getting up. Maybe she'd bake some of those sugar cookies with a big raisin in the middle. Nobody could make them as good as Ella could. Sam picked an evening to go over to the Judd farm when he knew Old Bill would be off to the cockfights with his lady friend. He also knew the other two brothers gallivanted to town every night after the chores were done. Ella wanted to go with him to Lula's. She watched as he harnessed the roan and backed him up to the buggy. "No, Ella, you stay here and tend to your knittin'," he said, frowning at her. "Bring out the cookies you want to send to the little boys."

    She sputtered as she walked to the house to get the box of cookies. Sam didn't talk much, but when he did, she listened. Sam hadn't told Ella how he worried about Lula. He was afraid she might turn out like Mrs. Judd, overworked and treated like a hired woman in her own house. Christ, he knew old Bill had been seein' that Abigale person long before his missus had that bad spell. Sam bit hard on his pipe thinking about this and then he snapped the reins and said, "Let's go" to the horses. He didn't have a quarrel with young Bill; hadn't talked to him much. But he heard that the boy minded his p's and q's and that was all he wanted to hear. Those little boys were good lookin' and acted decent. He smiled, thinking of Ella

The Family

saying, "Got more Fischer in them than Judd, Sam." She had been so pleased when Lula named the baby girl after her great aunt. The little boys were rolling around on the ground with their collie dog when Sam pulled up. He could see they were healthy and well taken care of. He handed them the box of cookies and got a big grin from both of them. He found Lula and Bill in the kitchen and she hurried to fix him a cup of coffee, always happy to see her pa's kind face. Bill shook his hand and pulled out a chair for him. Bill was always a little uneasy with Sam Fischer after being told before the wedding, right in front of his pa, that he'd string him up in the hay mow if he didn't get his ass over to see Lula. He had been surprised when his old man agreed with Sam, but he had and that's the way things turned out. He had just been telling Lula he had gotten a belly full of his pa when Sam pulled up. Sam removed his hat and accepted the coffee, noticing how tired Lula appeared. He decided to spit out in a hurry what he'd come to say.

"Wanted to tell you folks, Jess Franks was telling me his cousin told him they were doing a lot of hirin' over there in Rochester, Michigan. Woolen mill and knitting factory goin' good. They're even lookin' to hire railroad crews." Sam somehow knew Bill had a hankerin' for railroads and trains. He guessed someone had told him that. "Is that right, Mr. Fischer?" Bill's face lit up as he asked this. "Yep," Sam answered, "growing fast and furious over there in Rochester, they say. If I weren't so blamed old, I guess I'd have a curiosity to go see what's goin' on." He took a swig of coffee. Bill was looking at Lula and smiling. He knew he was right. The boy was interested! He didn't stay long. He left feeling satisfied he'd given Bill and Lula something to chew on. It was early fall when Bill approached his pa about leaving the farm. The beans had been taken off the fields and most of the harvesting had been done. He and old Bill sat in the kitchen one evening while Lula nervously washed dishes. Bill came right to the point: "Pa, me and Lula, well, we think it's time to move on, Pa." The old man had been drinking that day and his face was flushed from the swigs of whiskey that he had always said "keeps the ole heart a pumpin'." Now, he couldn't seem to grasp what young Bill was talking about. "What in hell you sayin', boy?" he asked, his voice booming. "Well, Pa," Bill gulped. He usually listened to his pa, never talked to him. "They're hirin' over in Rochester, Michigan. I always did have an urge to work the railroad, Pa. Me and Lula think we should get out on our own. You got Seth and Georgy here." The old man's face was like a thundercloud, with the veins in his neck protruding.

"I got what here?" he bellowed. "You mean those two

scallywags, who have to have their asses pushed every minute to get any work done? You know, you and Junior and Jake could keep them in line. All they can think of is shittin' round downtown trying to find trouble. You ain't goin' nowhere, boy. I need ya!" Bill jumped up, knocking a glass to the floor. He raised his voice, "We're leavin', Pa. Gonna take the train next week." The old man could see young Bill was determined. His shoulders slouched and he thought about the changes there would be. And, Christ, what about the woman's work? Abigale couldn't do it. Lula had done everything. Jesus, he had depended on Bill and Lula to keep things running smooth. What in hell would he do now? Abigale, she'd be leavin' if things changed too much. He couldn't lose Abigale. He started to say more and then stopped. He slammed his fist on the table. "Can't I talk you outta this, boy?" he asked. He had a humble tone in his voice now. "No, Pa," his son said. "We need to make our own way. Have our own house. A home for the younguns, like you did, Pa." The old man couldn't listen to any more. He shoved his chair back and walked to the screen door. He turned around to Bill and Lula. He realized he sorta admired them for what they were gonna do and he also realized he envied them for being young. But what would happen to his farm, his shrine? He had cleared the land, pulled stumps, carried rocks, worked his ass off in the scorchin' sun. Slept in his clothes on lotsa nights, too tired to pull them off.

All the neighbors envied his farm. He was the master of it all. He had been prepared to give all his boys a piece of his labor. Now this was happening. He saw Bill and Lula's faces staring at him, wanting him to approve of what they were going to do. He remembered when he left his pa and ma and the sad looks they had given him. He spoke quietly, "Go if you have to, boy." He closed the screen door behind him and moved wearily toward the barn. He wasn't young anymore and he still felt betrayed by the seeds of his own making: Junior, Jake and now, Bill. It wouldn't be long and maybe the other two would get the itch to leave, to see new places, new people and make their own way. Well, he still had Abigale, for a while anyway. He knew he was going to get real drunk tonight. Maybe he'd sleep in the barn so he could smell the sweetness of the hay. His big roomy barn, the biggest in the county. Built by him and his sons, who were the greatest, the strongest, the best and could whip any troublemaker. God, he felt like hell! There wasn't a lot of packing to do for the move to Rochester. Lula's ma had sent over the trunk her Great Aunt Olive had given her. Lula had played in it as a child. She had liked the curved ornamental top and she would open the trunk and sit in it, pretending she was floating on

The Family

the ocean. She remembered this now, as she carefully placed their freshly ironed clothes in layers in it. Her ma had sent some pretty linens and Lula appreciated that. After all, they had no possessions to speak of. They had lived in Old Man Judd's house. All they had were her and Bill's clothes and the children's. This was the entire collection of seven years of marriage. She kept busy waiting for her pa to arrive to take them to the train station. She dressed the baby, fussed at the little men to get ready and then hurriedly packed a lunch for them to eat on the train. She felt excited and a bit scared, but Bill smiled all the time and that made her feel better. Her pa pulled up as she wrapped the last of the sandwiches and placed them in the wicker basket.

Lloyd and Ralph felt kinda bad about leaving the farm and uncles they were so fond of. They had spent the night in the barn, listening to advise given to them from Seth and Georgy. It all boiled down to: "Don't take no shit from nobody," and "You're the best, cuz you're a Judd!" The boys had grinned at each other when the two uncles had flexed their muscles and told them this. Now, they sat at the back of Grandpa Fischer's wagon and swung their feet waiting for the trip to begin, thinking of the great train ride they would be taking. They were finally all loaded and ready. Old Bill watched from the doorway, swearing under his breath, as the wagon creaked its way down the driveway. He had given young Bill a hundred dollars, shook his hand and that was it. He would miss those two little men runnin' and jumpin' around the yard with that flea-bitten dog of theirs. He hadn't had his breakfast yet and he felt terrible. He could hear Abigale moving slowly around the kitchen and he could smell burnt bacon. Things wouldn't be the same with Lula and Bill gone. He knew that for sure. He thought of baking powder biscuits Lula baked for them for breakfast every morning and the honey she put on the table to eat with them. The bacon was crisp, not burned and the eggs were splattered just right with bacon grease. Christ no, it wouldn't be the same. He turned from the doorway and watched Abigale try to break an egg into the smoking frying pan. Sam had handed Lula an envelope with some money in it, as they were ready to board the train. "Here's a little somethin' you can tuck away, as you might need it sometime. Jess Franks says there's a boarding house there in Rochester. Maybe Bill would want you and the family to stay there awhile, till he finds a job."

Lula hugged her pa, noticing his kind face, which was now sad looking. She held on to him as long as she could, her face against his mackinaw coat, which smelled like hay and other barn odors. Her ma had stayed home. Lula understood why. It would have been

Doris P. Burke

too painful to see them leave, knowing it was the best thing for them. She wiped her tears away and boarded the train, carrying Olive. She waved to her pa and wondered if she would ever see him or her ma again.

The Family
Chapter Six

In 1907, Rochester, Michigan was a flourishing town. People had drifted in to find jobs at the paper mill, the Western Knitting Mill and the woolen factory. The farming country was decent on the outskirts of town. The old farms were there, as well as new farmhouses and barns that were being built. The businesses set up on Main Street were satisfied with their locations and remained extraordinarily busy. The livery stable kept its rigs in good shape, greasing the wheels and polishing the exteriors, the lively horses were brushed and combed daily. Discussions were heard frequently about the new motor cars - the Franklin Stearns and the Peerless - being built, but no one believed they would own one of those horseless carriages. Eight passenger trains a day stopped here, in the ever-growing Rochester, and on October 20, 1907, the Bill Judd family arrived on one of them. Lloyd and Ralph pressed their noses against the window of the train as it chugged its way to a stop. The boys had liked the ride. The steaming black engine with the great whistle impressed them. They had whispered to each other the entire trip and had come to the conclusion that, if they didn't become major league baseball players, they would be engineers and go like hell down the tracks, blowing that loud whistle all the time. Bill was enthused about the train also. As he stepped from the train, his thoughts were of how he would do almost anything to work on the crew taking care of the tracks which led the gigantic monster across the countryside.

He helped Lula, with the baby in her arms, off the train and then he stood observing the town they hoped to call home. He wasn't used to towns like this. It was bigger by far than the small burg of Perrysburg. Lula had told him about the boarding house her pa had mentioned. He decided they would go there and stay until he found them a home. Lula stood holding the baby, her back beginning to hurt from the weight of the big girl. She watched as Bill talked to a man with a rig about taking them to the boarding house. She felt disoriented. She wasn't used to being out of her kitchen there on the farm. She noticed the women sitting on benches in front of the station. They looked so well dressed, some with parasols held over their elaborate hats to keep the bright October sun from their pale faces. Their coats were fur-trimmed and expensive looking. Some of them reminded her of Abigale, the ones with the gaudier clothes.

Doris P. Burke

She glanced down at her coat, which didn't come together in front. She had gained weight, she knew, and this was the same coat she had when she had lived with her ma and pa. Her boys made a good impression, with their short wool pants she had made and their black stockings under the new black button shoes the uncles had bought for them. And Bill was quite handsome in his black and blue mackinaw and felt hat, which he wore on a jaunty angle. She saw some of the ladies smile at him as he walked by them. She was proud of her family and of Bill, who was going to make a new home for them here in Rochester. Bill made the arrangements with Mr. Swayze, the rig owner, to pick up their trunk later that day. He would first take them to the boarding house. Mr. Swayze, a friendly man with red beard and mustache, helped Lula and the baby into the buggy and told the boys they could ride on the step on the back.

He pointed out different businesses as they rode down the wide main street, which was lined with majestic oak trees. "This here's the fastest growing town around," he said proudly. "Why, I remember when this was just a paltry place. If you blinked your eyes you was through it. Now look at it, folks. Right there is our Clarion Newspaper Company and Finks Hardware, where they got nuts and bolts and wash tubs and washboards and ready-made horseshoes." He seemed to be enjoying his task as a self-appointed tour guide and he wiped his hand across his mustache and continued. "We've got us Doc Spencer to bring the younguns into the world and we got, right over there, Tuttle and Sullivan, the undertakers, to see that the old folks get a decent burial going out. He was informative, telling Bill the D.U.R. was hiring crews for the railroad. "And right over there," Mr. Swayze continued, still pointing, "is Korff Meat Market. Why, I tell you folks, their bacon and ham is so lean you gotta throw some lard in the pan to fry it. Over there is Starring Drug Store. They got stuff in there that cures lumbago, headaches, back problems, gassed up bellies and any pain in the behind. And our grocery store on the left, well, if they ain't got what you want to eat, you shouldn't be eatin' it. And for men only, we got Wilcox's Stag Restaurant and Poolroom, where you can play hide-and-go-seek from the little woman, and she can't get in the door to find ya!"

He continued his information on the town until they pulled up at the boarding house. It was a rambling, paint-less building, off by itself, overlooking the woolen factory and the paper mill. Not much to look at, Lula thought, as she stood up to step out of the buggy. But, she smiled, we won't be staying here long, so it will be fine. She had thought of a white house with a big kitchen and

The Family

backyard for the children to play in and she and Bill would be happy always. Bill paid Mr. Swayze fifty cents for his trip and thanked him for all the information he had provided. He didn't leave yet. He asked, "None of my business folks, but are you here to apply for the job of cook and manager of this here establishment?" He was peering at Lula with a quizzical look on his face. "They're in dire need of a good cook. I hear tell they got seven men living here and the management moved right out in the middle of the night, left town, took a bunch of silverware and good china. Old Man Jenkins, he's the owner, why's he madder than a bull locked out of a cow pasture. The men staying here are complainin' the food tastes like hog swill. He's got a hired girl cookin' and makin' beds. She ain't no cook, they say. He has to come up here every morning to get her outta bed. He's probably in there right now a jawin' at her. Men threatenin' to leave, if things don't get better." He kept studying Bill and Lula's faces and then spit out some tobacco juice and started talking again. "He's got nice rooms for the cook and family. You might wanna check with him 'bout this here job. Course, don't wanna tell you what to do, but there ain't many places to rent here in town. Good job for somebody." He smiled, seeing the boys running to the yard in back of the boarding house, where they could see the smoke rising from the factories down below. He flicked the reins to the horses and they started to move back the way they came. He hollered, "Good to meet you folks and, by the way, free room and board for the cook and family. Also heard Old Man Jenkins might sell." He waved his hand, spit again and was gone, leaving Bill and Lula to ponder over everything he had told them.

Lula spoke quietly," Bill, it is something to think about. You know I can cook. I've been doin' for a bunch of men for a long while." She suddenly felt tired and the baby was fussy and wanted to nurse. He shook his head in agreement. "We sure gotta find some place. We'll talk about it to Mr. Jenkins." They knocked on the door. Lula noticing the dirty marks on the door and windows. "Land sakes," she sputtered, "They sure do need a woman around here." They heard the door being pulled open with a flourish and a short, elderly man stood there, a frown on his thin, wrinkled face. "What ya want?" he asked, still scowling, looking from Bill to Lula and then to the wriggling baby. Bill put out his hand. "I'm Bill Judd and this is my wife. Mr. Swayze said you're looking for a cook and manager for your establishment." Jenkin's face changed to a hint of a smile and he stretched his hand out to Bill and gave a weak handshake and invited them to step in. Lula couldn't believe the

Doris P. Burke

cluttered kitchen she was seeing. A young girl was peeling potatoes at the sink, amongst the heap of pots and pans piled high around it. Wiping the sleeve of her dress across her eyes often, she appeared as if she had been crying. Jenkins escorted the family to the living room and Lula was thankful to sit down in a battered rocking chair. Jenkins asked, "You folks looking for a job?" Bill spoke quickly, "Well, I'm wantin' to hire in at the D.U.R., but my wife here, she's a darn good cook. We're looking for a place to stay. Got two boys and this here little girl."

"Good cook, huh?" The old man stared at Lula, noticing she was young and healthy appearing. The man was desperate, Bill could tell that. He never asked another question. His distress look changed to a grin. "Show you the rooms," he said, walking with a slight limp toward the back of the boarding house, expecting them to follow. There were three bedrooms. Room enough for the family. Lula glanced around, seeing the rumpled beds and dust clouding the tops of the dresser and chest of drawers. She wondered how anyone could live in this mess. She asked Jenkins if there were clean linens for the beds. He pointed to a basket filled to overflowing with wrinkled sheets. "Right there, ma'am," he answered, hoping she would be satisfied with the rooms. She had Bill help her pull the sheets tight on the beds, trying to get some of the wrinkles out of them. She nursed the baby and then laid her on one of the clean beds before she hurried to the kitchen. It was bothering her terribly to think of the disorganization there. The hired girl, Wanda, had the pots and pans washed and was staring sadly at the potatoes with the dazed expression of frustration on her face. Lula stirred the embers in the stove, piled wood into it from the wood box and asked Wanda to start slicing potatoes. A couple of hours later, the men who lived in the boarding house arrived. They were tired and dirty from a long day at work. They stood at the door and sniffed the air, noticing a delectable aroma. Mr. Jenkins was limping around, greeting them with a smile on his usually frowning face. He waved them to their chairs at the long dining room table. He seemed to be enjoying the surprise he had in store for them.

They found long pans of scalloped potatoes, crisp and golden on the top, and platters of ham simmering in brown sugar. Corn muffins as big as baseballs were served in a napkin-lined wicker basket, with melted butter ready to pour on them. Cucumbers and onions were swimming in the rich sour cream Lula had found at the back of the icebox. And, for dessert, she served the best peach cobbler, the men agreed, they had ever laid bite to. Old Mr. Jenkins introduced Lula and Bill to the group of men as the new managers

The Family

of the boarding house. He was indeed enthralled with Lula's efficiency and even helped her carry the dirty dishes to the kitchen. He had tasted her food and truly believed, as her husband said, she was a good cook to say the least. Bill was pleased with all the praise given to Lula and he was proud of her. She had been taken for granted, he knew, back on the farm. His old man and his brothers never, ever complimented her on her efforts. He guessed he never had either. She certainly was a good mother to the little men and his little Lady, he thought, watching her move around the unfamiliar kitchen, checking each cupboard for what it held. He realized his pa must have known she would be a good wife. And she certainly had been. And so, by that evening, the Bill Judd family had settled into their new residence in Rochester, Michigan.

Doris P. Burke

Chapter Seven

The next year was busy at the boarding house for the entire family. Mr. Jenkins was pleased with the management and especially with Lula. He was amazed at her efficiency and neatness. He noticed her blonde hair was always pulled back in a round bun and her house dress, and the starched apron she wore over it, was pressed. She was short and plump, but she moved like a sleek mountain lion. He had bought paint for the outside of the building after she smiled and mentioned it would look so clean if it was painted. She managed to get Bill and the boys to paint it a sparkling white to show off the glistening windows she insisted the boys wash regularly. The beds were kept clean and were appreciated by the tired men who crawled in them at night. Jenkins paid Lula a small amount of money each week and he had watched her put it in a sugar bowl, pushing it away to the back of the cupboard. She would look wistful, saying, "You never know when a rainy day might not be far away."

Jenkins lived by himself down the street in a small house. He had never married. He had bought the boarding house as an investment ten years before. For the last five years, it had been filled to capacity with men who drifted in, found jobs and stayed. The boarding house was a good income for him. He was getting old and with the good management he found in Lula, he could sit back and watch his bank figures grow if he wanted to. He didn't need to walk the short way to the boarding house every day, but he did. He liked to watch Lula knead the dough for the delicious bread that would rise in the warming oven of the stove. If she made cookies, he got to taste the first one off the pan. When she churned, he'd help her, never seeming to notice the ache in his leg that bothered him most of the time now. Lula stayed busy every minute, but she listened to Jenkins' stories of his early years in northern Michigan, when he had lived with his pa and ma and life was hard. She didn't say much, but her face showed sympathy and kindness as he talked. She was a jewel as far as he was concerned. He couldn't say that for Bill, though. He had noticed he was gone more and more, hanging around downtown at the Stag Restaurant with the regulars that were there every day. No, Old Jenkins didn't need to even check up on anything at the boarding house, he knew it was being well run. He did anyway, because he liked to watch Lula and think about how it

The Family

would have been when he was a young fella and if he could have found a nice little woman like Lula. In the evenings, he would sit in his old wicker rocker on the porch at his house, stare up at the boarding house and wonder what Lula looked like with her blonde hair down and in her night dress. He knew he would never know. Bill had gotten a job on the railroad crew. He liked it, never had been afraid of hard work. God knows he'd worked his ass off on the farm. He was soon regarded as one of the best on the crew. He had made acquaintance with the gang at the Stag restaurant, heard all the gossip there. It was a great place to hang out after work. He had never been able to do that before. Even before he had married Lula, his pa had kept his sons' noses to the grindstone most of the time.

    He didn't miss his old man. He felt free of him. He did miss his brothers, though, especially Junior and Jake. He found himself bragging about them: They were the greatest, the strongest and the best, he'd tell people. The more he drank, the more he talked about his brothers. He seemed to be getting opinionated about other things, too, and began to be louder and noisier to anyone who would listen. At the boarding house, when the subject of schooling came up, he agreed to send the boys to school for awhile. He told Lula, "Them boys will learn to read and write and that's all they need to know." He scowled at her, expecting her to disagree. Lula knew Bill and his brothers had been pulled out of school to help on the farm. He proceeded to tell her this, his voice becoming louder as he talked. "I know which way east is and which way west is and north and south. That there history and geography is a pain in the ass. Boys don't need to know 'bout that shit. Learning to be men, that's what's important. And workin', like me and my brothers had to." And Lula knew that was the way it was going to be. He had never mentioned buying a house anymore. There had a been a few for sale, Mr. Swayze had told them. When she told Bill, he would frown and say he didn't want to talk about it. He had allowed her to buy a few pieces of furniture to put in the parlor of the boarding house. This gave her pleasure, polishing the wood on the red velvet settee with the curved arms and the matching straight-backed chair. Mr. Jenkins had told her she could have the old grandfather clock that sat against the wall in the parlor, with its years of grimy dirt embedded in the wood. She scrubbed it carefully with naphtha soap and then used linseed oil to bring out the beauty of the wood. The floors in the parlor were cleaned and dusted until they shone, to set off the first furniture that actually belonged to Lula and Bill.

    She was proud of her parlor and she wished she could have an

Doris P. Burke

organ to put with her other pieces. She decided she might buy one with the money her pa had given her, but of course, she would have to ask Bill. She knew he might think an organ was an unnecessary piece of furniture. She did so hope he would let her. One evening as she was turning the sheets down on the bed, she decided she'd better tell Bill of the baby she was sure they were going to be having soon. She was really quite pleased, being as Olive would be two when the baby would be arriving. Lloyd was eight and Ralph had just turned seven. Olive needed someone to play with. The boys were involved in school and had many friends, they didn't have time for a baby sister. "We're going to be havin' another youngun, Bill," she announced, letting her hair fall from the hairpins she was removing. She glanced at him, waiting for the surprised look he always got on his face when she told him of having another baby. She expected him to be pleased. He did love his Little Lady. "For God sakes, woman, ain't we got enough to take care of?" His face took on a mean look she hadn't seen before. Before she could answer, he was snoring. She decided he was tired. Her poor Bill worked hard. She knew he would be pleased after he had rested. She lay down beside him and stretched her short legs. She hadn't been feeling the best. Sometimes she felt like she had never left the farm. The work was always there and the men, just like it had been on the farm. She would be all right, though. The baby growing inside her was slowing her down a bit, but she'd be all right.

    She turned so she could see Bill's face in the moonlight. He was beginning to resemble his pa all the more the older he got. It went through her mind as she lay there, how Old Man Judd used to rave and rant about everything. She closed her eyes, assuring herself her Bill would never be like that. As she dozed off, she realized she had crossed her fingers. Myrtle Eunice was born when Lula was approaching her 23rd birthday. It wasn't an easy birth. Even though she was smaller, the baby was turned around, coming breech. The labor was long and hard. Doc Spencer finally managed to get her out, involving excruciating pain for Lula. Doc Spencer advised Lula to take it easy after that. There had been a disturbance in her womb area and healing would be slow. Lula smiled and thanked him kindly for his concern, but she had no intention of taking it easy. She had so much to do, not only with the everyday cooking and cleaning, but now there would be diapers to soak, to scrub and to hang on the line. The little men helped take care of Olive, and the boarders, noticing Lula's white face, gallantly carried their dirty dishes to the sink and rinsed them. Mr. Jenkins insisted Wanda work for a while. Without asking for help, Lula was

The Family

helped. For the first time in quite a long time, Lula felt someone cared. Bill did seem pleased to have another girl baby and he called her Babe from the minute he laid eyes on her tiny, delicate face with the dark wavy hair surrounding it. He immediately started bragging to his newfound friends at the Stag Restaurant about his daughters, who were the prettiest, the smartest and the best. He spent hours now at the Stag Restaurant, drinking, gossiping about his work with the railroad crew, and playing poker. He was making a fair amount of money and used a large amount of it buying drinks for himself and his friends. Many evenings, it would be way past suppertime before he staggered home to the boarding house.

Lula kept his supper warming when he didn't arrive to eat with the other men. His temper flared often now and she sent the children to their rooms early, so as not to see their pa in a raging mood. He would eat silently and it frightened her when he watched her move around the kitchen, completing her chores for the evening. She was timid about asking him anything when he was in "his mood", as she called it. For years to come she would never undersand what had happened to her Bill.

Doris P. Burke

Chapter Eight

In 1912, Rochester was at its best. The wide streets were filled with the new and older model automobiles chugging noisily through the town, some backfiring, leaving smoke streams and the drivers tooting their horns at the slow-moving horse-drawn rigs. The businessmen smoked ten-cent cigars and talked of expanding their businesses. The new bank in town was lending money to anyone having a good-paying job and gave a large box of candy from the candy factory to any new account. The topic of conversation on the street or with any of the people who stood around the nickel-plated stove at Fink's Hardware was baseball; mostly of Ty Cobb, who could steal bases and make more hits than anybody. Or else of Christy Mathewson, the knock-kneed pitcher, who threw the beautiful curve known as the "fadeaway." The Judd boys hung on every word any stranger or wanderer had to pass on about what was going in the big league baseball world. They lived and breathed baseball. They had their own team, "The Rochester Grizzlies", and on a cool day in September, they were to have the playoff game with "The Rochester All Stars". The teams were tied ten games each and the competition between them ran rampant. Bloody noses and scratches, seen on many of the players from both sides, gave indication of the fierce battle yet to come in the playoff game. The Grizzlies were mostly farm boys, plus the Judd pair. The All Stars were the town's favorite schoolboys: the best, they figured.

The boys played their ball games on the property belonging to Mr. Hammond, the banker. They had diligently laid out the ball field. A little crookedly, maybe, the diamond shape a bit off-center, but they paced 60 feet by putting one foot in front of the other from one bag to another. Burlap bags filled with wood chips were used for bases. The day of the game, the wind was blowing leaves around, stacking them up in piles against the stump fences. The pasture was damp and here and there mud patches gave a slick appearance to the field. A crowd from town was gathering, some bringing chairs to sit on, others sitting on the damp ground. They were anxious to see the All Stars win the championship game. Some of the boys had visited Harry Farley, an old baseball enthusiast, at his shack on the outskirts of town. He had agreed to be the umpire for this very important game. Harry didn't do much anymore: couldn't, his feet were always swollen and his hands were crippled. He had a few

The Family

chickens that kept him in eggs and his ornery goat gave him enough milk, which he figured was good for his affliction. The boys liked to visit with Harry. He told long stories about the early years of baseball while he sat in his rickety rocking chair on the front porch and spit his tobacco juice on the squawking chickens that ran wild in his front yard. He felt flattered the boys had asked him. The walk to the field had been painful, but he was there. Now, as he looked out at the bunch of boys, who were shouting and jeering at each other, he had to grin. He had never seen such an excited bunch since he was in the crowd that watched Christy Mathewson pitch in the 1905 World Series. Mathewson had struck out 18 and walked one. "Play ball!" Harry hollered, taking his place behind home plate and leaning heavily on his cane.

"We can't play yet, Mr. Farley," Little Joe Brown yelled from his spot as short stop. "We gotta wait for the Judd boys. Ralph's our pitcher and Lloyd catches. They'll be here purty soon."

He squinted as he looked across the road coming from town. "Here they come," he said, jumping up and down. He could see two heads over the high weeds. The boys were running fast to get there. Herbie was at the pasture waiting for the game to begin. He held the two bats the Grizzlies used. Herbie suffered from a spastic condition, but most thought he was "teched" in the head. His head shook, his arms shook and he had quite a time keeping his legs moving straight. He fell down a lot and he'd clamber up and start again. Now, when he saw the Judd boys, he slobbered out, "Ah cleaned the bats, Lloyd." He was excited and staggered a little more. "That's good, Herbie," Lloyd replied, taking his place behind home plate and pulling on the worn mitt one of the boarders had given him. Mr. Farley stood right behind him, positioned so he could see the ball coming right over home plate. "Howdy, Mr. Farley, glad you could umpire for us," Lloyd said, pulling out a red handkerchief and wiping the sweat that was dripping down his face. Ralph threw a couple of warm-up pitches to Lloyd. Mr. Farley hollered again, "Let's play ball!"

In the outfield were three of the Simpson brothers, Calvin, Josh and Matt. Neal, the other Simpson brother, wandered back and forth around second base. Tommy Craft was on first, with Jase Brown on third. The shortstop was short indeed: Little Joe Brown, his legs resembling tree stumps crouched, waiting for that first ball to come his way. All were farm boys, except for Lloyd and Ralph. The oldest one of the Grizzlies was Neal Simpson, just turned 13. With everyone in position, the game was on, the crowd cheering on the favorites. Ralph spit on the ball, wiped it down his pants and wound

Doris P. Burke

up, sending it toward home plate. "Good one," his brother encouraged him. The All Stars batted one by one with Ralph striking out Sammy Johnson, walking Marsh Gregory and giving a hit to centerfield by Harry Wright. Lem Joslyn, next at bat, stood tall and powerful. He was the best player on the team. "Put it right over, Ralph boy," he chided, holding the bat firmly. Lloyd was frowning, making gestures at Ralph, trying to give him a signal. Ralph wound up and threw a fast ball low and inside. "Ball one," Mr. Farley called, chewing fast on his wad of tobacco. He was enjoying the game, except his feet were aching from standing. He shifted his weight, planted his cane deep in the soft dirt and leaned heavily on it. The enthusiasm of the boys was something to see. He pushed his wad to the other side of his mouth and called, "Ball two." Lloyd, crouching in front of Farley, made another sign and Ralph threw a curve ball over the plate. Lem swung at it. "Strike," was the call. The outfield had moved back, all the Simpson boys expecting Lem to connect with one of his sky-high hits. Over the plate came Ralph's fast ball and Farley called another ball. "Hell, that was a strike, 'iffen I ever saw one, Mr. Farley," Lloyd grunted. "Ain't no disputin' the umpire," Farley replied as the Grizzlies shout their disapproval.

Lloyd heaved the ball out to Ralph and watched as his brother grabbed some loose dirt, rubbed his hands with it, then wound up for the pitch. This time the ball came like a whirlwind and Lem swung hard. The bat connected and the ball went up and over Ralph's head, straight toward the heavens. The Grizzlies watched in dismay as Marsh and Harry came in home and Lem ambled around the bases with a smile as big as a baby's when its ma sticks a sugar tit in its mouth. The ball was found and thrown to the discouraged pitcher. The crowd was cheering for Lem. Ralph gave a hit to the next batter, but it was a fly ball caught by Josh. He struck out the next batter and the Grizzlies were up to bat. They managed to get two runs and the game went on. In the sixth inning, Lloyd brought in another run. In the first of the seventh, with the All Stars at bat, Lem slammed another hit and came waltzing home with the same satisfied expression on his face. The Grizzlies were upset, talking amongst themselves as they came up to bat in the last of the eighth. Herbie sat by the apple tree making moaning noises and shaking. Mr. Farley was getting tired. Now his back was hurting as well as his feet and legs. The score was 4-3 in favor of the All Stars. The crowd was noisy, rooting for the All Stars. Ralph and Lloyd were giving pep talks to their team. "You're up to bat, Joe," Lloyd said, slapping his short friend on the back. "Shoot that damn ball right over that old crab tree back there."

The Family

Little Joe grabbed the bat from Herbie's shaking hand and, with a determined look, stood waiting for the pitched ball. A slow pitch came at him. He planted his short legs solid to the ground and swung. With a smack, the ball when up over centerfield for a home run. The Grizzlies waited by home base to slap him on the back and two of the Simpson brothers carried him on their shoulders. He was a hero. Next, Josh Simpson had a base hit and his brother brought him in with a good liner to left field. The next batter struck out. Ralph hit a grounder to the short stop and was called out at first. Soon, three outs and the Grizzlies took the field with a one-run lead. "Let's hold the lead, fellas!" Little Joe yelled, jumping up and down at shortstop. Ralph, standing on the pitcher's mound, rolled the ball around in his hands and squinted at his brother. It was the first of the ninth. Lloyd called time out and ran to the pitcher's mound. "We've got to win this game, brother," he said to Ralph. "These smart guys will never let us forget it if they beat us!" He hung his head, looking at his battered mitt. "Ya wanna be like Christy Mathewson, don't ya, Ralph?" Ralph nodded in agreement and muttered, "We're gonna be good someday brother." Lloyd whispered, "Let's be good right now. Sling the ball fast and low." With that, he ran back to home and crouched behind Marsh, who was swinging the bat confidently. Ralph threw the ball like his brother told him and Marsh swung, his bat going right over the ball, again and again and was out. Another batter got a bunt to shortstop and Little Joe slung the ball to first for an out. Lem was up to bat, looking a bit distressed. This tickled Lloyd, it was what he hoped would happen: Lem had lost his confidence.

The crowd was quiet. The Grizzlies roamed the outfield wondering if Lem would connect with one of his famous hits. Ralph rolled the ball in his hands and smiled. He could see the tension on Lem's face. Ralph threw a fast ball at him and Lem connected for a foul ball. The next one he swung at, desperate now. It was a strike. Ralph knew exactly what ball he was going to throw at Lem this time. He wound up and pitched one fast and low, right over home plate. Lem stood there holding the bat as Mr. Farley called, "Strike!" Lem threw his bat and walked slowly toward his teammates. It was a great day for the Rochester Grizzlies. Mr. Farley realized he'd watched a damn good game as he started his long trek home. He had seen an 11-year-old boy pitch an exceptional game. For a few minutes there, in the excitement of the game, he'd forgotten how his legs ached and how his feet felt like they were burning up. The Grizzlies yelled and jumped their way back toward town. Ralph strutted as if he would sprout feathers any minute. Half-way back,

Doris P. Burke

Lloyd glanced around. "Where's Herbie, Joe?" he asked. "Thought he was with us," Joe answered, stopping to look behind them. "Let the little stumble-ass get back when he can," Ralph yelled from up ahead. "We ain't got time to wait for him. We gotta hurry up. We gotta get home before the old man does, Lloyd." Go ahead, you guys," Lloyd turned and said over his shoulder. "I'll find him." He ran back the way he came. Around the next bend in the road, he could see Herbie stumbling toward him. As soon as Herbie saw Lloyd, he started making moaning noises. Lloyd ran up beside him to hear him say, "Ah was trying to hurry, Lloyd." "I know Herbie. Grab a hold, I'll give you a ride." Herbie was as skinny as a picked chicken and was no weight to speak of on Lloyd's back. Herbie was so happy he kept saying over and over in Lloyd's ear, "We beat 'em good, didn't we Lloyd?"

"We sure did, Herbie," Lloyd replied, smiling as he hurried toward the boarding house with his friend hanging on tight, making happy noises.

The Family

Chapter Nine

Ralph was telling his ma about the game when Lloyd walked into the kitchen of the boarding house. She stood at the stove, stirring a kettle of stew. It was cool outside, but beads of perspiration were running down her face. The little girls, Lady and Babe, were setting the long table to feed the boarders, who would be pushing through the door any time now. Lady, who had lost the name of Olive a long time before, finished throwing the silverware in place and then remarked, "I wanted to see the game today, but Ma wouldn't let me." Her lips came out in a pout as she looked at her big brother for sympathy. "It was a good one," Lloyd answered, tickling her under the chin and then grabbing his baby sister, who was trying to get the plates to set evenly on the table. "Ma, you should have seen me pitch today," Ralph was saying as he pumped water into the wash basin in the sink and then began scrubbing his dirty hands with the brown bar of soap. "You would have been proud of him, Ma," Lloyd said, holding Babe and giving her a big kiss on the cheek. "That's all you boys think about," their mother scolded, opening the oven door and pulling out a pan of golden brown biscuits. "Get some clean towels out of the sideboard, Lloyd. Those men will be shovin' that door open any minute." She hurried to put another pan of biscuits in the oven and then covered the others with a clean towel.

She was thinking of Bill, as always, wondering if he'd be home tonight. Things had gotten worse for Bill in the last five years and worse for the whole family. No one could tell Bill what to do any more. Not Lula, or his boss down at the railroad crew, who still figured Bill was the best he had - when he showed up for work. Alcohol was running Bill Judd these days. It sometimes made him into a working fool, but most of the time it made him into a mean, disgusting human being. He loved his daughters and tolerated his sons. Nothing was too good for his Lady and Babe. He'd tell Lula to buy the best cotton cloth down at Tucker's Department Store and say, "Make something pretty for them, Mama. We've got the prettiest gals in all creation." She preferred to sew them up a decent-looking dress out of the nice, flour-sack material everyone used. Lots cheaper. But instead, she'd drag out her old Singer machine and spend her spare time sewing when she could have been relaxing a bit. She would carefully sew lace and ruffles on the

Doris P. Burke

dresses, hoping to please Bill. They became the best-dressed little girls in Rochester, with their hair done in long curls, which involved a tedious job for Lula, having to wrap each curl in tight rags to make them perfect. When Bill was halfway sober, he'd trot them downtown, showing them off to whomever he met. The boys were a different story. Boys had to learn to be men, he'd tell Lula, and he'd often whack them a good one, to toughen them up, he'd say. She tried to keep the boys away from their pa if she could. He wouldn't let them go to school anymore. Girls went to school, he told her. Boys had to work to become men. This was why Lloyd worked at the livery station for Mr. Swayze and Ralph helped down at Fink's Hardware. Lloyd was 12, Ralph was 11. Lula cooked, clean and washed clothes a good 14 hours every day. She knew she had to.

Sometimes Bill went on drinking binges and there wasn't any pay. Mr. Jenkins was still paying her what he could and she used this money for clothes for the children. She was thankful they lived at the boarding house and had a roof over their heads. Her dream of a home of their own was still just a dream and she didn't believe it would ever become a reality. It was getting dark as the first of the boarders started drifting in. They washed up at the sink, listening to Ralph tell in an excited voice about the ball game. They clapped him on the back. It tickled them to see how excited he was. Lloyd set chairs at the table and grinned, hearing Ralph rehash the game. He didn't care if Ralph didn't tell about Joe's home run. He knew he wanted the boarders to think he won the game by striking out the last batter. Well, maybe he did, Lloyd decided. The boys grabbed a plate out of the cupboard and dished themselves up a plate of the chunky stew. It smelled good and the boys were hungry after playing their game. Lady helped her ma put the huge biscuits on tin plates and then she plunked them in front of the men. The boarders sniffed the great aroma of the stew in appreciation. "Put the honey on, Lady," her ma ordered. "They might want some on their biscuits." Lula was red in the face from the heat of the kitchen and she kept pushing some hair back that had fallen from her bun. She dipped up more stew to refill the dishes the men had quickly emptied. Lloyd watched her from where he and Ralph sat at the small kitchen table. He was thinking how hard she worked and what a bastard his old man was. Most of the boarders ate in silence, others told stories about the day's happenings. A few worked at the cotton mill. The others worked on the railroad with Bill. They waited now for Lula to ask the same question she asked every night when Bill wasn't there.

The Family

She finally did, as she filled the biscuit plate again: "Was Bill at work today?" "Saw him this mornin' Mrs. Judd," Dan Quinton glanced up from his plate to say. She nodded and went back to the store to throw some more wood in the opening. Lloyd and Ralph jumped from their chairs to stand by their mother. "Let us go downtown, Ma" Ralph said. "We'll see if we see him." "No, you boys have work to do around here," her voice was husky. "Lloyd, you wait till the table is cleared and then take the rest of the stew to Cora's. She's been ailin'. No tellin' if they have a bit of food over there. Ralph, you get those peelings and scraps out in the barrel. Now, hurry along boys!" She was scared Bill was on another drinkin' binge. He'd been good for a month now. She counted on the calendar every morning. His last binge had lasted three weeks. What a nightmare! He'd come home after a day of playing cards and bullshittin' at his new hangout, Whipple's Tavern. His face would be puffed and red from all the alcohol he poured down and then he'd raise hell with her and the boys. The boys stayed out of his way, if possible. Otherwise, they were slapped and shoved while he roared, "Ya gotta be men, like me and my brothers. We were the best in the 'tire county. Beat the hell outta anybody." Lula was afraid of him when he was in his drunken rage. She didn't understand his need for drinking and had foolishly asked him why once. His face had gotten black with fury and he had grabbed her arm and squeezed it hard, saying, "Ain't none of your business woman, what I do!" She had been so frightened of the fierce look on his face, she never confronted him again.

Most of the time he passed out after he shoved some food in his mouth. Other nights, he would pull her into the bedroom, push her on the bed and get atop her, forcing her to put up with his disgusting sex. She always hurried to the kitchen afterwards, grabbing her douche bag to flood her insides with warm water, hoping she wouldn't get pregnant again. She wouldn't have minded another baby, but not with Bill's instability. She had to raise the children she had, with or without his help. The boarders knew what went on. They talked amongst themselves about Bill. No one would confront him. He was tough, backed down from nobody. He wasn't a big man, thin, but strong as an ox. When he was sober, they all liked him, but drunk, he was a cruel man. And drink? He could outdrink any of his cronies, who hung in the bars where he did. Lula glanced anxiously at the clock. Seeing it was near seven o'clock, she feared the worst. The boys helped her clear the table in silence, feeling what she was feeling. The little girls ran to their room, unaware of how their mother and brothers felt. They whispered to

Doris P. Burke

each other about what their pa might bring them. They loved their pa. He was good to them. Lula was remembering how decent Bill had been for the month he hadn't been drinking. He had even promised the boys he would try to see their ball game and told her she could buy the organ she had wanted. That had pleased her so much and he was like the Bill she had known. What had happened, she wondered. Lloyd picked up the dish of stew and the plate of biscuits his mother had ready for Cora and Herbie. It was getting chilly out, giving the promise of winter to come. He walked the few steps to Cora's shack, a dingy black weathered building where Cora and Herbie had lived since Cora's husband had fallen from the top of a barn and broken his back. He died soon afterwards.

Lloyd looked toward Main Street. He thought he might see his pa coming, but he didn't see anybody on the dark streets. He knocked at the battered door and soon Cora stood staring at him. He always felt a twinge of sympathy for her - a tiny bit of a woman with a distressed look on her face at all times. Never smiling, Cora's eyes showed a sadness that was hard to forget. Herbie was trying to put wood in the old heat stove as Lloyd entered. "Ma sent this stew and biscuits over, Cora," Lloyd said. "Heard you were sickly." Cora stepped aside and he made his way to the stove. "Hey, Herbie, let me give you a hand." He grabbed the wood from the floor and threw some on the smoldering embers. He stoked the coals and soon the wood began to fire up. Herbie was always glad to see Lloyd and it showed as he staggered to an old chair, his face squeezing into a smile. "Good game, eh, Lloyd?" he shook out. "Good game, Herbie," Lloyd answered, brushing the dust from his hands. "You got enough wood, Cora?" he asked, looking at the small pile by the stove. "There's more outside," she answered, setting the dish of stew on the table. "I can bring it in when we need it." "I'll get it," Lloyd offered, noticing how peaked her face was. He found the pile of wood and loaded his arms full. Cora held the door for him and he watched Herbie trying desperately to push some stew in his mouth. Cora hurried over to help him. Lloyd felt better to know they had some warm food and enough wood to tide them over. He tried to watch out for them, even if his pa told him to mind his own business. Lula sent food over often and once in a while she would have Cora iron shirts for the men and pay her out of the money she received from Mr. Jenkins. Wood was dropped off at Cora's shack by farmers passing by. No one stopped to talk, but the pile was never empty.

Whenever Lloyd had time, he tried to help Herbie to read. He knew he wasn't stupid, like most thought, even if he staggered and

The Family

shook. His mind wasn't affected by his affliction. "Isn't his fault he's that way," Lloyd would say to the other boys, who tended to make fun of him. He'd even given a couple of black eyes to some smart guys calling Herbie stupid. He figured if he could just get Herbie to readin', life would be better for him. He could find another world in a book. Lloyd left Cora's and wandered back to the boarding house, hoping his old man was there so his ma would feel good. Ralph was sitting at the table wiping a bat with a dirty cloth when Lloyd pushed the door open. He was still talking fast to their ma, telling her about the ball game. She stood at the sink filling the coffeepots with water to be ready for the morning breakfast. "Let's go to bed, Ralph," Lloyd suggested, washing his hands at the sink after his ma moved away. "It's early," Ralph frowned. "Ain't going to bed yet." "Yes we are, gotta get up early," Lloyd answered, swinging his head toward the bedroom. He wanted to get Ralph alone so they could sneak out and find the old man, if possible. Ralph got the idea and he tossed the bat to the corner of the kitchen. "Pick that bat up, sonny," Lula scolded. The noise of the bat hitting the wall set her nerves on edge." He smiled at his mother, "O.K., Ma, can't get away with nothin' around here." She dabbed her face with a muslin napkin. She never could stay mad at Ralph. He had a crooked little smile that spread to his eyes and seemed to touch her heart. She smiled back at him and said, "You boys get to bed." She didn't want them up when Bill got home. It would be better if she went to bed too. She glanced at the clock again. It was eight-thirty. The boys both gave their ma a kiss on the cheek and Lloyd pushed Ralph toward the bedroom.

The minute they closed the door, Lloyd told Ralph what he had in mind. Ralph asked, "For Christ's sake, what we gonna do if we find him? He'll kick our asses good." "I wanna see what the old bastard is up to," Lloyd answered, pulling his sweater over his head. They shoved their bedroom window up and jumped out into the quiet moonlight. They hustled as fast as they could toward the lights downtown. They met a few people walking and they ducked behind a tree until the people were gone. Ralph was scared they would meet their pa and he mentioned this to Lloyd. "Shit, he's so pie-eyed by now, he wouldn't know his own sons from a block of wood," Lloyd told him. They stopped first at the Stag Restaurant and climbed on a garbage barrel so they could see through the window. "He ain't in there," Ralph whispered to his brother.

"Look at your boss, Mr. Swayze, Lloyd. He looks like he swallered a red pepper. Look at his face!" They both grinned and jumped down. They headed straight for Whipple's Tavern. They were sorta enjoying their night excursion. Their ma never let them go downtown after dark. They kept whispering and laughing quietly as they made their way toward the tavern. They couldn't find anything to stand on when they found the window at the back of the tavern. "Get on my shoulders," Lloyd ordered. "Then tell me what's going on in there."

    Lloyd finally got Ralph balanced so he could peek through the window. "Can't see him yet," Ralph said quietly. "Oh, yep, there he is. Why, the old fart's got a woman sitting on his lap. Jesus, Lloyd, I think he's got his hand on her crotch. She's wriggling like a worm on a hook! Why, the old bastard! He slobbering all over her!" Lloyd backed up and leaned down so Ralph could get off his shoulders. "That's just what I thought," Lloyd muttered. He wished he was a couple of years older. He would have busted through the door and kicked the shit out of old man. They walked slowly along the street toward home, Lloyd asking Ralph to tell him all over again what he had seen. They both agreed their pa was a real asshole and they agreed they would never tell their ma what they knew. "Ya know Ralph, as soon as we get old enough, we'll take ma outta here, away from the old man. She don't need this shit," Lloyd said, feeling so damn disgusted. "When we get in the major leagues, we will," Ralph said, nodding in agreement. They crept into their bedroom window, both wondering how their old man could do this to the ma they loved. They went to sleep with the picture of what had happened still in their minds. Lloyd, hearing a noise, woke up in the night. He listened and decided the old man had finally found his way home, probably pissed up to his ears. He closed his eyes and thought, ta hell with him!

    Chapter Ten The next morning Lula was busy in the kitchen pouring pancake batter on the hot griddle when the boys came out of their bedroom. The boarders sat at the long table, eating the piles of pancakes she had put in front of them. Pa was nowhere to be seen. The boys were glad. "Get a plate, boys," she fussed. "Hurry, you'll be late for work. Your pa left early. He said he was sorry he didn't get to your ball game." They looked at each other, knowing full well their pa never said that, never said he was sorry for nothin'. They knew their ma was covering up for him like she always did. They grabbed a plate from the stack on the table, threw some pancakes on it, poured syrup over them and started wolfing them down as fast as they could. "We gotta go, Ma," Ralph said, spitting some pieces of pancake out as he talked. She handed them their lunch pails and they stumbled to the door. Lloyd whispered to Ralph, "Ma ain't ever going to believe the old man is full of shit, even if

The Family

she sees it with her own eyes." The mornings were always the same for Lula. She washed the pile of dishes and dried and then helped the little girls dress. She then started her bread. This morning, she kneaded the soft dough and thought about Bill. He said he was going to work, but was he? He had fallen into bed about midnight, not saying a word. She had listened to his loud snores most of the night and the smell of booze was overwhelming. She had hardly slept at all.

Now, she suddenly wondered where Mr. Jenkins was. He always came every morning, rain or shine. She wished he'd come. It took her mind off of Bill, to hear his stories of his young years. She walked to the window and peered toward his house down the way. It was just getting light out, so she could barely see the house itself. A dim flicker shown through the front window, she could see that. She went back to her kneading, turning the dough over and over. It was strange, she thought. Mr. Jenkins should be up and around by now. She decided she'd wait awhile and then walk down if he didn't show up soon. She separated her dough and put each chunk in the tin bread pans, smoothed them round and placed them, covered, in the warming oven. She moved to the bedroom to see if the girls were contented. They were playing with their china-faced dolls their pa had insisted they have because they were pretty, like his girls. She told them she would be outside for a few minutes and she grabbed an old sweater and went out into the brisk fall air. She had a feeling of apprehension as she strolled toward the small house. She stood at the door, noticing there was no sign of Mr. Jenkins outside. She knocked timidly. She had never been down to his house or inside and glanced around as she stood there. The paint was chipped and the porch boards squeaked under her feet. There was no answer to her knock and she heard no noise from within. She turned the knob and entered. The liniment smell was strong. She remembered he used it often on his lame leg. Her eyes wandered around the front room. She observed the curtainless windows and the drab colors of his settee and chairs. One chair sat by the window, with a lamp burning next to it. There was a good view of the boarding house from the window. She wished she'd offered to make curtains and helped him more. Maybe she would suggest it to him.

She called, "Mr. Jenkins." She knew she was going to be embarrassed when he came from his bedroom and found her there. It was so still and she felt frightened when she heard no answer. She had to get back to the boarding house before long, the girls would be wondering where she was. She thought of how tired Mr. Jenkins appeared lately and he had mentioned he was getting old. She knew

Doris P. Burke

he must be in his late seventies. Maybe he was sick and couldn't get out of bed. She moved cautiously toward the door she figured was his bedroom and noticed it was slightly ajar. She pushed it open. He lay on the four poster bed, a patch quilt coverlet over him. She moved closer. His eyes were closed and she couldn't hear any breathing except for her own. She knew her friend had died here alone in the little house he had told her was the home he'd always wanted. His wrinkled face had a contented look. She felt a lump rise to her throat. She would miss him so much. He was the only friend she had found in Rochester. She picked up a few clothes lying near the bed and laid them on a chair, then hurried through the front room. She'd have to get in touch with the undertaker. She heard a horse whinny as she walked out the door. It was Mr. Swayze coming up the street with his rig. He saw her and flicked the reins to the horses. When he stopped beside her, he could see the distressed look on her face. She told him what she had found in the little house. "I'll take care of things," he assured her.

    She nodded, then turned and walked slowly toward the boarding house. Things wouldn't be the same, she knew that, and maybe they would have to leave. She would think about that later. Right now, she really wanted to have a good cry. The shock of finding him dead was starting to bother her. She realized she was wringing her hands like a child. That was enough of that! She had things to do. There were beds to make, clothes to scrub and the endless chores she did every day. The grocery store would be delivering the flour and sugar she used so much of and supper plans had to be made. She stood in her organized kitchen, her eyes moving to the churn. She thought of yesterday, when Mr. Jenkins had patiently turned out the rich, creamy butter for her, while she kneaded the bread he was so fond of. She felt a pull at her heart, thinking of the goodness he had shown her. She used her apron to wipe away the tears on her face before she went into the girls. The day of the funeral she insisted the boys go and dress in the best suits she had pressed and ready for them. She dressed the girls in their ruffled dresses and placed silk ribbons in their hair. They would all be presentable and show respect to Mr. Jenkins for his farewell. Bill was sober and was glad to take the day off, he told her, and acted quite sincere when he remarked Old Jenkins hadn't been a bad sort. The funeral was in the parlor of the undertaker's. Mr. Swayze had insisted he would pick up Lula and the family and take them in his rig to the funeral. He was waiting for them as they all emerged from the boarding house. He had been friendly with Jenkins. Though he was kind of a funny old codger, he had liked him. He put on the best suit he

The Family

had, which Lula noticed was a bit wrinkled. She wished she could have pressed it for him. The undertaker's parlor had very few people there when they arrived. Lula saw Mr. Hammond, the banker, and two men from the boarding house, apparently taking time off work to attend. She realized not many people had known Mr. Jenkins. He had kept to himself in his house and at the boarding house.

The preacher had a shiny, black suit on and a holier-than-thou look on his face, as he stood by the plain wood casket. He started the sermon in a loud, booming voice. "O Lord, if this man be a sinner, have mercy on his soul!" Lloyd and Ralph covered their mouths as he continued. They though he looked like he was going to burst with his own enthusiasm. His eyes bugged and his arms flared and he acted like he was going to piss his pants, Lloyd told Ralph later. The preacher didn't talk long, he just said, "I hope all sinners will get on their knees and accept God." The boys covered their mouths again, wanting to bust with laughter, when the fire-and-brimstone preacher looked right straight at their pa, who was squirming in his seat. The sermon over, they all filed past the casket. Lula stood for a moment gazing at the face she would see no more. She was disappointed the preacher hadn't said one pleasant word about her friend. She knew the preacher hadn't known him, but he could have asked her and she could have told him many things. Mr. Hammond stopped her as she came through the door of the funeral parlor with the little girls, clinging to her skirt, afraid of the quietness there and of the still body in the casket. He tipped his hat, saying, "Mrs. Judd, if you have time, will you stop at the bank? It won't take long." He was a large, observant man with proper appearance. He noticed her worn coat that didn't come together in front and the less-than-fashionable paisley print dress under it. Most of all, the tiredness in her eyes bothered him.

He startled her with the question and she glanced around for Bill, who was glaring at the preacher because he was telling boarders to repent before it was too late. "I suppose we could," she answered. "I do have things to do." She felt very self-conscious in the presence of this well-dressed man who was speaking to her. She pulled on her coat, suddenly aware of her appearance. Mr. Swayze heard the conversation as he waited on the rig. "You go right ahead, Missus, I'll take the children up to the boarding house and come back for you." He seemed to have a knowing look on his face and she wondered what he knew. She told Bill what had been said. His voice was loud as he asked, "What in hell does he want?" "I don't know, Bill," she answered, wishing he'd quiet his voice, but was afraid to say so. They followed along the street to the bank. Bill

Doris P. Burke

looked longingly at Whipple's Tavern when they passed by. He would have given anything for a shot to wet his whistle. Lula had never been in the bank before and she was impressed with the neatness of the surroundings and the well-dressed employees. She felt quite out of place, but Bill smiled and tipped his hat to all the ladies and acted as if he did business there often. They were escorted into Mr. Hammond's office by a sedate young lady who seemed dedicated to her lucrative job. Hammond had papers on his desk. He stood up and politely waved them to a chair and began talking in a friendly, but business-like, voice. "It seems, Mrs. Judd, you were held in high regard by Mr. Jenkins. A documented will was made by Mr. Jenkins, leaving the boarding house and the small white house where he resided to Mrs. Lula Judd."

Lula's hand went to her heart and she realized she had been holding her breath as he talked. She felt a bit faint for the first time in her life. Bill was staring at Hammond, a smile starting on his face. He asked, "Is that the truth? Are you sure?" Hammond cleared his voice and peered at Bill through his spectacles. "It certainly is, sir. We have some legal papers for Mrs. Judd to sign and then the property will be hers to do whatever with. Jenkins wanted it that way. Said there isn't a finer woman than Mrs. Judd. Of course you are very aware of that, I'm sure." Hammond had heard rumors of Bill's carousing and drinking and now frowned at him, saying, "The property is in the name or Lula Fischer Judd, only!" Lula was still in shock at what had been said and she had a hard time speaking. She had no idea Mr. Jenkins would do this for her. She found her voice at last and murmured, "I knew he had no kinfolk, but this is more than I could accept." "No way not to accept it, Mrs. Judd," Mr. Hammond said. "It is yours, we have it all here and legal." He smiled at her, noticing her tired eyes. He felt good to be telling her of the will. He continued, saying, "He left quite a sizable sum of money to be used for a new ballpark right here in town. He was quite a fellow. Folks didn't know him very well. Apparently you did, and were quite a good friend. He told me that." She could feel the tears starting and she reached in the pocket of her coat for the lace handkerchief she kept there.

Lula and Bill left the bank, Bill grinning like a Cheshire cat and tipping his hat to a passersby and holding on to Lula's arm like he never wanted to let go. They were now property owners. He was going to be an important person in the community and he would sure have liked to have a drink to celebrate. He didn't give a damn. He thought about that pompous Hammond making such a point of saying it was in Lula's name only. What was hers was his. She

The Family

knew that - or she damn well better know it. And so, the battered sign that said, "Jenkins' Boarding House" was taken down and replaced by a newly painted and printed sign reading, "Judd's Room and Board." The Judd family moved into the little white house with the backyard for the children. Bill had painters come and put a new coat of white paint on the house and even hired carpenters to build on a fancy parlor in which Lula would keep the brand-new organ he purchased for her. He quit his job at the railroad, saying, "There is too much to do at the boarding house. Have to help Mama take care of our property." The rooms the family had occupied at the boarding house were turned into more rooms for boarders. The boarding house could now accommodate twelve. Bill used some money the boarders paid to buy a used 1908 Model T Ford with a fancy convertible top, and he was seen often driving through town with a cigar in his mouth and a smile on his face. He was a business-man and a property owner with prestige. He was the greatest, the strongest and the best!

Doris P. Burke

Chapter Eleven

In 1915, Rochester was still growing. There was a new grocery store advertising rendered lard, flour bagged in the newest print material and juicy dill pickles that would make your taste buds sit up and take notice. There was an exclusive millinery shop for the fashion-conscious woman and a haberdashery showing the latest in suits for the big-city look. Filling stations had sprung up out of nowhere, providing gas for all the automobiles moving through the busy town and repair shops were there to fix them when they took the notion to stall. The talk on street corners was always of the great Ty Cobb and of the many bases he stole. Playing for the Tigers in nearby Detroit, he was revered by most. Newspapers were read and the conflict in Europe was discussed. People were shaking their fists, threatening the unseen enemy with what would happen to them if the United States entered the war. Rochester was a busy, vocal community. The Judd boarding house was full to overflowing and was considered the place to stay if you wanted good food and a clean bed. Lula had built a fine reputation, being called the best cook in five counties by anyone sampling her food. She was admired and respected. She was now able to hire Wanda to help with the never-ending cooking and cleaning. She had Cora do most of the ironing. She had even saved enough in her sugar bowl to buy a brand-new Supera washing machine from the Sears and Roebuck Company.

She still felt tired most of the time, but the burden had been eased. Bill was still a problem with his drinking and she wondered if he would ever stop. He made a pretense of helping at the boarding house, delivering the necessities Lula needed. He was good at that. He traveled back and forth downtown, making sure he had his whiskey bottle with him for a nip, now and then. He still hung out at Whipple's Tavern, often way into the night. Life was good for Bill. He made sure he was there at the boarding house to collect the money from the boarders, shoving a large amount in his pocket for future drinking money. The rest he gave to Lula for the upkeep of the place. He was healthy-appearing, not a wrinkle on his face, a slight tiredness the only after-effects of his drinking. He was being consumed by alcohol and it seemed to agree with him. Lloyd had grown tall, with dark hair and a slim, strong body. He worked at the woolen factory now, because Mr. Swayze's rig business had dimin-

The Family

ished a great deal with the automobile boom. Ralph, with his light hair and stocky body, resembled the Fischer side of the family. He kept working at the hardware, liking the contact with people. They were grown up now, they told each other: Lloyd 15 and Ralph 14. They were men and being men, they knew for sure that they could never become the disgusting person their pa had become. They had listened to their ma cover up for him for years. Saw her face crumble when he didn't come home and saw bruises on her arms from his abuse. They had watched him drive through town, chewing on a cigar and tootin' the horn at any nice-lookin' woman on the street. They had heard people talk about him and whisper about him, but nobody had confronted him. He was a tough guy and a horse's ass all at the same time. Rochester had changed, the boarding house had changed, but their old man, they figured, was the same. They stayed out of his way and wanted him to stay out of theirs.

Lloyd was a reader, buying a book a week out of his paycheck. He read on his lunch hour at the factory or anytime he could. Treasure Island and Huckleberry Finn were favorites and so were all of Zane Grey's westerns. He was helping Herbie read and was succeeding, making Herbie shake with enthusiasm as each word came to him. This pleased Lloyd and as he promised, another world was within reach for Herbie. The evenings Lloyd spent at Cora's were interesting and he felt rewarded with just the happy expressions on Herbie's face as he delved into the school of learning. As sort of a reward for Herbie's efforts, Lloyd always stopped on his way home from work and purchased a pint of ice cream to be eaten after the reading lesson. Herbie's face would pucker into a smile and he'd stammer, "You're the best, Lloyd!" Besides baseball and reading, girls had entered the picture for Lloyd and Ralph. After an evening of surveillance of the eligible females standing in front of the ice cream parlor, the conversations in the boy's bedroom at home turned to sex. Most nights, loud laughter was heard coming from the boys, who were growing up. It was Ralph who urged his brother to tell him of each girl he'd had behind the bleachers at Jenkins' ball field. Especially, he wanted to hear about Sally Mae Pinkerton. "You, and Joe and Jase have had it into her, huh, Lloyd?" he asked, lying in his long underwear on the bed one night. He waited for his big brother to tell him some good stuff. "Come on, tell me about it," he begged. "Is it true she don't wear no bloomers and she greases her crotch with Vaseline?"

Lloyd waited until Ralph was about to explode with his thoughts of what went on and said, "No bloomers, slippery as a greased pig, ya gotta get right at it or you're gonna miss. Why, I tell ya, Ralph

Doris P. Burke

my man, Jase said he slipped right off one night and 'bout broke his old donager in two on a board laying there. Said it got sore and black and blue. Thought it might fall off." Yep, the laughter of the boys was heard by all, even up to the boarding house. The men lying on their beds would smile and remember when they were young fellas. They figured that much laughter had to be about sex and girls and they knew the Judd boys were becoming men. Sally Mae Pinkerton lived with her pa in three rooms above Whipple's Tavern. Her ma had left the year before with a man who frequented the tavern. She ran right off, leaving Sally Mae and Seth to fend for themselves. She took her best red dress, her new hat with the yards of netting, everything out of Seth's billfold and her douche bag. This left Seth to raise his daughter, who was the spittin' image of her ma, right down to the pouting lips. He vowed he would try his best to keep her from turning out like her ma - a hussy with a capital H, as far as he was concerned. Sally Mae was 16 and a knowledgeable girl. After her pa had left for work every morning and before she left for school, she had watched her ma get ready for her day of carousing. Her ma had pulled on her black stockings, placed her red garter on above her knee and smiled, as if she had a little secret. Then she would slip on her brightest dress, being careful not to disturb her tight red curls. She'd pinch her cheeks until they had a nice glow and then she was ready for her day of fun. Sally Mae thought her ma was beautiful and she wished to be just like her. She resented her pa's old-fashioned attitude. In fact, she didn't blame her ma for leaving him. He was an old fogey and didn't deserve a beautiful woman like her ma. She wished her ma had taken her along with her. Sally Mae had to stay here in these god-awful rooms, with the god-awful ugly wallpaper and listen to her pa say god-awful dumb things.

She tried to outwit her pa anytime she could. When he'd asked her how school was going, she'd reply, "Real good." Then she would show him a paper marked "A", one she had marked herself. When he asked to see her report card, she would smile and say, "Pa, they don't have report cards no more." He believed her; wanted to believe her as he looked into her small round face surrounded by curly red hair and the deep blue eyes that were identical to her ma's. She was tiny and helpless and needed him to protect her from the evil of men. That's what he thought. She knew she had her pa wrapped around her little finger and she loved it. After he left for work, she went to school if she felt like it. Otherwise, she did as she pleased. Sometimes she walked down to the woolen factory to see if she could catch a peek of Lloyd Judd sitting outside at dinnertime.

The Family

She had feeling for Lloyd and she knew he had no idea of her affection. She'd been behind the bleachers with him and, of course, other boys. The other boys didn't matter, she liked Lloyd. She sneaked out every evening after her pa, tired and sweaty smelling, fell asleep on his bed. She'd stand at his bedroom door, seeing his mouth wide open and snoring so loud it made her ears ring, and she'd think he was the dumbest, most ignorant man she had every seen. Then she'd quietly close the door and go out to try to find some fun.

   Sometimes she would meet a couple of friends who liked to hear her wild stories and she made up more and more to satisfy and entertain their young minds. It was always on the same street that they waited for the boys to show up and then the giggling and whispers started, each girl picking out the one of their choice and hoping the one they picked would take a shine to them. If Lloyd didn't show up, Sally Mae felt bad, sorta, but there were others there to entertain her. She'd even been behind the bleachers with Lem Joslyn, the most popular boy at Rochester High. She thought he kissed like a slobbery pig and she always giggled when she thought of Marsh Gregory, whose penis resembled a short, fat sausage. They were all right for entertainment, but she liked Lloyd. She lie in bed one night mulling things over in her mind, while her pa snored in the next room. It annoyed her lately to have Lloyd ignoring her and not spending time downtown. She heard he was spending time with that idiot Herbie. She couldn't understand why anyone would spend time with someone who didn't know nothin'. She heard, too, he was sorta sweet on Mary Miller. She couldn't understand that either. Mary, with the flour-sack dresses and the stiff-braided hair and the space between her teeth. Why, she looked like a jack-o-lantern with braids. All these things she had heard bothered her. She knew there had to be a way to get Lloyd to like her. She thought about the nice house he lived in. She had walked up that way one day and had seen the boarding house and his ma shaking rugs in the doorway and his little sisters playing in the backyard. She noticed what pretty clothes they wore. She'd seen his pa driving around in his fancy car and she figured they must be prosperous. Not like her life, the awful rooms they lived in and her pa just making enough money to feed them and buy her some cheap clothes that she hated. She had to have a plan to get Lloyd. Knowing what a great talent she had for outwitting people, she could think of something. Coming to that conclusion, she closed her eyes and went to sleep.

   In the next few days, Seth Pinkerton found himself concerned about his daughter. She would stay in bed in the morning, saying

Doris P. Burke

she was feeling poorly and believed she had a stomach ailment. He would fret, insisting she see the doctor. "No, no, Pa," she'd say. "This will go away. I just feel tired." She would give him a pouting smile and he would feel assured it was something that would pass. He would stand at the door, ready for work, and she would wave goodbye and then lie back on her pillow, looking helpless and puny. He didn't know that after he left, she'd jump out of bed and head to the kitchen cupboard to find some food for her growling stomach. She'd laugh, thinking of the concerned look on her pa's face. This morning, she figured her plan was working good as she pushed oatmeal cookies into her mouth. She was hungry. She had refused the supper her pa had fixed the night before and also the breakfast eggs he had offered to cook for her. Finding her hand mirror, she peered at herself. She hadn't combed her hair in three days or washed her face. She did look bad and that's the way she wanted to look. She smiled at her reflection. She was going to outwit her ignorant pa again, and other people too. She felt confident that tonight would be when it happened. She sat at the window and watched people walking down the street. Ralph Judd hurried by. He was nice looking, she thought, but not as nice looking as his brother. She got up and moved to her bed and climbed in, pulling the covers over her. She'd sleep all day. Tonight would be busy. Lloyd and Ralph had some practicing to do. They hadn't thrown a ball or caught one in a week. They headed for the ballpark right after supper, playfully shoving each other and making jokes as they tripped along.

A gang was there with bats and balls and they proceeded to run onto the field and do their own thing. Girls were there too, watching their favorite fellows. It was fall and a brisk breeze with a darkening sky gave indication a rainstorm was brewing. The boys ran off the field and gathered in back of the bleachers, some smoking cigarettes, others kidding each other about some girl they had seen there. They all started elbowing each other as they noticed Sally Mae walking slowly toward them. She was taking her time getting there and the boys wondered who she would pick to be with tonight. Ralph was excited and shoved his brother. He hadn't been there this late before, his ma always telling him to get home and help with the chores - Lloyd being excused because he was older. Now, Ralph waited to see what the big guys did. Mary Miller and several girlfriends had come to the ball field to watch the practice. Mary liked seeing Lloyd and Ralph. They were friendly, well-liked boys. Now, she watched Sally Mae coming toward the group and she wondered what she was up to. Most of the girls at school had no respect for Sally Mae. In fact, they tried to avoid her if possible.

The Family

She was known for her lies and exaggerations. The small groups of boys moved apart when Sally Mae stood in front of them. They waited with an expectant grin. She scanned the crowd and spotted Lloyd standing beside Mary and Ralph. This provoked her and she pushed her way toward him, saying "There you are, Lloyd. I hurried to meet you. I've been feeling so awful, you know that." She stood beside him, taking his arm. He tried to move away, but she held on tight, smiling up at him and then her bottom lip came out in a pout. She said, "I'm going to tell pa about our secret in the morning."

"What secret?" he asked, jerking his arm away and wondering what in hell she was talking about. "Why, you know," she whined. "The baby we're going to have." There was complete silence through the crowd. Hearing this, everyone was stunned. She kept talking in a childish voice and then pulled a hanky out to dab her eyes. "Pa will be mad, you know that, Lloyd," she said. "We'll just have to go on with our plans." Lloyd was speechless. He could feel Ralph's eyes on him and Mary moved away. Everyone waited for him to say something. He couldn't, the shock was there. He turned and walked fast across the ball field. He knew Ralph would be right behind him and he started to run. This was something he didn't know how to cope with. He had to get away from there and think. It was raining, a steady downpour. He felt disoriented, running this way and that down the street to his house. He hoped he hadn't heard right, but he knew he had. She really had said, "baby." Reaching the door of his house, he grabbed the knob, opened it and glanced around quickly. His ma wasn't there, nor the girls. They must be at the boarding house. That was good. He hurried to his bedroom and then heard the front door shut with a bang. It was Ralph, he knew. He stood in the doorway, staring at him. "Jesus, Lloyd, is she nuts?" he asked, water running down his face and his eyes as big as saucers. "I don't know, but I gotta get outta here," Lloyd answered, throwing clothes in a satchel.

"Joe and Jase say she's full of shit, Lloyd. She lies like hell and besides, where ya gonna go?" Ralph sat down on the bed and watched his brother pushing clothes haphazardly into the bag. "Outta here. Maybe to Aunt El's. Don't tell nobody Ralph. Christ, I can't think straight!" "I'll go with ya," Ralph said, starting to grab some clothes from a drawer. "No, ya gotta stay here and take care of ma and the girls. Never know what the old man will do when he hears about this. Might take it out on ma." Lloyd turned to his brother and put his hands on his shoulders. He knew Ralph would do anything for him, same as he'd do for his younger brother. "Don't tell

Doris P. Burke

them nothin', even if the old man threatens to whip ya. Hell, we've been whipped before. Just say ya don't know nothin'. Promise me, Ralph." "Don't worry," Ralph answered. "Ya ever comin' back? What about our ball playin'? We gotta play ball!" "We will. This has gotta blow over. I'll see ya sometime." Lloyd answered, squeezing his brother's shoulders and flinching at the look of sadness in his eyes. He grabbed the bag and rushed to the front door. He started down the path that was away from Main Street. He heard a yell and he turned around, the rain pouring down his face. "Junior took Jake with him," Ralph's voice was shrill. Lloyd lifted his arm and waved at his brother. Then he turned and hurried down the path to somewhere.

The Family

Chapter Twelve

The wind came up, sending sheets of cold rain splattering against Lloyd's body as he found his way along the path taking him to the main road leading out of town. He pulled the collar of his mackinaw jacket closer to his face and held his head down and wished he'd brought his stocking cap. He'd travel toward his Uncle Frank's place. He knew how to get there. He remembered the time his pa, wanting to show off his new automobile and brag about how prosperous he was, had loaded the whole family up to go over there. He figured it was about 15 miles. He'd have to get out of the rain for the night somewhere, but he wanted to get down the road a ways first. He felt sick to his stomach thinking of all the shitty stuff he'd heard and the look on Sally Mae's face. She looked like a pouting little girl, not like a 16 year old. Christ, she'd been with most of the gang there. How could she know whose baby it was? His mind was going fast and furious as he pushed against the whipping wind, trying to get down the muddy mess of a road. He knew there was a gravel pit nearby. Shouldn't be too far. He could get out of the wind there. Sure enough, he saw the high sides of it in the darkness and he ran, welcoming the site. He would burrow down in the sandy gravel. Wouldn't be comfortable, but it would be warmer. He found a spot caved in a bit and he pushed his body into the dampness. He has tired and devastated from all the events of the evening. He put his hands over his ears. He could still hear her words.

He slept some during the night, waking often to the depressing sound of the cold autumn rain. He opened his eyes to the bright morning sun sending a hazy glow through the gravel pit. He stretched, trying to get some feeling back into his cramped body. He had to get going. He could tell by the sun it was early yet. He was about three miles out of town. He had to hoof it right along before nightfall. His shoes made a squishing sound as he started his walk up to the road and even with the sun shining, he felt chilled. He took his wet mackinaw off. His shirt was damp underneath, but it felt better letting the warm rays dry it. He thought of the breakfast his ma would be putting on the table for him and Ralph and his mouth watered. His ma, he knew, would never understand why he had to leave, unless Sally Mae and her pa showed up to tell her. Maybe Ralph would get the word spread that he was gone before

Doris P. Burke

he got there. Good old brother Ralph. He'd do a lot of talking, but he wouldn't tell nobody where he was, he knew that for sure. He remembered he might have a piece of peppermint candy in the other pair of pants in his satchel. He stopped and fumbled through the bag, finally pulling out a sweet, sticky piece of peppermint. The candy tasted good and gave him something to suck on as he tripped along. He thought of his little sisters and how they liked the candy he often brought home to them. God, he'd miss them. An automobile came down the road now and then and he'd hide behind a tree when he heard the noise, hoping it wasn't his old man out looking for him. He didn't want anybody to find him.

By late afternoon, he knew he was getting close to his Uncle Frank's place. He'd been moving right along and the tiredness was taking hold. With no food or drink, his body was rebelling a bit. He stopped in the middle of the road and peered ahead of him. It was dusk and he could see smoke rising slowly above a clump of trees. He stood there thinking about what he'd tell his aunt and uncle. It was quiet and a rabbit running from a bush startled his thoughts. He hung his head. He'd heard pa say many times, "Frank and Eleanor live their whole life by what the Good Book tells 'em, but no where in that Good Book does it tell Frank how to farm. Him and Eleanor are gonna starve to death, just readin' that Good Book." He couldn't tell them of his shame, but he had nowhere else to go. He moved slowly toward the smoke stream, kicking a stone in front of him. His sinful way was eating him up as he thought about it. God, how did this happen? He was only 15 and his life would be ruined by this little whore of a girl who somehow got it in her head she wanted him. He, who wasn't old enough, or smart enough, to have a family! Hell, he wasn't no man like he and Ralph thought. He was a scared kid with 25 cents in his pocket. He should have gone to the hobo camp and stayed with them, jumping a freight train later. He coulda been a bum. He felt like a bum. He was tired and hungry like a bum. He wiped a tear away with his shirt sleeve. He wished Ralph was with him, talkin' and swearin'. It always made him feel better to have Ralph around. He took a deep breath, pushed his thick hair back with both hands and entered the long, rut-filled driveway to his aunt and uncle's place. Frank Hamilton watched the figure coming up the driveway. He couldn't make out who it was. He was on his way to milk the three cows. He stopped and turned to holler to his wife, "Ellie, there's somebody comin', better set another plate on the table, probably somebody looking for work. Can't let 'em go away hungry." He entered the barn, knowing he had to get those restless cows shed of their milk.

The Family

Lloyd had seen his uncle. He felt shy and scared about facing him. They were long gone from Perrysburg before he was born. He had never known them - hardly at all — except for the time he had driven over with his pa and the family. They hadn't stayed long that day, the old man in a pucker to get home. He knew they didn't have children, or he guessed they had a boy who died. His ma had told him that. The yard was neat and clean, the house, small and homey appearing. He stepped to the front door and lifted his fist to knock. It was pulled open before he could. His Aunt El stood looking at him and her face broke into a big smile as she said. "Lloyd! It's you! Why, look how you've grown. Come in, boy, don't stand there. Did you walk all this way? You must be dead on your feet." No "why he was here" questions were asked. Before he knew it, he was sitting in front of the wood stove, his shoes off and his damp socks soaking in the wash pan in the sink. His mackinaw jacket hung on a hanger behind the stove drying. Aunt El was emptying his satchel, straightening his rumpled mess of underwear and pants. He'd hardly said a word since the big bear hug she had given him. He had a lump in his throat for the first time since he was five, when he and Ralph had to bury their pup dog. Aunt El wasn't built like his ma, he noticed, as he listened to her chatter. She was tall and slim like Grandma Fischer, but he remembered his grandma having a haughty, distant look. Aunt El resembled his ma in the face. The goodness was there and beamed out at you. He felt welcome, tired and oh, so hungry. She read his thoughts, saying "My goodness, child, I'm glad I made that stew today. It will perk you up. When you get rested a bit and your uncle gets himself in here, you can eat till your belly pops out."

She asked about his ma and the children, all the time bustling about, setting the table, pulling biscuits out of the oven that looked exactly like his ma's and telling him she hoped he'd come to stay awhile. He felt warm and sleepy and had almost forgotten his troubles because of this woman, whom he hardly knew. He wondered, though, what Uncle Frank would say when he saw him. The thought brought him back to the mess he'd brought with him. Maybe his uncle wouldn't look too kindly at him. He felt nervous again as the door opened behind him and he turned to face his uncle. Lloyd stayed six months with his aunt and uncle. In all that time he never felt he wasn't welcome. No questions had been asked. He became their son in a sense, the son who would have been his age if he had lived. His aunt told him, very matter of factly, the boy had been sickly since birth and had slipped away in his sleep to God. She was a deeply religious woman. Lloyd helped as a son would, milk-

Doris P. Burke

ing the cows, throwing hay to them and the two horses. This left Frank to do some of the odd jobs he had put off for so long. Lloyd helped with the fence fixing and the harness mending and he learned about the farming he was too young to learn at his Grandpa Judd's. He spent Christmas there at his aunt and uncles. It was a little sad for him not to be home and have his ma hurrying to see that there was presents for everyone under the decorated pine tree. The thoughts were of home, but there was warmth and caring in this small farmhouse. A present from his uncle was found under the tree. Lloyd knew, as he examined the pearl-handled jackknife, he would cherish it forever. His aunt presented him with a knitted sweater that was warm and comfortable.

It was winter and the blowing snow enveloped the house, turning it into a virtual igloo. Plowing through the drifts of snow to the barn was a chore, but he and his uncle would don their warmest clothes, looking at each other and laughing at their bulky selves. Frank had the same speech every morning in those wintry months, saying, "Let's go, boy. God is testing our manhood today." It was peculiar, Lloyd thought, that the work or the snow never seemed of any consequence. He found himself reveling in the cold and the surroundings. By noon on any given day of the blustery long days of winter, work was completed and the afternoon was ahead of them to do with as they wished. Often Frank would place the Bible on the kitchen table and stand with his arms folded, as if waiting for his congregation or classroom to be seated. Aunt El gathered her pile of mending and relaxed in her favorite rocking chair, while Lloyd plunked himself on the floor in front of his uncle and waited. At first, Lloyd thought the reading from the Bible would be boring and senseless and he was quite indifferent. Instead, he found it to be most interesting. He listened intently to his uncle's voice telling his interpretation of the well-used Good Book. It was never the fire and brimstone voice of the preacher back in Rochester. It was a kindly voice believing in the goodness of people. Uncle Frank was a man who practiced what he preached. Lloyd learned of the Bible from listening and often in the privacy of his room at night, he would read for himself. He turned 16 in February. Somehow he felt he had grown in spirit and mind. He felt this in a humble way, knowing his aunt and uncle had given him a new outlook on the life ahead of him. He knew he had to go back and face what was there.

The snow finally began to melt and left clumps of dirty white here and there. The change in the weather made it possible for the three of them to bundle up and climb into the buggy. Every Sunday morning, they headed for the little wooden church down the road.

The Family

The congregation had built it with care and with the sweat of their brows. When the traveling preacher couldn't get there, Uncle Frank took his place at the altar and gave the sermon. Lloyd enjoyed seeing the neighbors, who greeted him with warmth and friendliness. He sang the hymns and prayed with them and wished he was worthy of their kindness. He was never asked when he was leaving, or why he had come. Spring was right around the corner and he knew he had to leave soon. He approached his uncle one morning as they were doing the milking. "I think I should be going home soon, Uncle Frank," he said. He set the pail of milk down and hung his head as his uncle turned to him. "You think it's time, boy?" his uncle asked. "I guess I'd better. There's a problem back there and it's time I faced my problems." His uncle put his hand on his shoulder. "You're a good boy, Lloyd, and the Lord will help you with your problem." Frank's face was somber, his eyes sad, as he watched Lloyd struggling to make the decision. He thought of how he and Ellie would miss this boy who had come to them and had brought them such joy. He had taken the place of their own child. He had no words to express how this boy had filled the void in their lives, but they had to let him go back to his own family and his troubles. Ellie would cry after he left, but she would smile and wish him well before he did.

Lloyd loved this man and the aunt, who gave him all the affection his own mother gave him. They were grand, wonderful people and he would miss them. "I'll be leavin' on the weekend, Uncle Frank," Lloyd said, picking up the pail of milk and walking toward the barn door." He had no idea what his old man would say when he showed up at home. He was liable to kick him out. Maybe he'd have to hop a freight train like Junior and Jake. He wandered toward the house, hesitant about telling his aunt of his decision. She was busy cleaning the less-than-dirty cupboards when he entered the kitchen. She asked when she saw him, "Why, are you through milking already, Lloyd? I swear, you can milk faster than anyone. You sure are a born farmer. Your Uncle Frank says that all the time." She chattered on, wiping the oilcloth-covered shelves and placing the sparkling clean glasses and cups back in place. He knew as he watched her he wasn't going to tell her. He'd let his uncle do that. Friday morning came in warm sunshine and Lloyd and his uncle started out the door of the kitchen to do the morning milking, both welcoming the brightness of the day to come. They heard the sound of an automobile grinding its way down the driveway. This startled Lloyd and he took a step backwards into the kitchen. He hoped it wasn't who he thought it might be. He saw his uncle raise his hand

Doris P. Burke

in greeting as the automobile came in view. He could see it was his pa and Ralph. "Ralph the traitor" ran through his mind, but he stepped out to face them for the first time in six months. His pa seemed to pay no attention to him and proceeded to shake hands with Uncle Frank, while Ralph jumped from the car and stood in front of him. The same grin was there that Lloyd remembered so well. "Hey brother," Ralph said, excitement in his every move. "Boy, have I got news for you."

He followed Lloyd toward the barn, ignoring his brother's frown. "Jesus, Ralph, I told you not to tell the old man where I was. Do you want to see me get my ass kicked right here in front of Aunt El and Uncle Frank?" He opened the barn door and turned to look at his brother, waiting for an explanation. "You ain't gonna believe what happened, Lloyd," Ralph said. "I'll tell ya. Listen, it's the only reason I told the old man where you was." "And what would that be," Lloyd said. "It better be good, or I might have to break your neck!" Lloyd moved into the barn and grabbed the milking stool and positioned himself beside the restless cow. Ralph was still grinning, knowing his brother was about the explode. He started talking fast. "Ole Sally Mae came up to the house the next morning after you left. Had her pa with her and he was madder than a wet hen, Ma said. He wanted to know where ya was and Ma told him she didn't know. Ma had been bawling and didn't want to talk, so she slammed the door in his face." Ralph took a deep breath and hurried on with his news. "Well, the old man found out what was goin' on down at the bar. Made him so damn mad that the little whore - he called her that - had accused you. All the men down at the bar knew about her. Guess the only one that didn't know was her pa. Anyway, Pa waited at Whipple's for Sally's pa to come find him." Ralph was getting more excited all the time. Now he was pacing back and forth by the cow.

"And, Old Man Pinkerton came to the bar and you'll never believe what happened, Lloyd. He started to tell Pa about how you violated his precious daughter and now she was gonna have a baby. Well, Pa listened for a minute," Ralph took another breath and grinned so big it spread clear across his face. "Mr. Swayze was tellin' me about this. He said Pa grabbed Pinkerton by the shirtfront, lifted him up and threw him right out the door of the bar. He yelled at him to tend to his little whore of a girl and don't be comin' round and accusin' none of his boys. "Well, the next day, the fellas at the bar looked out the window and old Pinkerton was adraggin' Sally Mae by the arm, right down to the doctor's office. It didn't take long for everybody in town to hear that Sally Mae wasn't havin' no

The Family

baby. She made it all up. Her pa moved them right outta town. They ain't there no more, Lloyd. That's why I told the old man where ya was. He wants you to come home and so does Ma. Poor Ma, she bawls when she peels the potatoes." He stopped talking and waited for his brother's reaction to his great news. Lloyd held his head down and watched the white milk squirt into the pail. He felt so damned relieved, he couldn't think of anything to say. He lifted one udder and squeezed it hard, sending warm milk right up into Ralph's eye. They both laughed, Ralph wiping his face with the sleeve of his coat. "The old man said to let ya stay here at Uncle Frank's," Ralph said. "He told Ma it would do ya good to learn some farmin'. That's why we haven't showed up till now. Ya gotta come home now, Lloyd. Jesus, I've missed ya! We gotta get to practicin' our ball playin'. I've been working on my curve ball, but I need ya to catch it for me. Go get your damn clothes and we'll get outta here. Ma will quit bawlin' if ya get home where ya belong."

They headed home. Lloyd and Ralph bounced around in the backseat of the chugging automobile. Lloyd was trying to forget the face of Aunt El as she came toward him to say goodbye. It was a forced smile she gave him - he could tell by the quiver of her chin - but the good wishes shown in her eyes and the love was in the hug she gave him. Uncle Frank had shaken his hand and whispered, "Remember, boy, God will be with you. You have the heart of a saint." Bill talked a steady stream all the way back to Rochester, never mentioning the Pinkertons. He went on and on about Lloyd finding a new job, his voice becoming harsh at times as he took swigs from the whiskey bottle he carried with him. The boys sat in the back seat staring at their Pa's new fedora and listening to him telling them, "Gotta work, be men. Work never hurt nobody." They wanted to laugh. They had heard this so many times from this man who didn't do a damn thing, only pretended he was helping their ma at the boarding house. Ralph was so glad to have his brother coming home again, he didn't care about the shit his pa was telling. They would get back to their ball playing, so they could be the best. After all, they were Judds. They were supposed to be the greatest, the strongest and the best.

Doris P. Burke

Chapter Thirteen

In 1917, to the United States the war in Europe was no longer just a bad situation far away. It became very much a reality when, on April 6, the U.S. declared war on Germany. America changed from a leisurely, calm country to one running at a feverish pace to win this war it was thrown into. The country was unprepared and hurriedly adopted a selective service act, requiring all men between the ages of 21 and 30 to register for the draft. Recruiting posters appeared everywhere, with a picture of Uncle Sam announcing, "I want you." Soldiers and civilians alike sang George M. Cohan's "Over There" to let the world know the Yanks were coming and the enemy beware. Ships and planes were built fast and furious. People were urged to save food and "meatless" days were promoted. Gas was rationed to civilians. The good times were shut down until the enemy was defeated. The Americans rose up together as a nation. Rochester became quiet, as more of its young men enlisted to fight for their country. The merchants on Main Street complained of a bit of slow business, but not many people thought of new hats or suits when their sons were fighting in a foreign land. It became a subdued town with whispers and fears of a loved one losing his life and the sadness of it happening becoming real. There was a show of patriotism and for most, it was there at its best. And so, for a year, the war raged on.

Life went on at the Judd boarding house. Men came and went, but there were always more men stopping to stay for a week or a month and there were those who stayed for years. Lula kept busy and had become resigned to the fact her Bill would never be any different. She was glad the boys had grown to be men and no longer had to be intimidated by their pa. The girls were becoming young ladies and the prettiness was there - Lady with light skin and green eyes, Myrtle with the dark curls surrounding her face. Lula was proud of her good-looking family and doted on them, knowing they could do no wrong. Lloyd and Ralph, in 1917, talked of joining the army constantly, but knew their ma wouldn't lie for them about their age. It was frustrating for them to watch the older boys they were acquainted with go off to war. They had to be content to stay on their jobs and read of the war in the daily paper. They both had hired in on the railroad crews. The work was sweaty and a test of strength, leaving them dead tired at night. They pushed them-

The Family

selves to practice their ball playing and they did. The dream of being a major leaguer had never left. Lloyd was still helping Herbie with his reading when he could, lending him books and feeling happy to see the calming effect it had on him. He would listen patiently as Herbie would stutter out the knowledge he had found in a book. Cora felt Lloyd had brought a miracle to her handicapped son and she became more alert, losing some of the desperate look in her eyes.

Herbie had learned about Tom Sawyer and Huck Finn and all the adventures they experienced. They were his favorite and he did so wish he could live in their world of rafting on the river, of Injun Joe and of pirates. How he would like to meet a real pirate. He felt brave now. After all he had read of their experiences, he knew something of the world, but he needed to explore. He wished he could walk better - darn his legs going this way and that. His balance was poor, but he knew he could get to Miller Pond if he tried real hard. Lloyd had told him about the swimming and fish there. He knew the way, he'd go on the day his ma went to the boarding house to do the ironing. He wouldn't even tell Lloyd of his plan. He would tell him after he explored by himself. This excited him. His ma, afraid he would get lost or hurt, would never let him go alone anywhere. He was a man now, as old as his best friend Lloyd. It was time. Friday morning came, the day his ma did the ironing. He let her help him eat breakfast. He had a heckuva time finding his mouth. Most often it frustrated him, but this morning, he felt good. It was going to be an exciting day. He watched his ma gather some clothes she would wash in Mrs. Judd's washing machine. He was ready, had even made a hook outta the end of a coat hanger. He hid this in his hat. It wouldn't be long now. He was going to have a day to remember, an experience he could tell Lloyd about. Maybe he'd write a story and surprise Lloyd. He grabbed his pencil and a piece of paper lying by the chair. He wished he could print better, but his hand shook so much. He started way up at the top of the paper, because he knew his hand would jiggle its way down. He printed: "To Lloyd, my best friend, my excitin' experenc'." He covered this up with his hand as his ma laid the book he had been reading next to him. She squeezed his hand and told him she'd be back in the afternoon. His head shook as she smiled at her and then she was gone out the door.

Cora was late getting back to the little shack that afternoon and she worried about Herbie not getting his dinner. The ironing had been long and tedious, so many shirts for the boarders and the hanging out the washing had taken forever. Lula had sent roast beef and

Doris P. Burke

potatoes home with her for supper. It would taste good, and later she would please Herbie with the sweet apple dumpling Lula had insisted she take. Cora had felt better lately. She liked to see Herbie reading and telling her of the stories. It had become a new life for her and her son. Lula paid her for the help with the washing and ironing and now she was able to buy a few pleasures. It felt satisfying to walk in the food store with money in her pocketbook. For so many years, she had relied on the kindness of neighbors like Lula and the farmers, who dropped off wood, eggs and side pork. She was proud to be able to take care of her poor boy, whom she loved as much as any mother with a perfect child. Now, she pushed the door open, wanting to surprise Herbie with the delicious supper she had brought. He wasn't in his chair by the window. She glanced around the room. A chill ran through her. He wasn't there. His bed against the wall was empty. The book he had been reading lay on the stand unopened. She started to whimper. Where could he have gone? He never went alone, he couldn't. She suddenly thought of Lloyd. Maybe he had taken him for a walk, but then he wouldn't do that without telling her. She went outside to look around the shack. It was still light out, being early summer. She didn't find a sign of him anywhere. Her heart beat against her chest so hard she felt faint. She ran as fast as she could to the boarding house. She'd have to find Lloyd; he'd know what to do. She burst through the door, scaring Lula, who stood at the sink washing dishes. "Where's Lloyd? Cora screamed as Lula stared at her.

"He's down at the house reading. Cora, what's the matter?" Lula asked, standing in front of the hysterical woman and grabbing her shoulders. "Herbie is gone," Cora sobbed. "Lloyd will have to help me find him." "Sit down, Cora. I'll call the boys, they'll find him," Lula said, trying to comfort the woman. She found the boys and they listened to Cora tell of the missing Herbie. Lloyd felt frightened too. He knew Herbie had never been on his own before. Someone always helped him get to the ball game - usually Joe and Jase, who let him ride on the wagon they brought into town, knowing he liked the bouncy ride and the trotting horses. Lloyd and Ralph left the frightened Cora with their ma and hurried outside into the quiet evening, not knowing where to being looking. "Where in hell do you think the stumble-butt has gone to?" Ralph asked as they stood studying the surrounding area. "How would I know? But let's get to lookin'," Lloyd answered. "You head toward downtown, ask people if they've seen him. I'm gonna head out toward where we used to play ball." The sun was going down, leaving shadows on the road as Lloyd walked along fast, checking every

The Family

tree and ditch to see if Herbie had fallen and might be lying there. He was coming to Miller Pond. He stopped, remembering about how Herbie had stuttered out about going fishing and how much he'd like to do that.

"Jesus, I hope he didn't come out here alone," Lloyd muttered, thinking of the high bank all around the pond. He felt fear run through his body and he ran as fast as he could toward the pond. He reached the bank of the pond and he stood scanning the sandy area at the edge of the water. He saw him. He felt a stab of pain at his heart. A crumbled body lay just beneath him down the high bank. He knew Herbie was dead before he slid through the sand to reach him. Ralph, his pa and Mr. Swayze came to the pond and saw the scene below them. Lloyd sat holding Herbie's body, rocking it back and forth. They could hear the distressful moaning from Lloyd. It was the first time Ralph couldn't think of a thing to say to his brother as they carried Herbie to the car. They all knew the fondness Lloyd had felt for the boy and they rode silently on the way back to town. The doctor examined him at the funeral parlor and it was determined Herbie had died of a brain hemorrhage almost immediately upon falling. It was a sad finding to realize Herbie had only wanted his time alone to prove to everyone he could be independent for a day. The funeral parlor was filled to capacity the day he was to be buried. Bill had driven out to Frank's at Lloyd's request to ask him to do the service. Frank and Ellie both came. Frank stood by the casket, looking out at the sea of faces in front of him and he spoke, "This boy, or I should say, this man has reached the most wonderful place, there in heaven, where he will be whole again. If I close my eyes, I can almost see him running to the Lord and thanking him for letting him come to this beautiful place. He is now free of pain and of his burden." Frank's gentle voice seemed to bring comfort to everyone there, especially Cora. She lifted her head, letting the tears of grief flow freely down her face. But then a smile appeared as she pictured her Herbie running through green pastures for the first time.

It brought comfort to Lloyd to watch Cora become transfixed with his uncle's sermon as well as the rest of those attending the service. He looked around at the farmers and their wives, who had given kindness to Herbie and Cora when they were in need. He didn't know why God had called Herbie to him, but there must have been a reason. It was an enlightening day for those who had known and liked Herbie. There was a loss, yes, but Frank in his wisdom gave everyone a hope of a life hereafter that would be glorious. They filed from the funeral parlor, the young and the old,

Doris P. Burke

with a little brighter light in their eyes. It was a sermon to be proud of, and again Lloyd was indebted to the uncle who had given him courage to face his problems. Lula put on a lunch at the boarding house after Herbie was put to rest. Even Bill attended, greeting the people and acting like the husband she had wished for. He had a glazed look in his eyes and Lula was sure he had been baffled by Frank's sermon. She noticed later he made a quick exit out the back door - she figured to his bottle, wherever he had it stashed. She knew her Bill couldn't comprehend talk of the Lord and she did feel sorry for him. The Judds had never stepped foot in church and she wondered if they ever would.

The Family

Chapter Fourteen

In 1918, while the war in Europe was still raging on, Walter Judd showed up at the door of the boarding house with a grin on his face and a line of bullshit that charmed even Lula. Walter was the son of Old Man Judd's older brother Wilton. His first words to Lula were, "Pa said to look up his favorite brother's boy, the one with the pretty little wife, and I do say, Aunt Lula, you are just as pretty as they said." Lula blushed, wiped her hands on her apron, pushed some stray hair back into her bun and invited the grinning face into the kitchen. When Lloyd and Ralph walked in that evening, Walt was sitting at the table devouring a piece of their ma's hot apple pie. They stopped talking when they saw this tall fella with a lean, tanned face and a crop of sun-bleached hair. Walt, his mouth full of pie, blurted out, "Howdy cousins. Your mama said you'd be comin' right along." He jumped up to pump their hands, squeezing them so tight they both were glad when he let go. He had come to get a job on the railroad, he told Bill that night.

"Don't like that there farmin', Uncle Bill," he said. "Why, by golly, Pa worked us so hard the bottom of my feet has darn near worn right off. Why, if I'd stayed on that farm much longer, I'd be just awalkin' on my bones." This made Bill laugh right out loud at the look on the boy's face. He thought he resembled a cat that swallowed a canary. And so, Walt came to live at the boarding house. Lula fixed a room off the kitchen she had used for storing her flour, sugar and other supplies, saying, "Goodness gracious, there's lotsa room for these things under the cupboards." It took her and Wanda three days to make room in the cupboards, but everyone liked Walt, even Wanda. She liked his big grin and the flirty looks he gave her when no one was watching. Life at the boarding house was never the same after Walt arrived. He was full of fun, a storyteller, a joker and as lovable as a cub bear. Lloyd and Ralph took to him like a long-lost brother, including him in their ball practice, finding out he could hit and catch a ball like a Judd. He found a job on the railroad, working side by side with Lloyd. They talked of girls and new clothes they would buy when they went to Detroit to see Ty Cobb play. On November 11, 1918, the war in Europe came to an end and on that same day Onalee La Preze walked into the heart of Lloyd. The celebration of the armistice went on in full force on the streets of Rochester. Everybody hugged everybody. Lloyd, Ralph

Doris P. Burke

and Walt took advantage of this by grabbing each pretty girl passing them as they stood in front of the hardware. It was a relief. Knowing the Americans had won the war and the boys would come marching home where they belonged brought excitement felt by all. Two girls came toward them. They were laughing, both seeming to enjoy the celebration going on around them. Walt grabbed at the dark-haired girl. She backed up, still laughing, but she shook her head, telling Walt. "No, we don't know you, sir." "Well, you soon will, darlin'," he answered and tried again to put his arm around her. "Leave her alone, Walt," Lloyd cautioned him.

The girl glanced at him as if to thank him. It went through Lloyd's mind that he had never seen anyone so pretty. She had a round face with pink cheeks on porcelain skin, her hair was dark and glossy. She had a slim body with delicate hands. He stared at her. She seemed embarrassed and she lowered her eyes. Ralph broke the spell by blurting out, "Where you girls from?" His eyes were going to the other girl, who was flirting with him, giggling with her hand over her mouth while she fluttered her eyelashes. "We've just gotten here, we're going to work at the cotton mill," she answered, after moving her hand from her mouth. "Well, that's swell. Could we show you girls around?" Ralph asked. There was nothing like new girls in town for him. They were a challenge. He smiled his best, the one that most girls thought was the cutest they'd ever seen. He waited for the girl to answer, already deciding this little filly would be the object of his attention for the evening. She wasn't pretty like her friend, but that was all right. He had found out the homely ones gave their all just for attention. He didn't care if she was knock kneed and pigeon toed. He might take her down to the livery station. He had a key, the one Mr. Swayze had given Lloyd when he worked there. A romp in the hay would be good and he liked the smell of the stable. And so he kept smiling and she kept giggling and soon he had her by the arm, and walked her slowly down the street through the clamoring crowd. He might have to buy her an ice cream cone, but that didn't cost much. Then, maybe she'd be ready to gallop and he'd sure be ready to ride.

Walt had a chubby, red-cheeked girl cornered up against the hardware building and was telling her stories of his great strength, flexing his muscles and grinning all the time. She was responding by feeling his arm and saying, "Wow!" This left Lloyd alone with the pretty girl, who made him feel all tongue-tied. He had never felt this way in his life. He could always come up with a line of bullshit, like Ralph and Walt could, but all he could see was this sweet girl in middy blouse and dark skirt, who seemed out of place in the

The Family

confusing surroundings. He wanted to tell her this. He wanted to take her by the hand to some quiet place and just look into her eyes and ask her if she would be his forever. She kept her head down, but he looked close at her face and was relieved to see a touch of a smile there. He finally found his voice and spoke quietly, afraid to make her feel uncomfortable. "So, you and your friend are going to work at the cotton mill," he said. She nodded, " Yes, we just arrived a week ago from Mesick. We heard there were jobs here." Her voice was beautiful, he thought, everything about her was beautiful. He wished Walt would take his plump girl and disappear into the crowd, so he could be alone with this dream of a girl. She spoke again, "We found a room at Mrs. James' house. I wish Mandy wouldn't have left. They lock the door at eleven." She appeared distressed and she stared at him for some reassurance. "It's only nine-thirty." He pulled out his pocket watch and showed her the time. "That was my brother she went with. I'm sure that he'll see that she gets back to your room in time."

He wasn't so sure that Ralph would be so cooperative, but he wouldn't tell her that. He hoped his brother wouldn't be a horse's ass. "My name is Lloyd Judd," he hurriedly said. He wanted to tell her all about himself and he wanted to know everything about her from the time she was born. He had never felt this way before. He offered to walk her back to Mrs. James' rooming house. He wanted to protect her from the rowdy young smart guys he knew would be roaming around. He felt like he wanted to protect her always. She shyly agreed. In fact, she was glad he offered. The new surroundings made her a bit nervous and this man seemed so sincere. His eyes had a humble look and this pleased her. He placed his hand on her arm and guided her through the excited groups, who yelled and hooted remarks to him. He knew right where Mrs. James' house was and he was glad this was where the girl was staying. Mrs. James was regarded as strict but kind to her roomers. As they approached the street where the rooming house was located, it became quiet. The throngs of people were all on the downtown streets. He suddenly realized he didn't know the name of this pretty girl and he wondered if she would tell him or was he just a safe escort home for her. He'd have to ask her. He wanted to see her again. God knows, he wanted to see her again! She felt all warm inside with Lloyd's hand on her arm and so comfortable as she strolled beside him. He was nice-looking, so tall and dark, with a shock of hair over his forehead, and such a gentleman. He wasn't like any of the boys she had known back in Mesick. They were silly and overbearing. She didn't know how she knew, but she was sure he would

Doris P. Burke

never hurt her in any way.

She peeked over at him. The moonlight shone on his face, a good face, she decided. Feeling very content, she pulled her jacket close around her body. It was a nice night to be 18 and alive. She was so glad she had come to Rochester. Lloyd was thinking the same thing. It was great to be young and alive as he strolled along beside this girl, who made him feel so good. God, how Ralph and Walt would laugh if he mentioned he had fallen in love at first sight. He wouldn't tell them, he knew that. The assholes would have a fit, especially Ralph. He'd say, "Gonna be a lot of women, brother, when we get to the major leagues. We can have 'em all." He shook his head, trying to shake the thoughts away. He realized they were standing in front of the rooming house and she was looking at him. She spoke: "Thank you so much for walking me here." She turned to walk up the path to the house. He couldn't let her go like this. He spoke fast, "What is your name? I'd like to see you again, if you would allow me." She slowly turned toward him. She tried not to seem pleased, that wouldn't be ladylike. Her mother had always said, "If they want to come courtin', don't make it easy. A lady is as a lady does." She thought her mother old fashioned in a lot of ways and now she had met this very nice man and her mother's words didn't seem important, to say the least. She wanted to see him again, lady or not. She knew nothing about him - where he worked or where he lived, where anything - but what did it matter? His eyes told her he was an honest man. She replied, " My name is Onalee La Preze and I work until five o'clock every day. I will be here after that."

He let out a sigh of relief. "I'll be here tomorrow evening, Onalee." He turned and headed back downtown. He wanted to jump in the air for joy or yell to the heavens. Instead, he just kept smiling as he pushed his way back through the crowds to where Walt stood. Walt had a flock of girls lined up. Each came forward to feel his muscles and then he'd give them a big kiss on the cheek. Lloyd stood watching, laughing right out loud at his cousin's line of shit he was giving the girls. He saw Ralph pushing his way toward them with a disgusted scowl on his face. He yelled, "Jesus, what a cookie that was! You'll never believe what happened." He stood in front of Lloyd frowning. "Why the dippy dame. I had her in the hay and she was gigglin' and rollin' round and the minute I started unbuttonin' my pants, she jumped up and screamed and ran out the damn door. I guess she thought we were gonna play hide-and-seek or some damn thing. Crazy dame!" Lloyd was thinking what this would do to his image, having a brother about to jump on this friend

The Family

of Onalee's. "Quit your belly-aching, Ralph, Jesus! Why didn't you take one of those girls Walt has got feelin' his muscles? There are nice girls around, ya know? Who don't wanna be attacked." Ralph was surprised to hear this coming from his brother. Any other time they would have had a good laugh, but now he was giving him hell for doing what they all tried on any one of the girls, who were fair game.

Lloyd felt frustrated. He hoped Onalee wouldn't think he was some kind of animal. Of course, he had been, just like Ralph. He didn't know why he was feeling so protective of this girl he hardly knew. It was strange and he could still see her face. Her lovely face. That had sent him on his heady feeling. Love. What the hell was that? He'd never loved anybody, only family and Uncle Frank and Aunt El, but that was different. He wished them all the best - that was the feeling. This was different. This girl he wanted to hold tight in his arms, take her away from all people, wanted her to be his forever. He'd work his ass off for her. Ralph was staring at him and asked, " You sick, brother? Maybe you should go home and climb in bed. You look funny." Ralph didn't wait for an answer. He had his eye on one of Walt's harem. He decided he'd try again.

Doris P. Burke

Chapter Fifteen

It wasn't easy to court Onalee. Lloyd found that out in a hurry. Obstacles were everywhere. She was hesitant at first, after Ralph's attempt to seduce her friend, but she soon realized Mandy should have known better than to get herself in such a situation. She was thrilled to have Lloyd show up at Mrs. James' to see her, with his hair all combed neatly and wearing a freshly laundered shirt and with such a charming smile on his face. The kidding he was taking from Ralph and Walt was getting on his nerves. It came mostly from Ralph, who couldn't believe he was so smitten with this dark-haired girl. He even tried to talk him out of it by saying, "Jesus, Lloyd, we got ball playin' to do, places to see. What the hell, there's a million girls with dark hair and big eyes. Get her in the sack and forget her." He wanted to hit Ralph in his big mouth, but he didn't. After all, he used to talk just like that. The more he saw of her, the more he wanted to. She wasn't unnoticed by other guys in town and this was threatening to him. It was especially the tough guys who were comin' in from nearby towns who had their eyes on her. He found out she was being harassed every time she and Mandy strolled downtown. This bothered him and he knew it had to be dealt with. The biggest offender was Jake Farrand, who thought he could get any girl he wanted. He was tall, good looking and could charm the bloomers off most of the girls. Well, not his girl, Lloyd decided, looking into the shaving mirror one evening. He about cut his Adam's apple open thinking about it.

He finished his shaving and grabbed a clean shirt out of his drawer. He started to sing, "Girl of My Dreams," as Walt waltzed into the room, saying, "Ya don't sing good, cousin, but ya sing loud!" Lloyd laughed and finished buttoning his shirt while Walt lay down on his back on the bed and stretched his long legs the length of it. Lloyd knew something was coming and he waited. "Heard somethin' ya might wanna know," Walt said, and then yawned, knowing full well Lloyd was gonna listen attentively. "Spit it out, Walt," he said, walking to the mirror again to comb his hair. "Well, heard Jake Farrand and his bunch of tough friends are gonna grab Onalee right away from you Saturday night." Lloyd turned toward Walt and scowled, "Where ta hell did ya hear that?" "Jase Brown was tellin' me the other night downtown. Said one of Jake's friends was laughin' 'bout it, didn't know Jase was a friend of yours.

The Family

Sounds like there's goin' to be hell to pay, cousin. We gotta think of a plan ta make those smart assholes laugh out of the other side of their soon-to-be-battered-up mouths." "You're not serious, are ya Walt?" Lloyd stood over him peering down into his face, hoping this was a joke he and Ralph had cooked up. "Hell yes! I'm serious! Jase said they were after you and were gonna grab Onalee right out from under your nose. That Jake, he's a bad one. Jase says he's raped girls before, beat 'em up. We gotta get him good, gotta have a plan." After his long speech, Walt closed his eyes. Lloyd yelled at him, "For Christ's sake! I know what the plan is gonna be. I'm gonna kick the shit outta him."

Lloyd could feel his heart starting to pump fast with the thought of Jake even touching Onalee. "I know how you feel, Lloyd, but we gotta keep him away from even seeing Onalee," Walt opened his eyes and grinned. "I got a plan all figgered out. You just gotta keep your wits about ya. Don't go bustin' out lookin' for the horse's ass. He's gonna come to us." With that, he closed his eyes again and waited for Lloyd to ask him what the plan was, and he knew he would. "What the hell is your plan?" Lloyd was about to burst and he paced around the room, wanting to hit something. "Just sit down and calm yourself, cousin. First we gotta get Ralph, Joe and Jase and some more of your friends in on the plan." "This is my problem, Walt. Ain't nobody else's," Lloyd ran his hand through his hair and shook his head. "Don't want you guys to get involved." Walt sat on the edge of the bed, staring up at Lloyd. He had a serious look on his face that was very seldom there. "It IS our problem. We don't beat up on women. If they aren't agreeable to our advances, then we walk away. This asshole has gotta be kicked out of town or the girls here will never be safe. And we gotta see that it gets done. So, this is our plan." They talked for an hour. Lloyd even laughed a little upon hearing what Walt had up his sleeve and he finally agreed it might work. It was Thursday evening and he had to hurry over to see Onalee to tell her what would be happening on Saturday night. Walt stood at the doorway ready to leave.

"Me and Ralph will take care of all the particulars. You just fill your little lady on it and be ready Saturday night for the fireworks to begin. By the way, how big are the Simpson fellas?" Lloyd grinned thinking about his friends, the Simpson farmers. "The smallest one is Calvin. I'd say he was six-four. The other three look like giants. Muscles, they got! Tell Ralph to ask them if they're in good shape, that'll make them laugh." Walt felt excitement in his every movement. Lloyd grabbed his jacket and hoofed it fast toward Onalee's place. There was gonna be a hot time in the old town Saturday

Doris P. Burke

night! It snowed Saturday morning, a light, wet snow, leaving the streets slushy and slippery. It wasn't the best day to be down at the ball field. Ralph slung pitches to Lloyd while Walt watched from the bleachers. There were rumors going around town from everyone in downtown Rochester that the Judd men were up to something, but no one knew exactly what. Anticipation seemed to fill the brisk cool air. Soon there were others sitting on the bleachers watching the pair throw the ball back and forth. Walt heard the whispers behind him and around him. It made him grin even more. By late afternoon, the three made their departure and the crowd watched them leave, still wondering what was going to happen. After a satisfying supper at the boarding house, they hurried down to Lloyd and Ralph's room, where the plan was about to be put in motion. "The guys all ready, Ralph?" Walt asked, carrying a brown paper bag into the room and setting it on the floor. "As ready as rain," Ralph answered, sitting down in a chair and pushing it back against the wall. He wanted a good seat to watch his cousin in action.

Lloyd lounged by the door. He, too, watched as Walt pulled a black skirt out of the bag and started to pull his pants down. "Borrowed these things from Wanda, said she wouldn't tell Aunt Lula nothin'. Besides, I told her I'd tickle her fancy sometime," Walt chuckled, and then pulled his long underwear off and stood naked. "You guys are starin', cuz ya never saw a body like this in your life, have ya?" Ralph's chair came down with a bang. He laughed until his sides hurt and finally manged to blurt out, "You ain't no Greek god, Walt, but ya got quite a hammer there!" They all had a good laugh while Walt pulled long black stockings on, twisting them around the calf of his leg. He covered the lower half with the full black skirt that came just below his stocking tops. With a flourish, he put on a bright red wool sweater. He then stood before them. "Whatcha gonna wear on your head?" Ralph asked, trying to keep his face straight. "Why, this here pretty babushka, belonging to Lloyd's beloved Onalee." He tied the scarf under his chin and smirked, "I'm almost ready, men. Let me get my galoshes on." Lloyd was like Ralph: He could hardly keep his face straight and he couldn't help but say, "You're the ugliest damn woman I've ever seen! Be sure and keep your head down or you ain't gonna fool nobody." "Don't give a hoot what you guys think of me, just be sure and keep your hand off my knee, cousin, while we're waitin' for big Jake to show up. Hand me my coat, fellas, we got a battle to fight. Hope I don't tear up Wanda's stockings."

It was a cold dark night and Lloyd and Walt slipped quietly

The Family

through the streets, ducking behind trees when a car came chugging by. They didn't want anybody to see them until they got themselves seated on the bleachers. This was where Lloyd and Onalee spent most of their evenings and the biggest share of the town people knew this, including Jake and his buddies, who often cruised by shouting insults at Lloyd. Dark was good, Lloyd figured. No one could tell it wasn't Onalee unless they got up close. When they did get up close enough the surprise would be in the person of Walt. They weren't seated long, Walt hunching toward Lloyd, when a car came slowly toward the ball field. They couldn't see who was driving until it stopped in front of the bleachers. A whisper came from Walt, "I think the enemy is about to attack, sweetheart. Wait till ya see the assholes' eyes." Six of them came out of the car in a hurry, shouting and yelling and throwing beer bottles every which way. They ran fast toward Lloyd and Walt, Jake leading the pack. Lloyd and Walt waited until they were almost on top of them before Lloyd stood up. Jake shouted, "Gonna beat your ass, Judd, and your girl is comin' with us." "Over my dead body," Lloyd replied. He got a good swing at Jake and it rocked him back three steps. Meanwhile, Walt was on his feet, startling the shit out of the other five, who stopped in their tracks. "Come on fellas, you're used to hittin' women. Take a swing at this one," Walt encouraged and then waited until the shock wore off. Then he stepped off the bleachers and knocked down the one he was closest to. The others rushed toward him just as Ralph, the Simpsons, Joe and Jase appeared from behind the bleachers. Jake Farrand and his friends stopped again, seeing the size of the Simpson brothers.

One of them hollered, "We ain't got no quarrel with you guys!" The Simpsons had the other four cornered and proceeded to knock their heads together, Calvin saying, "Thought there was gonna be men here tonight, Lloyd. These are a bunch of pantywaists." Lloyd was on top of Jake, pounding his fist into his face, when Joe and Jase pulled him off, advising, "Don't kill him, Lloyd, he's got to drive and his buddies to hell outta here." Jake staggered to his feet and along with his bruised and dazed friends tried to hurry to the car. Walt yelled to them, "Ya get back to your own town and don't come creepin' round here no more or next time ya won't be able to crawl back. Do ya hear me, ya bunch of bullshit?" The tires squealed as the car headed toward the road going out of town. Walt sniffed and wiped his coat sleeve across his nose and then said, "Jesus, I think that guy got a swing in. I gotta bloody nose and I think I ruined Wanda's stockings."

Doris P. Burke

Chapter Sixteen

After the war ended, Rochester became a bustling town again. Lloyd continued to court Onalee and everyone knew the inevitable would happen. Lula wasn't happy about the situation. Her boys were the light of her life and she felt protective of them. Another woman was an interference she hadn't foreseen. Ralph wasn't happy, either. The brother he depended on to lead them to the major leagues didn't need a wife, she'd be in the way. He found himself frowning at her when Lloyd brought her to the boarding house or to their home. He talked about it to Walt one day. "Christ, Walt," he said, "She's gonna ruin everything. The next thing ya know, they'll have a raft of snotty-nosed kids. He'll be hobbled and tied like a goddamned steer. Where ta hell does that leave me? I gotta pitch, ya know I gotta pitch. It's my life!" Walt tried to tell his cousin the way he saw it, "Lookie here, cousin, it's like this. That there love is a funny durn thing between a man and a woman. Ya can go out there and have whoopie with a hundred gals, don't mean squat. Then along comes this one little filly. Some durn thing happens to your thinkin'. Ya just wanna pick her up and carry her off and keep her all to yourself. Ya don't care 'bout nothin', only this little gal." He was lying on Ralph's bed looking at the ceiling, while Ralph threw his ball up and down. "How do you know all this shit?" Ralph asked, turning to peer at his cousin with a disgusted look on his face.

"Don't know how I know, I just do," Walt answered. He didn't turn his head toward Ralph, just kept staring at the ceiling. "Why, you asshole, you been sneakin' over there to Oxford, haven't ya?" Ralph snorted, staring down at his cousin. "Somebody told me you had a dame over there you been sparkin'. What the hell's the matter with you love-sick fools? If that's all ya want out of life is raisin' kids and one damn woman, well I sure feel sorry for ya." With that, he turned and left the bedroom, leaving Walt still staring at the ceiling. And so, in August of 1919, Lloyd married Onalee and in September, Walt married Caroline, his girl from Oxford. Ralph was Lloyd's best man and did go to Walt's wedding, under protest. He felt betrayed by his brother and his favorite cousin. He hated the silly look they both had on their faces when they glanced at their brides. He muttered to himself often, while he shaved or anytime, saying, " The assholes are gonna be sorry. What the hell would

The Family

anybody wanna get married for? Screw 'em and leave 'em, that's what ya do. No bitch is gonna get a hook in me." He knew life would never be the same for him and his brother. The brother he had known was no more. As far as he could see, Lloyd had thrown away his chance for the good life in the major leagues. Well, wine, women and song sounded good to him. That was his goal. He was gonna be a major league pitcher. He'd be the greatest, the strongest and the best.

Doris P. Burke

Chapter Seventeen

By 1922, Lloyd and Onalee had two children and Ralph had been picked up by Port Huron to pitch baseball. Walt had moved to Oxford and he and Caroline had one boy. Lula and Bill still ran the boarding house and with them lived Lloyd and his family. Things were not all hunky dory, though. Lloyd still worked for the railroad and Onalee helped at the boarding house. It was not a perfect situation as far as Onalee was concerned. She knew Lula resented her and she never let her forget she was an intruder in their lives. Lula had never had competition for her son's affection and now it was here in the person of this pretty girl, who could barely boil water, let alone cook a substantial meal. As time went by, things became extremely worse, until Onalee gave the ultimatum to Lloyd. Her eyes flashing, she spoke low but firmly, "We have to take our family and move, Lloyd. Your mother has pushed me to the limit. She never lets me forget you're her son. My God, she won't even show me how to make gravy because she doesn't want me to make it as good as she does. And the children. She tries to take over there, too." By the time Onalee was through talking, tears were rolling down her face. The new baby, Lloyd Keith, started to cry and she hurried to the bedroom to pick him up, leaving Lloyd to sort over what could be done. He knew his mother resented Onalee. That was obvious. But he thought things would get better.

A month later, Lloyd and his family left the boarding house with bag and baggage in hand. They left, not unlike Lula and Bill had, when they decided to go off on their own from the farm in Perrysburg. Lula cried as she watched the old car Lloyd had managed to buy slowly creep its way down the road from the boarding house. Now both her boys were gone, leaving him with Bill, who kept the booze pouring into his gullet, leaving his senseless most of the time. As she wiped her face with the bottom of her apron, she thought of Old Bill and she knew exactly how he felt when she and Bill had left. She knew she had been bossy and possessive, but she had meant no harm to the girl Lloyd had taken for a wife. Ralph and Lloyd had been there to help her cope with her unhappiness over Bill. She had resented the intrusion, but she did love those babies, Marge and Keith, and she would miss them so much. Lady and Myrtle would miss them, too. She watched until she no longer could see or hear the rattling car. She had dishes to do and bread to

The Family

make and the never-ending jobs ahead of her to keep the boarding house running. Bill didn't even know Lloyd was leaving. He would be angry, she knew. She hoped he'd be home that evening for supper. It had been three days since he had showed up. She could only hope he wouldn't be in too bad of shape. She felt tired and depressed. What would life be like now? The girls needed her. They were her responsibility. She lifted her face from her apron. She still had her girls. Life would go on. Ralph was making his way through the minor leagues from Port Huron to Toronto to Springfield, Massachusetts. He wasn't making big money, but he was saving some. He went to parties and speakeasies, drank right along with the other guys, and women took a shine to him. It wasn't a bad life and he was doing what he always wanted to do: playing ball.

His dream had become real and he gloried in it. He kept in touch with Lula, sending her letters, telling her of what was said by managers and owners. He wanted her to be proud of him. He missed her and the girls. He always asked about Lloyd and wanted his mother to send him his address. He sent postcards to the address she sent him, but never heard back. He felt bad about that. Sometimes he dwelled on the way it used to be with his big brother. Then he'd frown and think, it could have been different. Now, he was tied down with two kids and working his ass off trying to make a buck. Ralph even missed Walt, the tall drink of water, who could make you laugh just looking at him. What a life those two were living, nose to the grindstone. He heard from Lula that his Grandpa Judd had moved to Lapeer, had bought a smaller farm and that Grandma Judd was with him. He laughed to himself, thinking about how his uncles used to talk about Abigale. He wondered how Old Bill got rid of her. He was curious to find out about all the uncles and where everybody had gone to in the past years.

Doris P. Burke

Chapter Eighteen

It didn't take Lady long to leave the boarding house. When she reached eighteen, she high-tailed it for Detroit and got a job in a dress shop in the downtown area. Lula had cried again, seeing another one of her children leave. This didn't bother Lady. She wanted the excitement of the big city and to heck with her mother's warning about the hussies who roamed the streets and the gangsters who owned the streets. She told her sister Myrtle, "I'll make my way into something big and then you can come live with me." Lady was a striking girl, with golden hair, green eyes and slim figure — a happy, carefree, good-time gal. She wore clothes well and often modeled at the dress shop for the clothes-conscious women who frequented the store. She was liked by the owner, who was a baseball enthusiast and listened attentively to her stories of her brother's accomplishments in the leagues. Life was good for Lady, but she needed more. She wanted fun. She had to find fun and the place to find it, she figured, was at the speakeasies that were everywhere. She did find a girlfriend in Mabel Fricke, who lived at the rooming house where she did. A pretty girl with dark hair, worn in the new bobbed look, she was a bit chubby, but carried it well. She kept herself girdled up to the point where she gave the appearance of a stiff mannequin. She was a fun girl, like Lady, enjoying the big city and looking for good times with whomever came along. They were a lively pair when they ventured out.

Their fun had been limited, mostly to movie theaters where they watched Rudolph Valentino make advances at a fluttery-eyed female or Charlie Chaplin in his role of "The Tramp." This was sorta fun, but they wanted to see the inside of the talked-about speakeasies, where the illegal booze flowed like water, and the bootleggers, who were there to see that it did. That would be the ultimate in fun. Weldon Van Hughes was the owner of the dress shop where Lady worked. He was a well-dressed elderly gentleman, who had lost his wife in the influenza epidemic. Her death left him devastated for a period of time, but he managed to keep the shop running, even adding more and more exclusive garments to please the wealthy. He liked Lady from the time she entered the store. She was full of life and such a beauty, without conceit. He felt she didn't realize how much she had to offer. In fact, she was like a little girl in many ways, her green eyes flashing with enthusiasm and excite-

The Family

ment at every new experience she encountered. He liked her, to say the least. Although he was old enough to be her father, he didn't feel fatherly toward her. He thought she was like a flower, not yet at its full bloom, but the expectation of great beauty was there. Weldie, as Lady called her boss, was the one to get her and Mabel into one of these exciting saloons. She knew he knew somebody, because he had talked of the evenings he had spent there. She approached him one afternoon when he sat in his office smoking his 25-cent cigar and blowing smoke rings above his head. He looked content and approachable. She flopped in a chair in front of his desk and stared straight at him. "Weldie, I've got a favor to ask." She smiled her most tantalizing smile. "Mabel and I have been wanting to see the inside of that speakeasy down there on Water Street, would you please take us?"

He watched her through the smoke that was now encircling her hair. She had been modeling a new design just in and he marveled at what she did for the flowered chiffon with dropped waist and the softly flounced hemline. He could see her ample bosom rise up and down with anticipation. "Oh, hey, Miss Lady," he answered, shaking his head. "That's no place for you. All kinds of riff-raff in there. Murderers go there, mobsters of all kinds." The more he talked, the more excited she became. This would be the fun she was looking for. God, how she'd like to see a real live gangster. It would be something to write and tell Myrtle, scare the bloomers right off of her. Her sister, who was afraid of her shadow and was so content to be there in Rochester, safe and sound, working at the bakery, seeing the same people every day. Lady couldn't understand her younger sister; no wish for adventure in her whole body. "We're old enough, Weldie," she pleaded, "Please, please, take us just once. We'll never ask again." She leaned toward him, putting her elbows on the desk and holding her face in her hands. He thought she resembled a pretty young girl asking to go out on a first date. She was hard to refuse. He sat listening to her and his thought went to the speakeasy where he'd been many times. It was classy, sort of, with glass chandeliers and white tablecloths, not the ordinary saloon with the girls in their sleazy cheap dresses slipping around searching for a customer, or the sloppy drunks reeking of the cheap booze they had belted down.

It wasn't a bad place and hadn't been raided. He liked to go there. The booze was Grade A quality and God knew with this shitty Prohibition it was hard to find good booze. He always slept better after a couple of shots of whisky; made him forget for awhile the never-ending ordering of merchandise and the never-ending bills that went along with it. He could almost see the surprised look on Sam's face when he appeared at the door of the saloon with two young girls on his arm. The more he thought about it, the more he grinned. The assholes would be jealous as hell. He shook his head, bringing his thoughts back to the girl in front of him, who waited for an answer. "Well, let me see here," he said, in a teasing voice. "Friday night might be OK. You think you could get yourselves ready by then?" Lady screeched, "You're the greatest, Weldie, I just love ya!" She ran around the desk and gave him a big kiss on the cheek. He wanted very much to pull her onto his lap and kiss her the way a man kisses a woman he's crazy about. He watched her dance out of the room and he hung his head. By Friday evening, Lady was just about as excited as she had ever been in her life. Weldie told her to pick out a dress to wear and to pick one for Mabel too. She had never had a beauty of a dress like the green, shimmering, sleek gown she carefully removed from the hanger and laid on the bed. She had plucked her eyebrows to a straight line, creamed her face till it glowed and then pulled out the bobby pins from her hair, leaving fascinating little spit curls surrounding her glow. Weldie had even let her take a wrap with white feathers up the front and around the neckline. Mabel appeared in the doorway just as Lady pulled the gown over her head. "Lady, I'm scared. What if they have a raid while we're there? Jail isn't a pleasant place, you know." Lady laughed at the distressed look on her friend's face.

"You look absolutely great, Mabel," she said. "Don't worry, Weldie says they've never been raided. They have an in with the police." Mabel sighed with relief and hurried to check her dress in Lady's mirror. She felt quite uncomfortable in the black satin dress with the flared hem. She had to wear her tightest girdle to keep the bulges from showing and the stays were pressing into her flesh, making her want to say "ouch" with every movement. She did think, maybe, the torture would be worthwhile as she admired herself in the long mirror. She turned to watch Lady slip her feet into the shoes that matched her gown. She wished she could be as confident and as pretty as her friend. It was going to be a night to remember. Weldie showed up in front of the rooming house dressed in his best black suit and driving his black Pontiac touring car. He observed the girls coming toward him. He smiled at their enthusiasm. They looked lovely, he told them, and helped both into the car, telling them not to snag the dresses because the next day they would be back on hangers at the dress shop. The girls were thrilled to be in the practically new automobile and to have such a distinguished

The Family

escort, they told him. They giggled and poked each other in the side all the way to the front of the speakeasy. Excitement was in the air, they could feel it. The saloon was quite inconspicuous from the outside. They had to go down a flight of stairs to a wooden door with a peephole opening. Weldie knocked and soon the small peephole was opened and a frowning, scar-faced man stared at them. "Tell Sam that Weldon Van Hughes wishes to enter with his two lady friends," Weldie said, in his best voice of importance. The man glanced from one to another and ordered, "Wait right here!"

Sam soon appeared, opened the door and greeted Weldie with a handshake and invited them in. The girls tried to control their excitement by taking deep breaths. Then they both said, "Wow!" at the same time when they entered the large room, which was bustling with activity. "This is beautiful," Mabel whispered to Lady. "The cat's meow," Lady whispered back. Lady raised her chin a little higher so the feathers from her coat didn't tickle her nose and make her sneeze. She and Mabel each took one of Weldie's arms and followed the barrel-chested man to a table by the dance floor. Gorgeous women were everywhere, surrounded by men in dark suits. The men did give a casual glance at Weldie and his two young lady friends as they walked by. Lady could feel curious eyes on them. She felt nervous, excited and sorta sick to her stomach all at the same time. She imagined she could see bulges under their coats and she wondered if there were machine guns under the tables. Weldie, being greeted by waiters and a few women, seemed to be well known and respected. He gallantly pulled the girls' chairs out and they were finally seated. Then they were able to take a look around. Lady asked, " Are there any gangsters here, Weldie?" "Probably is, " he answered, pulling a large cigar from his vest pocket. With a flick of his gold lighter, the cigar was soon sending fragrant odor around them. "Where? Where? Tell us!" Lady demanded, wriggling in her chair, her eyes roaming the room. "Well, glance over to your left, but don't stare." He was enjoying the envious looks he was getting from some of these tough guys.

"They say the big, burly character with the pin-striped suit on and the disgusting tie that doesn't match, well, that there thug worked for Al Capone, probably still does. I don't think they ever leave Capone, unless they're in a casket." Lady slyly turned her head to seem whom Weldie was talking about. The man sat with a group at a large, round table. There was loud laughter and remarks being made back and forth. His women companions wore fashionable gowns and some held silver cigarette holders and often took little puffs from the end, letting the smoke drift from their mouths to form lazy little rings around the jovial bunch. One of the men caught her eye as she stared. She quickly turned her head, embarrassed she was caught. She whispered to Weldie, "Who is the man with the slick-backed hair? He looks like Valentino with a funny eye." Weldie stirred his drink and whispered back, without glancing at the group. "That's Harry Mullins, big shot something or other. Nobody knows what kind of business he operates, does real well. Maybe in with the bootleggers, who knows. They say he has a mansion around here somewhere. Has a glass eye, damn thing stares right straight at ya, gives ya the creeps. Women seem to like him; always got a slinky dame stuck to his arm, but he changes dames as often as he changes shirts. He loves 'em and leaves 'em, I guess." Lady was fascinated with the goings-on at that table and she continued to sneak peeks as often as possible. She sipped the whiskey and water in front of her and realized she liked its taste. It tingled in her throat and gave her a thirst for more. Another round came and they all looked at each other, wondering who had ordered. Weldie asked the waiter, "Where did these come from? Don't believe we ordered another drink."

The waiter politely answered, "Mr. Mullins sent them over with his compliments." This startled Weldie. He had never had a drink bought by anyone other than himself here at this saloon. He glanced over to the table where Mullins sat. He was getting up and headed their way. The girls were beginning to smile more and more, the shyness disappearing as the whisky took hold. Lady had a flush to her cheeks and a sparkle in her eyes as Harry Mullins stood before them and introduced himself. And then he added, "I have never seen prettier ladies than you have here, Van Hughes. I wonder if I could join you." "Of course, sit down and thanks for the drink." Weldie was agreeable, but wary of this charming individual, whom he knew had his eye on Lady. Mullins pulled a chair out and gazed at Lady, noticing her white, flawless skin and her green eyes that seemed to shimmer like the dress she wore. He was intrigued with her, to say the least. Lady felt her heart beating a bit faster and she felt self conscious from his probing stare. His glass eye was indeed bewitching. She thought it gave him a distinguished appearance. Mabel was kicking her under the table and Lady glared at her, trying to get the message across to not act like an idiot. It worked. Mabel leaned back in her chair and quietly watched the man who had intruded on their first night at a speakeasy. She found him sinister and she couldn't understand Lady's apparent interest in him. She was actually blushing under his stare. Mabel moved her eyes to Weldie and saw he was glaring openly at Mullins and she knew for

The Family

sure what he had surmised was true: Weldie was in love with Lady, a woman young enough to be his daughter.

God, how she wished they hadn't come to his place. She shivered as she noticed the loud men, who were rubbing their hands boldly over the women's breasts, and the women, laughing almost hysterically. She wanted to go back to the rooming house and get out of the dress that now seemed ridiculous for her to be wearing. She hoped Lady felt the same way, but the dazed look on her face made her worry. Mullins graciously asked Lady to dance and she hurried to her feet, letting him take her arm and lead her to the dance floor. She was thrilled to her very toes to be in the arms of this handsome man, who was mysterious and charming. She forgot Weldie and Mabel completely: it was as if she were under the spell of this man with the bewitching eye. He held her close and she followed his steps around the crowded dance floor. A whisper came from him in her ear. "Could I see you again, away from Van Hughes? He acts like a protective father, do you know him well?" She nodded and answered, "I work for Weldie, he has a dress shop across town. He's a nice man." She really didn't want to talk about Weldie. He seemed dull and stodgy beside this exciting man, who was holding her so tight she could feel his heart beating against her breasts. She wondered why he had picked her out of this crowd of gorgeous women.

She felt flattered he had, and now he had asked to see her again. Mabel would be shocked, she knew. These thoughts were running through her mind as they moved through the couples on the dance floor. It was unbelievable he was interested in her, a small-town girl who had never seen the inside of a saloon before. The whiskey had left her relaxed and she let herself enjoy the moment, pushing away the thoughts of what Mabel would say, and of what Weldie would certainly say. She loved the smell of the shaving tonic Mullins used; it was masculine and so intoxicating. She wished this evening would go on forever. He spoke again in her ear, "Did anyone ever tell you how lovely you are? I'm sure they have. You make these other women look like little girls dressed up in their mother's clothes and not filling them out." He pushed away from her to stare into her eyes. He smiled an irresistible smile. She felt like she had never felt before. He made her feel beautiful and she closed her eyes, putting her face against his shoulder. The music stopped and he reluctantly led her back to the table. Mabel told him Weldie was in the men's room and she frowned as she watched Lady scribble her address on a piece of paper and hand it to Harry. He excused himself and was gone before Weldie returned from the men's room.

Doris P. Burke

There was silence in the car as Weldie steered through the back streets, taking the girls to the rooming house. He was seething with anger at Mullins for his obvious attraction to Lady. The nerve of the fool, he was thinking, to take advantage of this young girl, who didn't know a thing about life in the big city. He knew he'd have to have a long talk with Lady. The talk came the next day when he called her into his office. It frightened him to think of what might become of her and her apparent attraction for Mullins. It had been written all over her face. He spoke finally, as she relaxed in the chair in front of him. "My dear girl, I hope you aren't interested in that jerk Mullins. We know very little about him. He's a mysterious guy; in fact, he could be part of the Purple Gang, who the hell knows for sure? He was sitting with some of the booze runners. I do know that. We have to be careful in this day and age. They find murdered girls in back alleys, all over the city. These guys tire of them and dump 'em."

He watched her face, hoping his words were getting through to her, her dear face with the innocent eyes and trusting look. He loved her and wished she felt the same way toward him, but she was so young. God, how he wished he was younger and could court her and tell her all the things he wanted to tell her. He knew she would be stunned and probably laugh if he told her what was going through his mind. He was an old man, as old as her father, maybe older. He was a fool. "Dear Weldie, you are so serious," Lady laughed. "I'm sure I won't be found dead in an alley. In fact, I haven't heard from Mr. Mullins and probably won't." She looked away from his piercing stare. She did want to hear from the charming Mullins, but she didn't want Weldie to know that. He was so protective and she loved him for that, but she was young, she wanted to see life and feel it to the fullest. She didn't want to be like Myrtle, who was stuck there in Rochester bagging up those fattening baked goods and smiling at those overweight customers. Detroit was exciting. She had a peek at it before Weldie whisked them out the door of the speakeasy, acting as if the Purple gang was going to arrive and shoot everyone in the place. She was disgusted with Mabel, who was afraid of her shadow and talked long into the night of what she thought she'd seen. Weldie breathed in a sigh of relief when he heard she hadn't been in touch with Mullins. He grunted, "I know you aren't the kind of girl to be impressed by these idiotic men roaming around looking for an innocent target. You go back to work now, and show Mrs. Markus that new flapper dress with the fringe. If she can get her big behind in one of those, she'll be happy."

He watched her leave and he hoped she would remain the inno-

The Family

cent, wholesome girl who had stepped in the front door so full of life and ready to take on the big city. He put his head in his hands and stared at the clutter of paper on his desk. He was tired and depressed. Lady did hear from Harry and her life was changed completely, from the humdrum to the extreme. He took her everywhere. He bought her clothes, the best money could buy, reveling in the fact of how she was enjoying what he could give her. She was young and beautiful and he wanted to show her off to the world. She asked no questions; she was in love for the first time in her life. She didn't even know if he was married or had been married. It didn't matter. She quit her job at the dress shop. She had to get away from Weldie's probing questions and disapproving looks. She didn't see Mabel anymore. There wasn't time; she had to be ready when Harry called. He rented an apartment for her in a quiet neighborhood, taking her away from the rooming house and Mabel. She became a party girl, a mistress and she could down the illegal booze with the best of them. Harry even drove her to Rochester to visit her folks and Myrtle. She was surprised to find Myrtle had married, had a new baby and lived in the suburbs of Detroit. She was happy for her sister and reminded herself she would have to visit her and the family. She missed her brothers. She knew Ralph was headed for the big leagues and she was proud of him. It was Lloyd she missed the most - her big brother, who was kind and good. She heard from her ma he had three children and was farming. She couldn't comprehend being a farmer's wife and she shuddered thinking about it. No pretty clothes and nowhere to go. It wasn't for her.

    For the next few years, Lady did live life to its fullest. At least, in her eyes she did. She never tired of the continuous parties, of the bathtub gin made by the friends of Harry at their exclusive homes, with just the elite attending, or of the backroom of a speakeasy where someone had a still churning out moonshine. It was exciting to see the mobsters in each place, accepting her and Harry into their group. She was known as "Glass Eye's Lady." Harry was envied for having a young, lovely girl with a great personality. Even the women liked her and accepted her into their circle. She listened to their troubles and often comforted and sympathized with those who were not treated so well by their ruthless companions. Harry was always attentive and considerate. She did find out he was married, but the wife lived her life away from his, in the home he provided for her and his children. Lady resented to a certain extent the time Harry spent at his home, but he assured her if his wife would divorce him, he would be free to take her as his wife. She believed him. He was the man she wanted and she would wait. Her patience

Doris P. Burke

stayed with her in the years to come. It was as if she'd been hypnotized by this man with the fascinating eye and nothing else mattered. She loved him, completely, sincerely and absolutely. Sadly, her life with Harry would end, much too soon.

The Family

Chapter Nineteen

Things were never the same at the boarding house after Lady and Myrtle left. Lula found herself getting more discouraged every day with Bill and his antics. She began to fear him more and more. When the girls had been there he had at least tried to put on a good show in front of them. Now, he had no one to hide his disgusting ways from and he seemed to glory in flaunting them to her. The abuse went on, verbally and physically, when he was consumed with alcohol. She tried to conceal her bruises from the few remaining boarders, but they had eyes. She felt embarrassed and so ashamed for Bill and what he had become. She took care of him when he came staggering home from one of his long binges, sometimes having been on one for days with his moonshine friends. He was too sick then to cause trouble. She would pour tomato juice into a cup and force him to drink it and then hold a pan in front of his mouth while he threw it all back up. He moaned and called her name, asking for forgiveness and vowing to never do it again. For a month he would be sober, actually talking to her and asking about the children. She knew he missed the girls and even the boys to a certain extent. She was glad they weren't here to see the offensive man he had become.

Most of the boarders had left to find jobs in Detroit at the automobile factories. Her income was hardly enough to keep supplies bought, let alone keep Bill in the spending money he was used to. She felt alone and desperate. Something had to be done to get Bill back on his feet, but what? She had no friends to turn to. She realized the only real friend she had ever made in Rochester was poor Mr. Jenkins and he was long gone. Cora had moved to her sister's home in Almont and Wanda had found herself a good man and now had two children. The boarders she had considered friends had left, seeking new jobs and a new life. She heard from Myrtle occasionally, telling of the baby and of her husband's good-paying job. Lady sent postcards with just a hello and goodbye. Lloyd had his hands full with four children and with working a farm in Lapeer. Ralph was the only one who could help her. She sat down one evening after the chores had been completed and wrote a letter to him. Winter was coming on and she knew he would be free of baseball until spring. The winter of 1926 roared in, leaving snowdrifts as high as the automobiles that tried to chug their way through

Doris P. Burke

them. Lula felt helpless as she watched the last of her boarders leave. Her thriving boarding house had become a thing of the past. People were buying homes, making good money. She wished with all her heart that her Bill would take on a good-paying job and they could live in the little white house that now needed painting and repair. She knew it would have to be sold with the boarding house. Bill had debts to be paid, as well as taxes to be reckoned with. She sat at the window of the boarding house watching the snow accumulate in the driveway. Bill had been on a binge for a week now. God knows where he is, she thought.

It was evening and the wind and snow made it difficult to see the car that was winding its way up the hill. She hurriedly stood up to move away from the window and whispered in frustration, "Don't let it be Bill, not tonight, I'm too tired." She closed her eyes: She couldn't look out the window to see Bill fall out the door of the car and then stagger to the house, ranting and raving with every step. How could she cope with that tonight? She waited. She didn't hear any noise except the motor of the car. It became quiet and she heard two doors slam. She put her hand over her heart - maybe something had happened to Bill. He could be dead and someone was coming to tell her. Her Bill, whom she loved no matter what. She turned as the door opened. Two men stood smiling at her in the doorway. She gave a relieved sigh and hurried toward them. Her boys had come to help her as they always had when they were small. They stood tall and handsome, waiting for her to embrace them. "Hey, mother, what's to eat?" Ralph asked. She couldn't answer, the tears clouded her eyes and she tried to smile. She felt overwhelmed with happiness to have these two standing in her kitchen and to hear the same words Ralph always said when he was just a boy. Her sons had come because she needed them. They hadn't forgotten her. She felt a weight lift from her heart and she was so glad she had made that apple strudel. She had their coats off and her sons sitting at the kitchen table with a large bowl of the apple mixture in front of them before they had time to ask a question. She loved waiting on them and her eyes hardly left their faces as she poured steaming cups of coffee.

Finally, she sank on a chair across from them and looked into the dear faces she had so longed to see. Ralph had the appearance of prosperity in his clothes and mannerisms. She was so proud of him for pursuing his dream and she could hardly wait to hear of his accomplishments in the baseball leagues. Lloyd had a healthy look, but tired eyes, she thought. A large family already to take care of. How she wished she could see the new babies and could have been

The Family

there to help at the deliveries. Lloyd asked, "Where's the old man, Mother?" He had an idea where he was and so did Ralph. They had discussed the situation on the way to Rochester. It wasn't any different now that it had been 15 years ago. "He's off somewhere," she answered, glancing away from the probing eyes of her two boys. "Jesus, Mother, how long are you gonna put up with this shit?" Ralph snorted. "He ain't gonna be any different if he lives to be a hundred. You gotta get outta here, away from the old man. Lloyd and I talked about it. We'll find a place for you. You're not an old woman. You could have a good life outta here." They both sat waiting for an answer, Ralph frowning and Lloyd staring at his empty bowl in front of him. They were half-afraid to hear her answer, afraid it would be the same story they had heard so many times in their early years. She hesitated a moment before she spoke, looking from one to the other. She knew they were trying to protect her from the man she had protected them from. How she loved these two boys she had carried in her womb, and from the moment they lay as tiny newborns beside her, they had been such an important part of her life.

She bowed her head and let the tears flow into her lap as she whispered, "Bill is your father and my husband. No matter what he does or has done, I will always love him. He has this terrible curse of alcohol. He doesn't mean to abuse me, it's the curse doing this." She wiped her face with her apron, straightened her shoulders and held her face up to face her boys. The story was the same. They knew their mother hadn't changed either. She would always cover up for the old man and take care of him. They felt defeat again. Ralph's face reddened and he stood up to pace around the room. Lloyd stared at the door, wishing his old man would walk through it so he could shake the shit outta him. Ralph muttered, "OK, mother. This is the way it's gonna be. We're gonna sell this place. I've got my eye on a farm over in Lapeer. We'll buy that and the old man can get his ass to farmin'. It's not far from Grandpa Judd's place. I've been to see Grandpa. He's got a nice farm there and Grandma looks good. They asked about you." She could see her youngest son hadn't changed much in spite of the expensive jacket he wore and the freshly pressed blue serge pants and the fedora he had carelessly thrown on the counter of the cupboards. He still paced and swore, saying whatever came to mind. It even tickled her a bit to watch him. She really wanted to hear what her oldest son had to say, the sensible one, who was quiet and thought things through before he spoke. She noticed he was turning his coffee cup around and around on the saucer. He finally glanced up and asked, "What

Doris P. Burke

do you want to do, Mother? I do think Ralph has a good idea there, but it's up to you. I can't help with money. It keeps me busy just making enough to feed the family. Got four kids now, ya know. Wouldn't trade 'em for a million dollars."

This was the son she knew and loved. He said his piece and that was the end of it. She moved to the coffeepot and poured each another cup. She knew what she had to do. "We have to sell," she said. "You do what you think is best, Ralph. Your father won't dispute you, he has no reason to. He owes money to a half dozen people, mostly those drinking friends of his and bootleggers. He told me that. Demanded I give him some money. I don't have any and it made him angry. That's probably why he's been gone so long again, I don't know." They both watched as she rubbed her hands together in frustration. It was a scene they had observed before. Things hadn't changed. It was as if they were young boys again, feeling what she was feeling, watching her emotions, wanting to believe in a man who had never given any support or promise of a better life. They had quit believing in their old man years ago, but this little woman with the stamina of three women, had never lost faith in the man she loved. Ralph shook his head as he watched her. Lloyd stood up and moved toward the door. He was remembering when he and Ralph made a promise to get her away from the worry, sweat and tears the old man had put on her. It was no use. She would stay with him no matter what. She'd stay home and wait for him and suffer the consequences. So be it. He had a family to take care of and he'd work his ass off to see they had food in their bellies and clothes on their backs. His baseball dream was long gone. He felt good about Ralph making it. One of them had, that's what mattered.

Ralph grabbed his hat from the counter, stuck it on his head and grumbled, "I'll see about that farm, Mother. Tell the old man to find a buyer for this place, maybe one of his bootlegger friends would want it. You shouldn't have any problem selling the house. I'll get in touch with you. He laid some money on the table, kissed her on the cheek and followed Lloyd out the door into the snowy night. Lula stood up and walked to the window and watched the taillights of the car disappear down the driveway. She sighed; she was so tired that maybe tonight she could sleep. Her boys had been here to help her. Oh, how she loved them. Ralph did everything he said he'd do. He matched the money Lula and Bill had left over from selling the boarding house and the small house. It wasn't a lot after Lula paid off Bill's debts. But it was enough to buy the 80-acre farm. He helped his folks move into the house, saw that the

The Family

old man was sober and advised his Grandpa Judd to keep an eye on him. He left for spring training in Birmingham, Alabama in 1927. The minor leagues were driving him crazy. He was making some money and pitching well, but he wanted to rub elbows with the best: Babe Ruth, Ty Cobb and Walter Johnson. He couldn't let his chance at the major leagues slip away. He had to get there. He figured he could throw a curve ball and a fast ball as good as the best of them. Ralph was impressive-looking on the pitcher's mound. He was stocky and solid like a rock, with powerful shoulder muscles, and he was noticed by the crowds who came to watch the games. The women especially liked the smile he gave the crowd and the gesture of the cap coming off when they cheered him on a strike-out. He was drinking some, mostly in frustration, but it didn't interfere with his ball playing. He was always alert when a game started. This was his life and his dream. He knew he'd make it to the major league. He'd be there with the best of them, he'd show 'em. He'd work the minors for as long as it took, he told himself. He'd never give up this dream.

Chapter Twenty

In 1927, Lloyd moved his family to the Turrill farm in Lapeer. The owners were looking for a good man to work the fields, share the money from the crops and keep the place decent. Lloyd was glad to take over the farm. There was plenty of room in the house for the family and a big yard for the four children: Margie, Keith, Billy and baby June to romp and play. He and Onalee were proud of their family, but it was tedious work taking care of four kids just a couple of years apart in age. Onalee took it in stride. Washing diapers she knew well and in winter and summer they hung in the breeze on the clothesline. The baby, June, was a year old now and sitting at the table to eat with the rest of the hungry bunch. This helped, making it so Onalee didn't have to take time to nurse the little girl. Onalee and Lloyd agreed their children would have an education, no matter what. Lloyd brooded sometimes about his old man pulling him and Ralph out of school. He had finished the third grade and that was it, just learning to read and write. His children would learn about the world out there, history and geography. They would graduate from high school, with knowledge. He still had his collection of books he had bought over the years when he'd worked on the railroad and at the cotton mill. He was proud of his books and knew his children would read them eventually and enjoy them as much as he had. He thought of Herbie sometimes and how his face would crinkle into a crooked smile when he read from the same books and what pleasure they had brought him.

 The oldest girl, Margie, started kindergarten class the fall they moved to the farm. The entire family watched their mother help Margie with her hair and pull the newly made cotton dress over her white petticoat. She was seven and the first of the bunch to be off on a new experience. Onalee realized, as she brushed her daughter's hair, she would miss her a lot. She had been helpful, watching the other children and learning to put the clothes pins on the line just right to hold the diapers and other clothing in place. Now their firstborn was off to learn her ABCs. They all stood at the end of the driveway and waved as she walked, a little bit hesitantly, toward the schoolhouse, which was just down the road a ways. They stayed, still waving until she turned into the schoolyard. That afternoon, they were there at the end of the driveway to greet her as she came hurrying home to tell them of her first day away from all of them.

The Family

She answered questions, feeling quite important indeed to have all the attention bestowed on her from her mother and dad and mostly from her brother Keith, who would soon be old enough to start his learning. He kinda resented his sister getting all the attention. And as often as he could, he'd pinch her arm when he walked by her. She would yell for her mother and he was told to stop. This went on for many years to come. It seemed he enjoyed pestering his sister and in a way, she got satisfaction out of saying and doing things to make him pester her.

Lloyd figured he'd better try to keep in touch with his mother and dad, just to see if the move from Rochester was a good thing. The farm his folks had bought was north of town, not far from his Grandpa Judd's place. The fall months were not as busy for him: a few cows to milk, wood to be chopped for the cooking and heating stoves and the livestock to be fed - everyday stuff. This would leave him with some time to do some visiting. He would take the two boys with him, leaving Onalee home with the baby at her own liking, being as she didn't look too kindly toward Lula and Bill. Keith was five, Billy three. They liked to ride in the jumpin', rattlin' old car and it was going to be fun to be alone with their dad. "Just us guys," Keith told his mother, jiggling around in excitement when she asked who was going. It was a mild fall morning when Lloyd decided he'd make the trip to his folks'. The road was clear, they shouldn't have any trouble unless the tires on the car decided to give out. He cranked the car and it gave a shake and the motor started. He waited for the boys to come from the house and they finally appeared with mufflers wrapped around their beaming faces. He smiled, seeing them. It reminded him of him and Ralph, when they were young little men living at their Grandpa Judd's farm those many years ago. The boys jabbered the whole trip, whispering to each other about what their grandma and grandpa would look like. Keith had been just a baby when his folks decided to leave Rochester. A grandma and grandpa would be special to see, he told Billy, and he felt tickled that Margie didn't get to go. She thought she was something because she went to school. Well, wait until she hears about us seeing a grandma and grandpa, he thought. When they pulled into the driveway, Lloyd was glad to see Ralph had made a good choice. It was a small house that reminded him of Aunt El and Uncle Frank's. The barn sat behind the house a ways. Everything appeared to be in good shape.

The boys, with their faces pressed to the window of the car, waited expectantly for the appearance of a grandma and grandpa to come from the house. Lloyd stepped out and went around to let the

Doris P. Burke

boys out of the car. They both tumbled out, staring at the side door of the house, waiting for somebody to appear. It opened suddenly and there stood a short, round woman with a smile as big as all outdoors. With one hand she held the end of her apron and she dabbed at her eyes. With the other, she was motioning for them to come in. The boys were hesitant and held on to their dad's leg. She grabbed them both when they got close enough and hugged the breath almost out of them. They were in the warm house with their mufflers unwrapped, sitting in a chair with cookies and glasses of milk in front of them before they knew it. Their grandma crouched in front of them, peering into their faces, telling their dad how great these boys were. They liked this grandma. Lloyd left the boys looking at the pictures his mother had brought from the photograph album. He strolled to the barn where his mother said his old man was. He found him pitching hay to the few milking cows. They shook hands, Lloyd noticing his dad had no smell of booze on his breath and his hands seemed steady. This was a good sign. He hadn't seen him sober in a long time. They talked of farming, of baseball and of how Ralph was doing in the leagues. Bill mentioned Grandpa Judd, saying, "He's got a nice set-up over there." He leaned on his pitchfork and spat some tobacco juice on the hay in front of him. "The next thing for him is ta stay the hell away from here and mind his own p's and q's. Nosey old buzzard, ya know?" He frowned and wiped his hand over his mouth getting some stray tobacco juice off his chin.

"I've gotta get over there and see him and Grandma," Lloyd replied. He knew his grandpa had probably said something about drinking to his dad. They walked back to the house, his dad saying he wanted to see the two grandsons and especially the one who was his namesake. He greeted them like a grandpa should, lifting them up in the air and telling them what great little men they were. Lloyd even thought he heard a little choke in his dad's voice. He smiled at his mother and she smiled back, shaking her head, telling him things were improving. He thought to himself, "Maybe this is what the old man needed, a new lease on life." He certainly hoped so. They left after Lula was satisfied the boys' stomachs were full and their hands were warm and their feet were warm and they were smiling contentedly. The boys watched out the back window of the car, waving to their new Grandma and Grandpa. Lloyd was glad he had made the trip. He felt better seeing his mother happier than he had ever seen her. His old man had been such a son of a bitch, maybe in his older years he'd settle down and be a husband. He was thinking this as they made their way toward home. He knew Onalee would

The Family

be surprised to hear of the old man's new look. The evening supper was spent with Keith telling his story about the trip to Grandma and Grandpa's. "We had cookies as big around as a pancake, with a fat raisin in the middle," he said, staring at each face to see if they were listening. "And Grandma smelled just like those cookies." He talked and Billy would grin and nod his head in agreement. "And we gotta Uncle Ralph - he's a pitcher - and a Aunt Myrtle, with a kid about my age, who's a cuzzen, and a Aunt Lady, who's gotta funny name."

Keith felt very good to have everybody listening to him. He felt very grown up and important and he had one more thing to say. He took a big swig of milk and checked to see if the family was still listening. They were still looking at him, even Margie, with a scowl on her face. He was satisfied he still had their attention, so he spoke his last speech: "And Grandpa has some fingers missin' he lost on the railroad doin' somethin' and he chews tobacca and spits a lot and has tobacca juice all over his chin." He felt very smug as he glanced at his big sister. He knew she was disgusted because she didn't get to tell her long stories from school. She was sticking her tongue out at him. That was good, he'd made her mad. If he got close enough to her and his mother didn't see him, he'd pinch her a good one. He knew now he could tell a story too, maybe better than she could. He ate a biscuit with honey on it and grinned at her. He'd had a fun day. Lloyd and Onalee smiled at each other. Hearing the story was enough to make them laugh right out loud, but they didn't. He was only five and this was an important story for him to tell. Onalee lifted the baby from the high chair, put her on the floor and started cleaning up the dishes. Margie moved around the table to help, still pouting a bit about her brother getting all the attention. She hoped she got to see her grandma and grandpa soon, so her brother wouldn't act like a smarty pants. She felt a pinch on her arm and yelled for her mother, "Mom, he pinched me again!" Her face was puckered up and she was rubbing her arm. Onalee shook her head. Not only was he a storyteller, he was a tease!

Doris P. Burke

Chapter Twenty-One

Ralph had pitched his way through the minor leagues, and in the fall of 1927 he was sold to Washington. He had made it to the major leagues, the American League. He came back to visit in Lapeer, sporting a brand-new Pontiac, some new clothes and an attitude. He stopped at the farm long enough to tell his folks the news, then proceeded to roar his way to Lloyd's. He wanted his big brother to know, and maybe he'd even brag a little. He was riding high on his ego. It showed every time he opened his mouth. He massaged his pitching arm while he talked, telling of the great control he had accomplished with it. He told Lloyd of the women who were throwing themselves at him and of the assholes he'd had to contend with on his way up the ladder of success. Lloyd didn't mind hearing all this, but he did mind the air of sympathy Ralph seemed to project as he observed Onalee in her house dress and apron, the children hanging on her skirt, shy of the well-dressed man in their home. Lloyd figured it was stupidity on Ralph's part to feel sorry for him and his family. Lloyd knew, as he listened to his brother, he would never have the clothes, the new cars, nor the lifestyle, but he knew in his heart he had much more. It was there in the timid smiles the children were giving to this talkative man, whom they wanted to like because he was their dad's brother and he must be great because they thought their dad was the greatest. And there was Onalee trying to wipe the breakfast stains from her dress the children had left there. Sympathy wasn't called for and he did resent his brother's attitude.

He listened to the ramblings of Ralph and he even smiled to himself, remembering the ball game so many years ago, when the Grizzlies had beat the Rochester All Stars. He thought Ralph still sounded like that boy who had pitched a winning game. He was proud of his brother for sticking with his dream, but he wondered if that was all there was for him. He was living high on the hog now, but there was a life after the ball-playing and the women and the drinking and carousing. Lloyd shook his head to clear his thoughts. "Got a lot of work to get to Ralph," he said. "Got some beans to get off the field." Ralph stood up, grabbed his hat, still talking about the manager of the Washington Senators and followed Lloyd toward the door. He stopped long enough to tip his hat to Onalee, never looking at the children. He showed Lloyd his new automo-

The Family

bile, jumped into the driver's seat and tore out of the driveway. He was on a mission, Lloyd decided, to see how many people he could see and tell of his good luck. He realized Ralph hadn't asked how he was doing, what the children's names were, nor had he even mentioned Lula and Bill. He walked slowly toward the barn, wondering what had happened to the brother who used to give a damn about things. This guy was a self-centered asshole. He shook his head. He missed the brother he used to know.

Doris P. Burke

Chapter Twenty-Two

The spring of 1929 was busy for Lloyd and his family. Onalee was carrying the soon-to-be-born baby and the work was always there for her. Margie helped as best she could with the care of the other two little ones: Billy, to be five in August, and June, to be three in June. Keith was already milking the cows and pitching hay along with his dad. The fields were getting planted and optimism prevailed. The sewing machine buzzed evenings, Onalee making new diapers and trying to salvage pieces of the old ones. Clothes were mended and passed down from Keith to Billy and Margie's outgrown dresses were cut smaller for June. The baby would arrive in April, Onalee figured, and was assured by Doctor Best it would be around the middle of April. It was a race to get all the preparations ready. Lloyd was happy about the new baby. He had two boys and two girls. Another boy would be good, but it didn't really matter, he told Onalee. Another mouth to feed gave him more incentive to work harder and nights he would fall in bed dead tired, the buzzing of the sewing machine in his ears. The morning of April 20th started out damp and cool, with more rain predicted. Onalee woke up with a nagging backache. She realized the baby would probably be making an appearance soon. She hurried with breakfast, whispered to Lloyd he might want to get his mother and then helped the two youngest into their clothes. Margie and Keith were off to school, leaving Onalee alone with pains starting to wrap themselves around the lower half of her body. She'd had four: This was an old story and she busied herself doing the dishes.

By noon, the pains were there, but were not excruciating. She fixed some peanut butter sandwiches for the two little ones, made sure their glasses were filled with milk and she was able then to sit down with some effort at the sewing machine. She managed to get one nightgown sewn before she glanced up to see June nodding in her chair. Billy was soaking his bread in the milk that was spilled on the table and he gave her a toothless grin as she scolded him for slopping his milk. June was lain down for a nap and Billy played with a top, watching it spin around and around. By four o'clock, Onalee wondered where Lloyd was, and his mother. She was beginning to feel quite uncomfortable, with the pains grabbing more often. Margie and Keith opened the door minutes later to see their mother sitting in the rocking chair. This was a sight they had never

The Family

seen during the day before. She was always doing. They knew the baby she had told them about was likely to be coming soon. This was exciting and they needed no urging from their mother to help with the little ones. It did scare them some to be told their dad wasn't there, but they were assured he would be coming. And sure enough, just as Onalee had the sharpest pain yet, a car was heard and Lloyd rushed into the house, fearing the worst had happened. He had a flat tire on the way to his folks' and then had to wait for his mother, who bustled around pulling cookies from the oven, finding a box to pack them in and hurrying to find her flannel nightgown for the stay at his place. By the time he had her sitting in the car beside them, he was exhausted from her scurrying around. He'd had to stop in Lapeer at Doctor Best's office to tell him he thought the baby would soon be coming. The doctor was not there, so he scribbled a note, leaving it stuck in the door.

He felt nervous and guilty for leaving his wife alone for so long. His mother assured him, smiling at his somewhat white face, that babies would come when they were ready and if she only had a backache in the morning, there was time before the agonizing began. This didn't help him too much, hearing her describe the pain she had gone through having him - and she did go into full details. By the time he reached his driveway, he felt a little sick to his stomach and wished his mother would hush her mouth for awhile. Lula was pleased to see the grandchildren and she dabbed at her eyes as they stood peering at her. She was so busy checking each to see how they had grown, she hardly noticed Onalee, who sat in the rocker getting paler by the minute. When she did, she reassured her by saying, "We're here, Onalee. Don't worry about a thing. I'll take care of these children, you get in bed and rest. You have work ahead of you." Onalee peeked around Lula's short body at Lloyd. She hadn't felt too bad before they came. Now, she wasn't sure she felt better or worse to have this very efficient little woman taking over her kitchen and her children. Lloyd seemed to read her mind and winked at her. She did manage a touch of a smile as she grabbed the arm of the chair for support and raised herself. She headed straight for the bedroom. It would feel good to lie down where it was quiet, she thought. She knew the children would "ohh" and "ahh" over the gigantic sugar cookies Lula had brought. Hers never came out looking like Lula's, somehow they were lopsided and certainly not perfectly round, like Lula's, with a perfect raisin in the middle. She had to cut her raisin into pieces lots of times to make them go further.

She was thinking all these irritating thoughts as she lowered

Doris P. Burke

herself onto the comforting bed. She might even be able to get a short nap, she thought, before this active little dickens made its appearance. Not so, by six o'clock she was so restless she was pacing the floor of the bedroom, the pains getting closer and closer. She called Lloyd in to ask him if he thought the doctor would be getting there shortly. He didn't know but thought so. She certainly hoped so. She knew Lula was perfectly capable of delivering a baby. God, she did everything so well, a baby would be a simple chore. They heard a knock on the door. It was the answer to her question: Doctor Best was there. She felt relieved. Lloyd leaned against the outside door, smoking a cigarette while the doctor examined Onalee. He hoped she wasn't going to have a difficult delivery. She'd been through a lot carrying June, having an appendicitis attack when she was six months along with her. This had been when they lived in North Branch. He shuddered, remembering the doctor operating at the kitchen table, taking out Onalee's appendix, hollering for the nurse to give Onalee some morphine. There wasn't any because the fool nurse was addicted to it and used it for herself. He could still hear the screams. It had been hellish. Billy hadn't been a picnic either, coming out with the cord wrapped around his neck, blue and gasping for air. They dipped him in a pail of water until he cried loud and clear. Jesus, she'd been through enough. This would be the last baby. He wouldn't put her through any more of this horse shit. It was turning dusk when he entered the kitchen to see his mother setting the table and visiting with the doctor, who was drinking a cup of coffee. "She's coming along nicely," Doctor Best remarked. "Won't be long now."

He sipped his coffee and pushed his glasses higher on his nose as Lloyd stood there with a questioning look on his face. His mother put a cup in front of him. She could see he was upset. He never talked when he was. "Have a cup of coffee, son" she said. "Perk you up." He didn't sit down. He didn't need a cup of coffee. He needed this baby to get here. He wanted this over for Onalee. The wind had come up, blowing in a thunderstorm. It was going to be a dandy, Lloyd could tell from the zigzagging lightening he could see through the dining room window and from the thunder that came, loud and booming. The little ones had been put to bed upstairs. They would probably sleep right through the storm and the arrival of the baby. The other two, he bet, were parked on the stairway trying to hear what was going on. It was seven-thirty when they heard the moaning from the bedroom and Doctor Best took a last sip of his warm coffee and entered the room, saying over his shoulder, "I think we're going to have a baby here pretty soon."

The Family

Lula hustled into the room right behind him. Lloyd was left with his thoughts and worry. He paced, he watched the trees through the window bend over with the force of the wind, and he worried. His mother was in and out of the bedroom, carrying a pan of water and clean towels. She smiled encouragingly at her son each time she appeared and when she left again, she closed the door behind her, but not before he heard the moans. He'd been through this before and every time it had been the same, sometimes worse than others. This time was a pain in the ass. He felt terrible, not knowing how she was or how the baby was. The storm didn't help, that was a pain in the ass, too.

It was just eight o'clock when Lloyd heard the baby cry. Even with the wind blowing fiercely around the house, he heard the cry and waited, holding his breath, hoping everything was OK with the baby and Onalee. Minutes later, his mother opened the bedroom door, holding a wrapped bundle. "Nine and a quarter pounds," she said. "A nice healthy baby." She walked to the kitchen table and laid the bundle down, motioning to Lloyd to come see. He was so damned relieved it was over as he stared at the round, chubby, screaming baby. "Another boy." He found his voice finally. He was happy it was a boy. His mother laughed," Look again, son, she's fatty down there, but she sure ain't no boy. Look how strong she is. She's a Judd all right," she added proudly. Margie and Keith, sitting on the stairway, stared at each other. She said, "Good," and smiled. He said "Darn," and scowled. She thought, " No more of those hateful boys." He thought, "Another of those bawly girls." He was irritated at his sister's happy attitude. He reached over and pinched her skinny leg. She wouldn't dare yell for their mother now, she was busy. But she did. She hollered out, "Mom, he pinched me!" Onalee lay exhausted on the rumpled bed and heard her daughter. She spoke quietly to Lloyd, who stood looking down at her, "You've got to talk to that boy of yours."

Doris P. Burke

Chapter Twenty-Three

The stock market crash came in the fall of 1929. A frightened America faced a Depression that would strip people of their homes, their jobs and their dignity. Lloyd hated the news in every paper and he was thankful he was on the farm, so as to provide food for his family. This would be a struggle, but he'd do it one way or another. He heard about Ralph from his mother. He'd finally reach his goal - playing for the New York Giants, right there beside Walter Johnson. He was rubbing elbows with the best. For the first time, Lloyd was envious. He'd never give up what he had for Ralph's life, but he sure wanted to meet the players Ralph would be playing with and against. He still loved the game and always would. He knew Ralph would be home at their folks' off and on during the winter months. He wondered if he'd lost a bit of his obnoxious nature. He doubted that. He was probably worse, now that he had made it to the top. Well, damn it all, he told himself. Ralph worked hard to make it there. I'm proud of him. He decided the next time he got downtown he might brag a little about his younger brother to some of the cronies at the grain elevator. After all, how many had a brother playing in the major leagues? Yep, he'd do that, give him something to talk about. Better than groaning about the Depression.

He was thinking all this while he squirted milk into the pail. He looked across at his oldest son, who was working hard to get the old cow's milk to flow into his pail. He kinda hoped the boy wouldn't want to play ball. Ralph did show up late in October with a brand new Cord car, painted yellow, spare tire behind the front fender and a convertible top. It was a sight to behold. Lloyd thought his brother resembled a kid with a new toy as he slid out of the driver's seat. Ralph had a smile as big as the car. They shook hands. Lloyd admired the car, congratulated his brother on making it to the Giants and then stood, waiting to hear what he had to say. Ralph's smile changed to a frown as he spoke, "Wanted to tell ya, the old man has got a still set up in the barn. Found him layin' in the hay mow. Jesus, the old fart drank up a field of rye. Mother, she's upset, couldn't get him up. I managed to get the old fool into the house, told him I was gonna tear down that damn still. He thrashed around like he was gonna beat my ass. He's a sorry sight, Lloyd. Mother says let him sleep it off. When I left, she was putting cold

The Family

cloths on his head and he was moanin'. He ain't changed. Gonna kill himself drinkin' that shit. She said he'd been pretty good till a bunch of his asshole friends started hangin' around." Lloyd shook his head. He'd thought the old man had been more content there on the farm. Now he was up to his old tricks. Who could figure? Ralph added, "I'll be around awhile, but you'll probably have to check on him, so he don't beat the shit outta mother. I got some things to do. Say hello to Onalee. Good to see you brother."

    He slammed the car door, started to back up, changed his mind, came back to where Lloyd stood and yelled out the window, "If ya hear a car pulling in fast some night and heading into your barn, don't think nothin' of it. There's some ladies who might like to take a drive and, you know me, I always did like the smell of hay." He laughed hard when Lloyd ran his tongue over the cigarette he was rolling and said, "What you mean is, a good hiding place from some of those ladies' husbands. Better think about Junior and Jake." Ralph winked at his brother, "I'm not jumpin' out no windows." This made them both laugh. They wiped the water from their eyes as they thought about Junior running for his life. It was like they used to be - enjoying each other's company, thinking of those days when all they thought about was playing another game of ball. Ralph left, backing as fast as he could out of the driveway. He waved again, roaring the motor of his fancy car, still with a big grin on his face. Lloyd wandered toward the barn, still thinking of those early years on his grandpa's farm. His memory of the uncles was good: Big, tall guys with the stamina of horses. He wondered where they were. He guessed he'd never know, being as his grandpa didn't. He entered the barn still thinking about the uncles and Ralph. They were good memories, he decided.

Doris P. Burke

Chapter Twenty-Four

In 1930, a telephone was indeed a luxury. You could ring up friends and neighbors for information without going out into the blast of a winter freeze or a summer downpour. It was convenient and fun to hear a familiar voice through the small receiver. The Judd children took turns listening to Grandma's voice coming through. She sounded distant at times, but she could be heard. Lloyd was relieved to have a connection with his mother other than the inconvenience of climbing into the old car and hoping it would make its way to their place without flat tires or the motor acting up. A frantic call came from Lula on a cold winter night in February. Her voice was barely audible, but he could hear the fear in her whisper: "He's in the barn boozin', got the shotgun. I'm afraid he's going to come in the house with it. Can you come get me?" Lloyd knew Ralph had gone back to New York. It was up to him to help his mother. "I'll be there, mother. Lock the door. When you see my headlights, come out. The old man ain't gonna listen to nobody. Bring a satchel with some clothes. You'll have to stay awhile." Onalee watched Lloyd, getting ready to rescue his mother from the old man again, pull on his clothes. She asked, "How long will your mother take this from your dad?" She did feel sorry for her husband when he answered, "Till one of them is covered up with dirt." The frustration and anger was in his voice.

She lay back on the pillow as he left, hurrying out into the cold, blustery night. She thought of her folks, who lived miles away; of her gentle mother and her stern but dependable father. How she wished they could come to visit. She stretched and peered at the old alarm clock by the bed. It was two o'clock. She decided she'd better make up the davenport for Lula, she'd probably be staying a while. She knew Lula would give advice about the children, act as if nothing happened in front of them and then she'd try to take over the kitchen. She felt a little irritated and not too sorry for the woman who stayed with a man who was a horse's ass. She fussed with the cotton sheets, trying to get them smoothed out on the lumpy davenport. She put a clean pillow-case on the one extra pillow she had and fluffed the feathers as best she could. She thought of what a perfect housekeeper and cook her mother-in-law was. "Well, Mother," she whispered under her breath. "You'll have to sleep on mended sheets and a less-than-fluffy pillow and I'm sure you'll

The Family

notice all these things and I'm sure you might mention it." She realized she was talking to herself and she half laughed out loud. What a story she would hear tomorrow from her mother-in-law, who would whisper about the old man, so the children couldn't hear. Tomorrow would be interesting to say the least. She climbed back into the warm bed. Maybe she could get back to sleep before Lula arrived with satchel in hand and fear on her face. It was just as Onalee anticipated. Lula settled in, bringing her two nightgowns, three house dresses and numerous bits of advice.

The two youngest children had been sniffling with colds and a slight fever. Seeing to their needs kept Onalee busy. She did appreciate Lula's help to a certain extent. She observed her in the kitchen doing what she did best. She had bread all ready to put in the oven before Onalee had the children dressed in the morning. Of course, it would smell and taste delicious. She made her cakes by guess and by God, throwing flour and other ingredients in the bowl and beating the batter as fast as an egg beater. She could slice pork and bacon as well as any butcher and she cleaned shelves constantly, changing cups and glasses to different spots, clucking to herself all the while, saying, "Can't stand disorganized." She insisted on helping with the mending, frowning a little as she noticed Onalee's attempts. "Give me something to do in the evening," she'd say. "Hard for me to sit still and do nothing." The children liked their grandma there and especially liked the variety of cookies that now were always in the cookie jar. Onalee had a feeling Lula was up to something on a Sunday morning when she found her staring out the kitchen window at the chicken coop. "What are you looking at, Mother?" she asked, with somewhat of a sense of foreboding. Lula shook her head, "Oh, nothing. I was just thinking how good some chicken and dumplings would taste to Lloyd and the family." She peeked out the corner of her eye at Onalee. She knew very well that Onalee's chickens were her pride and joy. She kept them well fed so they would lay the eggs that were needed. "Well sure, mother," Onalee answered. "There is an old hen out there, isn't laying any eggs. I'll have Lloyd take care of her for you."

Saying that, Onalee went back to the children, who were whiny and cranky. Coming back a few minutes later, she doused a cloth up and down in a pan of water to soothe the fever June was showing. Out the kitchen window, she saw her mother-in-law running in a circle after her best, fat, laying hen. Before she could get to the door, she heard a squawk and she knew it was too late. Lula had chopped the head off the chicken and was hanging it on the clothesline. Onalee stood in the doorway watching her do this and then she watched her throw some water on the axe blade she had used to execute the queen of the coop. She was so mad at this woman who would do such an unspeakable deed. She would certainly tell Lloyd. She spent the rest of the morning in with the children. She couldn't bring herself to face Lula. She could smell the chicken cooking in the afternoon and she knew it would be delicious. But she knew she wouldn't be able to eat a bite, thinking of her poor hen that had laid such perfect eggs and was now being stewed up with dumplings. She was glad to hear a car pull in the yard a couple of days later and looked out to see Bill step out and walk toward the door. She quickly pulled the door open and noticed his unshaven face and bloodshot eyes. Lula had heard the car and she appeared from the living room with her satchel in hand. "Ready to come home, Mama?" he asked, standing with his hat in hand, waiting for her reply.

"I'm ready, Bill," she answered. "I'm sure there's a lot of work for me to do when I get there." She smiled at him, her eyes bright. Onalee thought she resembled a blushing bride looking with adoring eyes at her bridegroom. Onalee watched them get in the car and she wondered how many times in the coming years Lula would be making a frightened call to Lloyd. It was sad, ridiculous and a poor example for her children to see. She checked her kitchen and noticed the neatness there. Her mother-in-law was certainly three women locked in one short, chubby body. She had even scrubbed the kitchen floor, leaving a shine that hadn't been there before. She wondered where her stamina came from. She worked from dawn till dark and beyond looking for anything to keep herself busy. Onalee sighed and spoke aloud to no one. "I will never forgive that woman for killing my best laying hen. She could scrub every room in this house and it wouldn't help because I will always remember the smell of chicken when I see her again. And I will never forgive Lloyd for eating so much and saying the dumplings were as light as a feather."

The Family

Chapter Twenty-Five

By 1932, the Depression grew worse. Between 12- and 15-million industrial workers lost jobs and the outlook was bleak. Farmers and city workers alike were losing their homes for lack of money to pay taxes. The farm Lloyd and his family lived on was owned by a man who had made good investments. But even he was fearful of losing everything. It was a panic-stricken United States. Talk of the Depression was heard on the streets, in the homes, in every newspaper that was printed and blasted out from radio stations across the country. It was hard to keep a positive outlook. Ralph was still with the leagues and sent money home to his mother for taxes. Myrtle, Lloyd heard, had a new baby and her husband was holding on to his job by the skin of his teeth. No one heard from Lady often. Now and then she sent her little scribbles saying she was fine. It was hard for Lloyd to worry about his sisters and mother and dad when he had seven mouths to feed. Trying to provide for his family kept him busy from morning till dark. Onalee canned anything and everything she could find from the garden they planted. The children picked wild elderberries, wild blackberries and tossed hickory nuts into their lunch pails when they found them on the way to school. They spent many an afternoon gathering apples from the spindly trees in the dying apple orchard. Nothing was wasted. It was a war against poverty. It was downright aggravation, constant preparation and heartfelt determination to beat the Depression.

Farmers banded together to try to do with what they had, exchanging ideas, offering help; even outgrown clothes and shoes were passed from one family to another. Beans were traded for potatoes, wives gave recipes to one another on how to make corn meal go further and lard was used in may homes to replace butter on bread. Chickens were treated with care so they would provide the very-much-needed eggs. And so the Depression went on with everyone holding their breath to see what would happen next. It came in March, 1933, when a banking panic took hold and many banks closed their doors. Those that stayed open allowed a depositor to withdraw only small amounts of cash. Franklin Roosevelt took office as the nation's new president. He made his first inaugural speech to a frightened nation and when he said with confidence, "All we have to fear is fear itself," people listened and took heart. The banking crisis came to an end when he declared a "banking

Doris P. Burke

holiday" while all the banks were examined by treasury officials. Those that were found to be in good financial condition were then supplied with all the money they needed to reopen. The run on the banks stopped. The president went on with his New Deal program, by setting up the Works Progress Administration, known as the WPA, providing employment for many workers. The Civilian Conservation Corps, the CCC, was also set up to put young men back to work as foresters. These agencies helped to bring the nation back to sanity, but the Depression was still real.

The Family

Chapter Twenty-Six

A resolution proposing the repeal of Prohibition was made in 1933. This would hit the bootleggers right in the guts. Lady was still in Detroit with Harry when the talk of a repeal started. It was a real shot in the behind for those who were making millions, big macho money, in bootlegging and especially for Harry, who had profited a deal from such. He became disgruntled and often disagreeable with Lady as he dwelled on the thought of his lucrative business going down the drain. After all, he was supporting a wife, two children and a mistress; a wife who was used to a comfortable home and lavish lifestyle, and children who attended the best schools. Lady, his mistress, was wrapped in furs and wore only designer gowns and lounged with no worries in the cozy apartment he provided for her. It all came to a head when he listened to his wife, one morning at breakfast, tell of the poor people standing in soup lines waiting for a handout. He watched her lips as she talked, noticing the puckered mouth and the superior tone of voice. He thought of her prudish way when it came to sex. They hadn't slept together in years and he hadn't missed the skinny, stiff body or the almost flat pair of tits. She was about as sexy as a toad and her face resembled a perch swimming its way to gobble up a minnow. He wanted to jump and yell, "Shut your mouth, you bitch, we're gonna be poor too!"

He didn't say it. He would stay with her and the children. His kind didn't leave. The family was his responsibility; that's the way it was. Something had to be done, though. His bank account was dwindling as less and less business came his way with the speakeasies closing their doors. He had to get over his obsession with Lady, with her warm arms and soft, giving body. She cost him big bucks. No matter how he looked at it, she was expensive. He left the house and climbed in his two-year-old Lincoln and headed for Lady's apartment. He noticed it was eleven o'clock by his watch. She should be up, he figured. They had danced and drank until two in the morning. She had been complaining of a side ache often, but then she'd laugh and say the booze took it away. Actually, Lady had the pains more often than Harry thought. She couldn't tell Harry when he came, he couldn't see her like this. She always bathed and powder-puffed her best talcum over her body and slipped into her best negligee before he arrived. She made sure she looked her best for Harry, whether they stayed in the apartment and made love

Doris P. Burke

or when they hit the night spots. He had never seen her when she wasn't beautiful and enticing. The pains only became extreme after Harry had left, after their love making, when the booze started to wear off. She often threw up, each time bending over from the sharp stabs of pain running all through her stomach. Now, as Harry parked the car and walked slowly up the stairs to her apartment, he was only preparing himself to unload a sweet luxury. God, he hated to tell her things were over, but he had to, right now. He hadn't planned to find her this way. She was in pain. He could see that when he opened the door and saw her through the opening to the bedroom. He moved closer. She was lying on the bed, holding her side, her face distorted, showing her agony. He could tell she was almost out of it. She did not even acknowledge him.

He stood observing her a minute, noticing the uncombed hair and streaks of rouge. Without speaking to her, he called an ambulance and waited until it came. Then he climbed into his car and left. He was relieved to find it was easier to get rid of his obsession than he thought it would be. Lady had called Weldie before the pains had become intolerable. He would help her, she knew that. She was able to reach him in time, just before she seemed to lose her ability to function. She could hear noises and see an image of a face that didn't speak. In her fantasy, it was her mother, with all her magic cures, here to help her make this terrible pain go away. She felt tears running down her face, just before she lost consciousness. Weldie had hurried after he heard the weak voice on the telephone ask him for help. He pulled up in front of Lady's apartment as the ambulance was pulling away from the curb. He saw Harry going in the opposite direction, passing him, not looking either way. Weldie noticed he seemed to have a satisfied smile on his face. Oh, how he hated this man who had taken this girl hostage and used her. He followed the ambulance, not knowing what had happened or what condition he would find Lady in. She had sounded so sick and disoriented on the telephone. He found her at the hospital after telling a nurse he was a friend who would be there with her. He would notify the family of her sickness, he told the nurse. He wasn't prepared for her reply, "You should speak with the doctor who examined her." Her face had a touch of sadness.

Lady was in a room with the afternoon sun shining on her white face when he entered. He heard her shallow breathing and he reached for her small hand. It was cool. He felt helpless seeing her like this and he thought of the vibrant, vivacious girl who had entered his office those years ago. She had hopes and dreams of a good life. And it could have been, he thought. Jesus, why hadn't he shot that

The Family

son of a bitch? The doctor appeared at his side and spoke quietly. "There is nothing we can do. She has peritonitis, caused from a ruptured appendix. The poison is all through her body. Don't know why she didn't have it out. This didn't need to be. She will be gone soon." He shook his head. "There isn't time to get her family here, I'm afraid." The shallow breathing stopped as Weldie held her hand, the doctor still shaking his head. Lady was dead at 27 years old. Weldie left the hospital to call her mother and father to tell them of her death. He didn't know how to tell them: He even felt responsible to a certain extent for this happening to this lovely girl. If he hadn't been so damned old, he could have courted her, married her, taken care of her. He brushed the tears from his eyes as he drove to make a telephone call. Lula answered the telephone with wet hands. She'd been trying to wash some socks for Ralph and get them dry before he got the bug to leave. He'd been home for the weekend and was in a rush to be gone again. She said hello twice into the phone and finally heard a deep voice ask, "Mrs. Judd?" "Yes, this is Mrs. Bill Judd," she answered, wiping her other hand on her apron. She pushed the receiver closer to her ear. "This is Weldon Van Hughes, Mrs. Judd. Your daughter Lady worked for me at one time." He paused as she acknowledged Lady had mentioned his name. "Are you alone?" he asked.

"My son is here," she replied. Her heart gave a jump, the voice sounded so serious. "I hate to tell you this, Mrs. Judd." His voice broke as he said, "Your daughter died today at St. Joseph Hospital." He waited when he heard a gasp. The next voice he heard was a man's yelling, "What in hell did you tell my mother?" He explained as best he could to Ralph, telling him the hospital was waiting to hear from them about the arrangements to be made at a funeral parlor. Ralph thanked him for calling and in a hoarse voice said goodbye. He stood with his arm around his sobbing mother and wondered how this could have happened to his young sister. He called Lloyd and Myrtle after he got his mother quieted. His old man wasn't home, hadn't been there all weekend. He'd wait for Lloyd to come and then they would go find him. "Probably at the bar downtown," Lula sobbed out when he asked her where he'd be hanging out. "Poor Bill, he will be so upset." She managed to stop her crying for a minute to feel sorry for her husband. Lloyd and Ralph found Bill at the crummiest bar in the area with the crummiest woman in the area on his lap. He was slopped to the gills, they could tell, but he jumped up when he saw them, spilling the woman to the floor. "Here's my sons, folks, the gratess, the strongess, and the bess," he slobbered out, and then stumbled over his chair. They

Doris P. Burke

picked him up and half carried him to the car, disregarding his urging to have a drink on him.

They waited until they got him home and poured three cups of coffee down him before they told him about Lady. He didn't believe them. He hit out at Lloyd. Lula tried to tell him it was true; he didn't want to listen. "It ain't so Mama, boys ain't tellin' ya right." He grabbed her arms and peered into her face. He saw the truth in her eyes. The grief erupted and came pouring out, "Not my Lady, my Lady baby. Oh, ain't so, no, no!" It was the first time in many years - maybe the first time ever - Lloyd and Ralph felt sorry for their old man. Bill wouldn't listen to any more talk of his daughter. He staggered to the barn. He had whiskey there; he'd drink until he couldn't hear the voice in his head saying, "My Lady is dead!" Ralph was on the telephone to the local funeral director making arrangements to pick the body up at the hospital in Detroit. Lloyd went to the barn to find his dad and tell him. He found him sitting in the hay mow staring into space. He seemed rational until he muttered, "Get the car gassed up, son, we're goin' ta pick up Lady, bring her home where she belongs. Mama wants her here ta take care of her." Lloyd gently grabbed his arm, "Dad, she's gone. Mother can't bring her back. Come in the house where it's warm." Lloyd stared at the still, which gave out the booze that poisoned his old man's mind. Tomorrow he and Ralph would tear the damn thing down, he knew that. He got Bill back into the house and Ralph told of the hearse going to pick Lady up. The old man scrambled to his feet and yelled out, "Ain't no body snatcher gittin' ahold of my Lady. We're puttin' her right in the back seat of the car, bringin' her home. Mind me, boy. Kick hell outta ya, iffin' ya don't."

Lula led him into the bedroom, eased him onto the bed and watched his eyes go shut. Then she sobbed quietly into her sopping wet handkerchief. Their Lady was coming home for the last time. She had to get the house ready. By late afternoon the next day, the house was ready for the arrival of Lady. Lula had worked all night polishing and scrubbing until the parlor gleamed from her effort. Neighbors were bringing dishes of food and expressing their sympathy. They smiled at Ralph, stared at Bill and hugged Lula and said they would be back for the funeral. Lady was carried in by four men, her body resting in a mahogany casket. Lula fussed with her hair, held her hand and patted a dab of rouge to her white face. Ralph had ordered flowers and they were delivered by two cars. Roses were placed everywhere. The casket piece of six dozen roses surrounded the area and he insisted rose petals be spread to cover the floor in front of the coffin. Nothing but the best for his sister!

The Family

The parlor indeed smelled like a rose garden. He and Lloyd stood and gazed at their sister after everything was put in place, both thinking of the pretty little girl who used to pout if she couldn't be at their ball games back in Rochester. They remembered the lively, wiggly, two-year-old they took care of when Myrtle was born. And they remembered how she bragged to her friends about her great brothers. They studied her face and wished she could tell them what had happened. Ralph turned away, knowing somehow he would find out. He would ask that Van Hughes fella. He would know if anybody did. Yep, he'd find out something or damn well know the reason why.

Myrtle came the morning of the funeral with her two girls and short, portly husband. She cried when she saw her mother and held on tight to her fairly sober dad. The baby of the family had come home for her sister's funeral, with questions and wrenching sobs when she stood by the coffin. Her beautiful sister, whom she hadn't seen in five years, now lay still. Lloyd and Ralph shook her husband Art's hand, noticing he never took his eyes off of Myrtle. He seemed friendly enough; they had only met him once after he and Myrtle were married and that was only for a few minutes. He had whisked her away like they all had the plague and he didn't want her exposed. He was well dressed and so were the girls, as well as Myrtle in fur-trimmed coat and hat. He was doing all right, he told them, working his way up in an automobile factory. They told him they were glad he was providing a good home for their baby sister. After he went to stand by his wife, seeming to be guarding her, Ralph and Lloyd looked at each other and laughed. Ralph mumbled, "Guess he likes our sister. Hope nobody tries to take her away from him. He'd shoot 'em for sure." Lloyd smirked, "Don't know how he goes to work without her. I hope he gives her room to breathe." They stopped talking when Myrtle broke away from her husband and ran to them. She still had her brothers. Lloyd made the trip to the house to pick up Onalee and the children. When they arrived back at his folks' place, Walt and his family were there. Walt came right to Lloyd's car, lifted Onalee out and threw his head back and laughed when she insisted he put her down.

Lloyd was tickled to see his big bullshitter cousin with his tall son Fred and his twin boys who were just as fun lovin' as their dad. Onalee liked Caroline, Walt's wife, the one Ralph said, "Roped herself a wild stallion and broke him, turning him into a grinnin' plow horse." They reminisced about their young years and then Grandpa and Grandma Judd pulled in and there were hugs and tears and talk and more talk. It was a happy reunion on a sad occasion.

Doris P. Burke

The preacher showed up finally, looking pompous and proper, clearing his throat and studying the people who stood watching him step from his shiny car. Bill strolled toward him. He'd had a good belt from his hidden bottle. He grabbed the startled preacher by the arm and took him to the side of the house. Lloyd walked over to hear his dad say, "Don't wanna hear no damn preachin' about sinners. If I hear any, I'll send your ass down the road back to your congregation who think they're sinless. And ya can sprinkle 'em with your holy water till the cows come home. Ain't gonna help most of 'em. You just say somethin' nice bout my Lady. Then maybe you'll get your damn money." The preacher said nice things about Lady at the service. He seemed nervous and jittery and even stuttered a bit. Everybody wondered why, except Lloyd and Bill. Ralph didn't get in touch with Weldon Van Hughes until he was back in Columbus, Ohio. He'd made the circuit, playing with the Giants and then in St. Louis with the Cardinals. Now he was back with the minors again, trying to pitch his way back to the majors. He was bellying up to bars quite a bit, drinking shots of whiskey and washing it down with beer. He was still making money, had made some investments, but he was frustrated and depressed. He knew he could pitch a damn good game. He had never gotten Lady's sudden death out of his mind completely. They said she died from peritonitis. Well sure, he believed that, but why hadn't she seen a doctor?

On a night when he was dwelling on this, he made the call to Van Hughes. He heard a story he didn't want to hear from an old man who had loved his sister. He hung up the telephone with the man's words ringing in his ears. "I should have killed the son of a bitch," Van Hughes had said. Ralph held the receiver a long time after the voice had hung up. He wanted to head for Detroit and kill the son of a bitch too. He couldn't do that. Maybe he'd hire somebody. He had friends who would do it for a song. He couldn't talk this over with Lloyd. He'd say let it go, she's gone, can't bring her back. No, he couldn't tell anybody about this. The old man might hear about it and head for Detroit with his shotgun loaded. Shit, he'd walk if he couldn't drive the car. Hell no, he couldn't tell anybody. He wished he could have been there for her. She had always been vulnerable, looking for a good time. For her to get mixed up with a one-eyed bastard, though, with a wife and kids, was too much to comprehend. He'd have to let it go. He had to concentrate on his pitching. He threw the whiskey bottle he'd been swigging across the room. It knocked over the picture he kept on the dresser of him, Lloyd and the girls. He lay on the bed and thought of what life had brought to the four of them.

The Family

Chapter Twenty-Seven

Lloyd had a big move to contend with shortly after Lady's funeral. The Depression had taken its toll on the owner of the farm where he lived. New owners would be moving in. He had to find a place for his family. The word around was a fire had burned a house and barns on Golf Road, west of Lapeer. The property had been bought by the White Realty Company. A new house and barns were to be built by fall and they were looking for someone to work the farm. He had the job if he wanted it, but he had to wait until fall before he could move his family there. This presented a bit of a problem, but it was settled when a house was rented for him at Lake Nepessing for the summer. They could be close to the farm and watch the building in progress. It was great for the five kids to be able to spend the entire summer at a lake. There would be time to just enjoy themselves, swimming, fishing and having fun. They had never had the opportunity like this before. It was exciting to think about. But to Lloyd, it was a pain in the ass waiting all that time before he could get his hands dirty again. It was one of those summers when you got hot just sitting still. When the kids weren't in the water, they were thinking about it. It was something to have this gigantic water playground right there in front of them. The girls learned to dog paddle. The boys swam like fish, diving under the water to explore the bottom or doing belly splashes off the dock.

For the first time, Lloyd and Onalee were able to vacation. Of course, the work of washing the sandy towels and finding enough food to fill the always hungry children was still there for Onalee. She sat in the shade of the hickory tree often in the afternoon, watching her brood with anxious eyes, making sure she should count five heads. She felt a little sad to have left the neighbors from the Turrill farm area and she knew Margie, Keith and Billy hated to leave the school friends they had made. June was seven and would start kindergarten at their new school. Doris, the youngest, was four and didn't want to hear about school. She wanted her sisters and brothers to be home with her always and she pouted when they talked of going again. She wished the summer would last forever, especially now that her dad had time to splash in the water with them and give her and June rides on his broad back. It was a wonderful time. But then her sister June stepped on a piece of glass in the water and her

Doris P. Burke

mother started washing the blood from her toe. Her sissy sister tipped right off the stool and fainted from the sight of the blood. She thought her sister a real silly girl and the cut wasn't very big. Every evening after supper, they loaded up in the old car and headed down the road and up the hill to the farm. They were always anxious to see what work had been done to the house and barns. The boys and their dad inspected the barn, where new stanchions were being put in place for the cattle who would be feeding there. There was even a fenced-in pen for the restless bull, who would soon be snorting and stomping in it. The horses would be stalled on the opposite side of the barn, which led to the barnyard where the livestock could roam. There were two silos attached to the barn for the silage to be stored. It was a great barn, they thought, and they could imagine it filled with the new-mown hay and the granary bins filled with golden grain.

The sheep barn sat on a hill to the south toward the lake, brand new and just waiting for the wooly animals to occupy it. An old apple orchard, the tree limbs gnarled with age, led to the rolling hills that seemed to be endless. There was a lane on the west side of the horse and cow barn running the length of the new apple orchard, which was dense with every kind of apple tree, from early-bearing to late snow apples. Onalee and the girls walked through the soon-to-be-completed house, admiring the new cupboards in the kitchen and the good size of the dining room and living room. There was one bedroom downstairs and up the enclosed stairway to the top floor were four bedrooms. It was roomy and seemed to be waiting for a family to settle in and take away the quiet atmosphere. Outside beside the garage was the chicken coop. This made Onalee smile. She would have that filled with clucking chickens, laying those much-needed eggs. The family moved in late August, just before school started. They were there at the farm with 440 acres to work and explore. It was their home now. It was still Depression times and finding school clothes was not easy, but with patching and mending, all four were ready the day school opened. It would be a little jaunt to get there, down Golf Road to Old Lapeer Road to Highway M-21, where stood Clover School. It was a sturdy building with swings, a teeter-totter and a playground in the back for the ball games and the running and the fun times.

School starting was a busy time for everybody. Leaving the relaxed days of summer behind was kinda hard. Now, there would be studying and homework. The electricity poles hadn't been put through on Golf road, so the studying would be done by light from kerosene lamps. Lanterns would be carried back and forth to the

The Family

barn at night. In early September a barn dance was being planned. It would be a gala time. New neighbors, family and friends would be invited - anyone who wanted to come. This would be in the sheep barn. There would be dancing on the clean wood floor, lots of food, a good time. It would be a real shindig not to be forgotten for a while. Onalee's brother Lou and his wife, Myrtle, would come to help get ready, as well as Lula and Bill. Byron and Lena, Lloyd's uncle and aunt, lived just around the corner off Golf Road. They would come to help. Uncle Byron would bring the apple cider, hard and sweet. The fizzy hard cider, he assured everyone, would put a grin on their faces and a spring in their step. A barn dance to beat all was planned. The morning before the dance, Lou and Myrtle arrived. Onalee had the wood cookstove heating nicely. She already had fried cake dough rolled out and when Myrtle entered the warm kitchen, she was put to work. The heavy frying pan was filled with lard and heated until it was extremely hot, then a small piece of potato was put in to absorb some of the grease and the day began with the making of dozens of round, yummy cakes. Homemade bread was brought by Lula and sliced for the many sandwiches to be made. Onalee dumped cooked beans into long pans, added side pork to the top and slid them into the hot oven. Lena came with cookies of all kinds. They were busy women. The boys and Lloyd were in the barn putting boards on sawhorses for tables. Then Billy swept the quite-clean barn floor, sprinkled some wax to make it slippery and then he slid back and forth on it, liking his job. Smiling Max Henderson would be there to play the music for the dance.

Neighbors stopped by all day long, asking how things were coming along and taking sips of the tasty cider offered by Uncle Byron. A fun day, a get-ready day, was enjoyed by all. By nighttime, all preparations were finished. The next day would be work on the farm as usual, but then in the evening, the fun would begin. And then it started. The music was loud, made you want to move your feet and get with it. Everyone felt it, clapping their hands and shaking their legs as they moved around the slippery floor. The sheep barn came alive. The people came from the lake, from downtown, and from near and far. Farmer folks joined in to celebrate a new barn warming. The lanterns that hung high and low swung with the movements and the wicks flickered in time with the music. June and Doris' job was to guide the people who arrived in the darkness through the gate to the swinging activities. It was an important job, their mother told them, and they felt quite important carrying their lanterns and showing the way. When the last of the good old folks were there, the girls found a spot way up high in the

Doris P. Burke

loft of the barn and there they had a good view of their Grandma and Grandpa Judd doing the polka around the dance floor. It was fun to see their short-legged grandma move so quick to the music and their grandpa, with his face red and sweating, seemed to be having the best time of all. The party went on till the wee hours of the morning, with more people coming when they heard of the Judd barn dance. Grandpa Judd called for the square dance and the people began to allemande left and allemande right and stomped their feet, a crazy sight.

The two little girls were sound asleep in the hay mow and were carried back to the house by their dad and Keith. The fried cakes and sandwiches were eaten and the cider was drunk. The music played until the last of the tired dancers flopped in chairs and admitted they couldn't dance one more step. The stragglers reluctantly left, some a bit tipsy from the hard cider, but still grinning and saying what a good old time they had. The lanterns were blown out and the barn door was shut. It was quiet and dark again, but it was sure warmed up for those gosh-darn sheep.

The Family

Chapter Twenty-Eight

The days were lonely for Doris after all the kids went to school. Sometimes she played with her paper dolls, dressing them and undressing them, then standing them up to stare at them to see who had the prettiest dress on. When she tired of that, she put them all back carefully in the shoebox she used to keep them in and then she put them away in the closet. Today she was especially anxious for the kids to come home. Her brother Billy promised to bring her a bubble gum. She had seen them chewing theirs and oh, how she wanted to taste that sweet gum and chew and chew. Her dad had given her a penny and she had made Billy promise to stop at Clover's Gas Station with her penny and pick out the biggest bubble gum for her. In the afternoon, she got very sleepy as usual and she laid her head down on the davenport to take her nap. She had a bad dream about swallowing her gum. She woke up to hear her mother saying, "Are you having a bad dream? You're crying in your sleep!" Her mother stood smiling down at her, holding the basket she used to gather eggs. "Come to the chicken coop with me and help me," her mother said. "You'll forget all about your bad dream."

Doris hated the chicken coop and the silly chickens, but she wanted to be by her mother, so she slowly got up from the davenport and followed her. She really was afraid of those darn chickens. They were jumpy, pecking around things. She stood by her mother in the warm, smelly coop, holding her nose. Her mother reached under the first old hen and showed her the nice white egg she retrieved. "Now, you reach your hand under this little fat lady here and see if she laid an egg for us," her mother urged. Doris shook her head and hunched her shoulders in fear. "They don't like me," she said, backing toward the door. "Nonsense," her mother scolded. "You try!" She tried to be brave. She approached the clucking hen and put her hand under the feathers to try to find an egg. The hen pecked her hand and clucked louder. She ran for the door. She heard her mother mumbling, "Now what's the matter with you ladies?" Doris never did understand why the chickens liked her mother and not her. But she didn't care. She'd never have to gather eggs from those nasty, pecky things. In the late afternoon, she stood by the mailbox, looking down the road, waiting to see the kids coming. She was excited; she would have her first piece of bubble gum. She kicked the dirt around the post, she threw some little stones across

Doris P. Burke

the road to the golf course and she watched some men hitting the white golf ball toward the flag. She was getting impatient when she saw them coming. They were talking and laughing and walking slowly. She wanted them to hurry. She jumped up and down, waving her hand to them. They all waved, except Billy. He looked away, kinda shuffled, stopped and brushed some dirt from his pant leg. Finally all except Billy reached the mailbox. They said, "Hello there, what have you been doing?" They ran to the house to change their clothes and do their chores.

Billy came slowly, peering around at everything but her. Oh, she was mad at him. He stood in front of her and asked, "What are you doing, you little mutt?" He had that teasing smile on his face and she stuck out her lip in a pout. "You better give me my gum, or I'll tell daddy on you," she threatened. "Didn't have no gum today, so you ain't gettin' none," he answered, glaring at her. She was going to cry, she knew that. She was disappointed. She had thought about chewing that gum all day, even had a bad dream about it. She heard a laugh and saw Billy reach into his pants pocket. "Here, you little worm, chew before I chew it up!" He handed her the small, round piece of gum. She grabbed it quick and ran to the porch. She unwrapped it slowly and held it to her nose. It smelled sweet and good. She popped it in her mouth. It was sorta hard, but she kept chewing and pretty soon, it turned into sticky sweetness and then it became smoother and smoother. Her first piece of bubble gum. She knew she could blow great big bubbles, bigger than Billy and June could.

The Family

Chapter Twenty-Nine

Ralph came roaring into the driveway one snowy evening in December of 1933. He was still driving his grand-looking Cord car and the boys rushed out to check it over. This time, he wasn't alone. Onalee and the girls watched out the window as he helped a lady from the passenger seat. "Good heavens and look at me!" Onalee sputtered, pulling her grease-spotted apron off and smoothing her house dress down as best she could. Lloyd was in the barn, finishing some chores. She wished he was in the house so he could greet his brother. The kids stared at the lady with the pretty, wavy hair and the long-painted fingernails and bright red lipstick. She wore a fur coat and when she undid the buttons, they could see a shiny, silky sort of dress under it. Doris hid behind Margie and June. She had never seen a lady dressed so nice. She felt kinda scared, hoping the person wouldn't see her wild dark hair that needed a good brushing. Onalee liked Rosie right away. She was friendly and smiled often. "This is your Aunt Rosie, kids," she said to all of them after the boys entered the kitchen. She introduced each of them, pulling Doris out from behind the other girls and saying, "This is the baby, Doris." Her mother squeezed her arm and she knew she was supposed to be good.

Lloyd came in with the same surprised look on his face that Onalee had and then greeted his new sister-in-law. The women sat down at the dining-room table and visited. Lloyd and Ralph stood in the kitchen. Ralph said he'd be spending the winter in Lapeer and had an apartment in town for him and his wife. Lloyd was tickled that Ralph had finally taken a wife and he told him so. "Well, brother," Ralph raised his voice loud enough for the women to hear him. "She lassoed and hogtied me before I knew what was happenin'." Rosie heard him and waved her hand toward him, but she laughed a pretty laugh and Ralph laughed too. The girls thought it was swell to have a nice-smelling, new Aunt Rosie. The boys wondered why their baseball-playing uncle, with an exciting life, would want a wife to slow him down. Keith pinched Margie's arm when he walked by her just because she was smiling at the new aunt. Billy whispered to June, because she was smiling too, "She's sure got skinny legs, look at 'em." Ralph had come home with a big surprise for everybody and after they left, Onalee asked Lloyd, "And what did he say your mother thought of his wife?" She chuck-

Doris P. Burke

led, thinking of Lula, who was so possessive of Ralph. "Didn't say, but don't matter," Lloyd answered. But he, too, wondered how his mother would accept this lady. Ralph was there all winter, often roaring in the driveway to pick June up to come and stay with him and Rosy for the weekend. Sometimes Margie stayed with them and went to school from their place. At Easter, he brought colorful Easter baskets for all the kids. Onalee believed his new wife had mellowed Ralph, making a thoughtful man out of her brother-in-law.

    Doris listened to June tell of the pretty apartment and how Aunt Rosie would help her paint her fingernails and of the yummy chocolate candy always sitting in pretty glass dishes on the coffee table. She was sure she wasn't invited to her Uncle Ralph and Aunt Rosie's because she had ugly dark hair and ugly dark skin. She got so that when they came, she hid behind a chair and peeked out at them and wished she was a blonde.

The Family

Chapter Thirty

Slim came in the spring of 1934. He came sauntering down the road, right out of nowhere, to ask Lloyd if he needed a good hired man. Everything he owned was in a brown paper bag under his arm. Didn't consist of much: another pair of long underwear and a badly-in-need-of-mending plaid shirt and a razor. He was hired. The boys were in school all day and the pressure of work on the big farm was getting to Lloyd. He needed help and Slim was a welcome sight. He knew how to handle horses, knew how to milk and knew how to keep his mouth shut and work. He was a tall man, skinny, in his early forties, but looked older. His face was tanned with deep wrinkles. It was a face which gave the appearance of having seen things, both good and bad. A real reflection of the soul was there in his eyes. Onalee put him up in Billy's room, bunking the boys together in Keith's. The boys griped about it to each other and to the girls until they got to know Slim. Here was a fella who could tell them about the world out there, and he did. Every evening after the milking and the supper dishes were done, they all listened to his stories of the hobo camps and riding the rails. He showed them a scar on his leg from his ankle to his knee, taking his corn cob pipe from his mouth and grinning, saying, "Couldn't get my gol-darn leg pulled into the door of the freight car fast enough, 'bout tore it off." His stories made the boys' eyes big as saucers and the girls would cringe, thinking of the danger.

Sometimes he'd offer to stay with the kids while Lloyd and Onalee took a break and went to the movies. And with a pan of popcorn in front of them, the kids listened intently, watching the expressions come and go on his face, which was shadowed by the dim light of the kerosene lamps. He even recited rhymes he remembered, clearing his throat like a young boy at a school recital. His favorite came out loud and clear: "Clara the cow went amblin' round, Lookin' for somethin' to chew. She ate some green thistle, And now she just whistles, Instead of goin' moo, moo!" Sometimes, he would get a sad look on his face and tell of the hobo camps that were now full to overflowing with families who had lost their homes and how they would stop at the camps for warmth and food. "They huddle around the fire, each with a different story to tell. Their faces showed the defeat they feel. This Depression has touched everybody. I couldn't stand to see the little ones with the ragged clothes and shoes. Got right outta there." He would cough

Doris P. Burke

and change the subject, saying, "Here's a favorite: "If I was a hobo, I'd try to be, The best dern hobo you'd ever see. I'd eat my beans out of a can, And soak my feet in a rusty ole pan.

I'd tip my hat to a pretty little lady, And rest myself under a tree that's shady. I'd hop a freight with a grin on my face, And tumble right off at a likely place, And, when I'm old I could tell a tale, Bout those gosh dern hobos And riding the rail." The kids clapped at his rhymes, felt sadness when he looked sad and enjoyed him to know end. He had become a friend. And when they asked what place he had been he liked the best, he answered with a twinkle in his eyes: "I've seen those cowpokes ride their ponies, Seen and jawed with hobo cronies, Picked those oranges from fruitful trees, Watched the waves on restless seas, Had a taste of lobster meat, Seen men perform a dangerous feat, Climbed a mountain, cause it was there, Ran like heck from a big, black bear, I sure liked every place I've been, But my favorite place is where I am."

He said just what they wanted to hear and they all went to bed with a smile, knowing their friend Slim liked them best of all. He taught them to appreciate what they had as they listened to the stories of people who had nothing, of those who had lost hope in the country that was the land of opportunity. They believed as he did that life would be better for most in the years to come. The spring planting was done, even the radishes and peas were poking up in the garden when Slim decided he had to move on. "Got those itchy feet startin'," he told the family. "And when that happens, gotta get goin', Think I'll move up to one of those CCC camps. I'd like to see what they're all about. You got the boys home for the summer, Lloyd, good strong fellas, help you a lot." They hated to see their friend leave, but they knew he had to. He was a wanderer, an adventurer. He was a hobo. Lloyd insisted they drive him to the train in Flint and on a warm day in June they all loaded up in the old car. Slim held his brown paper bag with all his possessions, his freshly laundered underwear and his newly mended plaid shirt and his razor. They didn't drive right up to the train station. They stopped a ways back from that, while Slim jumped out of the car. He had his eye on an open door of freight car. He stood a minute looking at the faces of the kids and then, with a bit of a choke in his voice, he said, "Remember boys, you don't wanna be a bum. You go to school, be somebody and listen to your folks. You girls marry somebody who likes to work and take care of you." He turned and ran quickly toward the open freight car, made a leap and was in it. They watched as the train started to pull away. They saw a hand wave and then their friend was gone, down the tracks somewhere.

The Family

Chapter Thirty-One

The apples on the first tree in the orchard were ready. When they were ripe, they would yellow and mellow. Right now, they were about as big as a ping-pong ball, green, juicy and tasty. They were ready to eat as far as Billy, June and Doris were concerned. They had been warned by their mother, who spoke in a stern voice, "You kids don't eat those green apples. They are bad for you and for sure you will get colory morbis." They had heard the speech many times, even shuddered at the words colory morbis. Whatever the deadly disease was, they had no idea. It didn't scare them enough, they loved the green apples. On any given day, they would try to sneak to the orchard and indulge. One afternoon, they all managed to elude their mother and were sitting very contentedly with a pile of the little hard nuggets on their laps and a chunk of the cow's block of salt in their hands. The salt added just the right touch of flavor. They heard a noise coming down the lane by the barn. They scrambled to the top of the tree and watched. Billy whispered, "Jeez, here he comes!" He was the proper Mr. Williams, the lawyer for the company that owned the farm. Maybe he owned an interest in the farm, they didn't know. He showed up often, snooping, they figured. He wore a well-pressed suit, white shirt starched to the point of ridiculous and a tie matching the suit's color. His shoes were polished to the point you could almost see yourself in them.

He walked with each shoe pointing outward, which made him resemble a well-dressed penguin. The kids agreed on that. He was really a horse's ass all dressed up. They agreed on that, too. He opened the tool shed, peered in, then closed the shed door. He then stood by the barnyard. He seemed to be counting the beef cattle that roamed around bellowing and pushing one another. The girls giggled quietly when Billy growled, "I wish he'd get in the yard with the cattle and they'd shit on him." He just finished saying that when they saw their mother appear around the horse barn. "Be quiet, you little mutts," he warned. "She won't see us up here." They watched from their tree limb, hardly breathing. She approached Mr. Williams. "Have you seen the kids?" she asked. He tipped his hat and said in a positive tone of voice, "If you want to know where they are, Mrs. Judd, why they're right up in that tree there." "I knew it," Billy gave a sigh. "He's also a tattle-tale along with being a horse's ass." She was frowning and staring at the tree, just before

Doris P. Burke

she hollered loud, "Get yourselves down here, right now! Do you hear me?" Mr. Williams walked quickly back the way he came, but not before they saw a satisfied smirk on his face. Their mother lined them up: Billy first - spanked him - June next - spanked her, and when she got to Doris she was puffing a bit, so she just gave her a couple of little spanks.

Billy didn't cry, but he did think his mother had hurt him a little. June cried and Doris cried too, but just because June did, not because it hurt. She was glad her mother was too tired to wallop her hard. Their mother sputtered all the way to the house, shooing them along and saying, "If I catch you eating those green apples again, I'll have your dad spank you. My goodness, I've told you you're going to get colory morbis one of these times." There it was, the dreaded word, she said it again! Billy felt fine, June felt fine. Doris had a touch of a bellyache and wondered if she might be getting the terrible thing her mother threatened would happen. June and Billy were sent to pull weeds in the garden and Doris was sent up to her room to take the nap she always took in the afternoon. "You look peaked," her mother told her as she pushed her up the steps to the bedroom. Doris lay on her bed, her bellyache getting worse instead of better. Oh, she knew she had it! She turned over on her back and could hear the gurgling coming from her insides. This was it! Would she die laying right here on the bed, of the dreaded colory morbis? She couldn't tell her mother she was sick; June and Billy would pound her if she did. All of sudden she knew what she had to do, and right away! She had to go to the toilet! She sneaked down the stairway. Her mother must have been in the chicken coop, probably putting a splint on one of those pecky chickens' legs. She was always doctoring them up.

She ran like the dickens to the toilet, getting there just in time. She sat a long time, watching through the crack in the door to see if she'd see her mother. Her bellyache was coming and going, getting better the longer she stayed perched on the toilet seat. She didn't dare close her eyes; then she might be dead if she did. She kept them wide open, staring through the crack. She felt better after awhile. She stood up. She had to make a run for it before her mother saw her. She did. And after she was in her room with her head on her soft pillow and her blanket pulled up around her, she sighed. She was tired from her terrible experience. She knew she would never, ever tell anybody what had happened, not even June. She knew she had survived the dreaded colory morbis. She went to sleep thinking, "Billy wouldn't believe me anyway."

The Family

Chapter Thirty-Two

In the fall of 1935, Doris started school. She was six. This time she was sure she could stay awake during naptime. Last year, she had tried to start kindergarten, but at two o'clock she lay her head down on the small desk and went right to sleep. Miss Lucas, the teacher, told her mother and dad she should probably wait another year. This had made her very unhappy. She wanted to go to school with the other kids, it was lonely at home. She knew her ABCs and how to count to a hundred. She practiced at home, printing on a piece of paper from June's tablet. She felt a little ashamed when the kids told her she flunked kindergarten. They were all so smart in school; Miss Lucas told their mother that. Well, she'd show them she was smart too. She wanted so much to read those books of her dad's that the kids had their noses stuck in every night. Especially, she wanted to read Tarzan of the Apes. Billy had told her about the man who lived in the jungle with the apes. She wanted to read and read. She had a new dress for her first day of school. Her mother had made one for her and June. Her's was red with pretty flowers; June's was blue with a white collar. Doris really liked blue better, but her mother said red looked nice with her dark hair and blue went nice with June's blonde hair. Nobody ever thought they were sisters, they didn't look alike.

She knew she looked more like her big brother Keith and June resembled Billy. She would have liked to have had light hair, but her mother always said, "We like what we have." Well, that was fine for her mother to say because it didn't hurt her when either she or Margie brushed her hair. Her's was so tangled from being so thick, it pulled and made tears come to her eyes. It was fun walking to school with her brothers and sister. Margie had started high school, so she had to be taken there by her dad. They met other neighbor kids on the way and everybody kicked stones, threw stones and talked about what game they would play when they got to school. And when they got there, they played Red Rover or Pom Pom Poli Way and the little ones played on the swings. It was a good time before school started. The teacher would ring the big bell on top of the schoolhouse and they all hurried in to hang up their coats and take a seat. The kindergarten sat in small chairs at the front under the blackboards. This is where Doris took a seat. Miss Lucas found out Doris knew what she had to know about kindergarten, so she

Doris P. Burke

put her with the first graders. She felt quite grown up when she had a desk instead of those dinky little chairs and besides that, she didn't want anybody staring at her there up front. They had their reading books and she loved hers, seeing Dick and Jane and their dog, Spot. She knew she would be reading quick as a wink. Most of all she liked her Big Chief tablet, brand new, with all the sheets of paper clean and ready to be printed on. She could hardly wait to print her first letters on the white paper. School was going to be a great time. She was glad to be here with June and Billy and her big brother, Keith. Now she was a grown up, too. A Christmas program was planned. All the parents would come to the school and watch their children recite verses or be in a Christmas play. A couple of weeks before the big night, schoolwork was put aside part of the day for practice time - practice and more practice - until each one had his part memorized.

It was a nervous time for Doris. She knew her poem, but what would she do when she had to stand up in front of all those mothers and fathers and other people? She was scared to have eyes staring at her. Billy and June told her to quit being such a scaredy-cat when she told them. They acted so brave and she wanted to be brave, too, but she almost cried thinking about it the days before the program. They were in the play with other kids. She would be alone up there. The night of the event, the school was full to overflowing with all parents turning out to see their children perform. When her turn came closer, she felt terrible. She knew she would have to tell the teacher she couldn't do it. Before she could, she heard the teacher say, "Doris will recite a Christmas poem." She hesitated and sorta stumbled getting up on the platform. She looked out at the faces. Her mother was smiling and her dad was smiling and shaking his head, as if to say, "You can do it!" She took a deep breath and it spilled out. She kept her eyes right on her dad as she said: "I'm a chink, chink, China girl from far across the sea, So far away old Santee Clausee, can never findee me. I likee Christmas verlee much, it brings me muchee joy, To have old Santee come and fillee stocking with a toy. I hope he findee me so far across the sea." She held her breath and then everyone clapped. She felt happy to see her dad clap the loudest. It was a Christmas to remember, especially when the teacher gave all the kids in school a brand new pencil and a candy cane.

The Family
Chapter Thirty-Three

The weekends were fun in the winter: no school and most early mornings the sleds came out. Neighbor kids came from the lake, from around the corner on old Lapeer road and way over by the school. The golf course had a good slippery hill right across from the farm and you could hear shouts and screeches coming from the snow-covered kids all day Saturday and Sunday. If anyone got a pair of skis for Christmas, they were invited to join the crowd because everybody wanted to use them. They stayed out, even after dark when the moon was full and the air was so brisk their breath seemed to freeze as they puffed coming up the hill. By the time June, Billy and Doris got in the house, their socks were wet underneath the boots, the girls' snow pants were sopping wet and Billy, with his long underwear on, was truly soaked to the skin. Their mother sputtered and scolded and warned of getting sore throats or pneumonia. And of course, if they did get a sore throat, out came the flannel cloth with salt pork wrapped in it. Pepper was shook onto it and around the neck the whole thing went. After a couple of days, they said it felt better just so she'd take the smelly thing off! Wintertime did keep them busy sliding downhill, playing Fox and Geese, building a snow-fort and going to the movies, if they could find the ten cents it took to get in.

The kids relied on a big, old, warm piggy bank on top of the furnace. When the neighbor men came in the winter to talk with their dad about something, they always stood on the wide register that brought the warm air up from the wood furnace. They warmed themselves and talked. Uncle Byron seemed to always be pulling something from his pocket: a knife to clean his fingernails or a coin to show. With the pull from his pocket, sometimes coins dropped through the register. It wasn't only Uncle Byron, it was Uncle Ralph or any neighbor who happened to stop by. The ping! ping! the kids heard meant change, real money. Of course it was lost, thought the men who stood over the warm register. They would laugh and go on their way. Losing a few pennies didn't matter. But, after they left, when their mother wasn't looking, up came the register and one of the boys dropped down to the top of the furnace to find the coins. This helped to get them to the movies on Saturday night. The little girls, June and Doris, like The Shadow serial. They liked to be scared and liked the voice that said, "Who knows what evil lurks in

Doris P. Burke

the heart of man? The Shadow knows!" They were intrigued by the man dressed in a dark overcoat, with a hat pulled down over his eyes and a built-up shoe that made the sound, "clop, clop" when he walked. He was always on the prowl, trying to find a new victim so he could wring their neck or whatever. It was scary, it was weird, it was fun. The girls liked to play "clop, clop" in the barn where it was dark and shadowy. One afternoon they went to the barn to play their favorite weird person. It was a dreary winter day and especially cloudy. This was good, more scary. They had an old coat and hat of their dads. June would wear these and Doris would try to escape "clop, clop." The cattle were in the barnyard and it was very quiet and spooky in the pathways, from where the cattle usually were, to the horse barn.

Doris hid in the stairway and shivered. She could hear June dragging her foot and then she'd "clop" loud with the other one on the cement floor. No matter where she hid, Doris could hear "clop, clop" coming. She wished she could hear the cattle chewing their hay or the horses stomping their feet. There was nothing, only the noise of that foot clopping its way toward her. She was finally scared enough and she yelled to her sister, "Let's not play anymore!" June was scaring herself and she was glad to quit. They stood together by the stairway that led to the upstairs of the barn when they heard a noise coming across the floor above them. They stared at each other. It was a "clop, clop" noise! To say they were scared is an understatement. They were petrified with fright and stood tight together, Doris looking at her sister for reassurance. She noticed June's blonde hair seemed to be sticking right up straight and she thought it was from fright, not realizing it was left that way when June pulled off the hat. The noise kept coming and then started down the stairway. And just before they found their voice to scream, they saw the figure of their mother standing on the stairway peering down at them. She said, "What are you girls doing out here in this dark barn today, scaring yourselves?" She had a smile on her face and they realized she had heard them talk so much about "clop, clop" she was trying to play the game with them. She never knew how close she came to scaring her two little girls to death. It was the last time they played "clop, clop" and they didn't want to hear the words or see him in The Shadow serial ever again.

The Family
Chapter Thirty-Four

The kids could smell spring coming and see the tiny buds on the tree limbs starting to pop open. The grass had a tinge of green under the brown and there was a sudden urge to shoot marbles and jump rope. Rings were drawn in the dirt at school and the boys huddled in a circle trying to win some colorful agates to add to their collections. The girls had a rope measured just right to swing and you could hear the noise of the rope whirling and the voices singing: "My mother, your mother, lives across the lane, Every night they have a fight and this is what they say: Acca bacca, soda cracka, acca bacca boo, Acca bacca, soda cracka, out goes you!" Thoughts were of slipping off to the swamp and getting some those croaking bullfrogs with those jumping legs you could sizzle in the frying pan. Everyone tried to wait patiently for the field to dry out in the back of the school so the ball games could begin. It was the time of the year to be tired of studying and just wanting the sun to send its warm rays down so you could stretch your arms and body and welcome the start of a fun-filled summer. They wanted to shed their shoes and wriggle their toes, to be free of rubber boots and leather footwear; to throw their coats in the closet, not to think about them until next fall. Snotty noses would be dried up and you wouldn't have to carry a handkerchief stuffed in your sleeve.

Rejuvenation was starting, and oh, what a great feeling to be young and alive. Soon there would be the fragrance of lilacs making you sniff in appreciation. It was the summer of 1936 and Billy, June and Doris had a nice surprise come to live with them on the farm. It was Molly. She was about 46 inches tall, had big eyes and was white with black spots. Big brother Keith had raised a calf to be sold at the livestock sale and instead he exchanged it for the lovable little Shetland pony. The three looked kindly toward their big brother after that. Molly was washed and curry-combed and her mane was brushed. They were very proud of their pretty little pony. It wasn't long before Billy was doing like the cowboys, jumping from side to side, the rear, and right up on the patient pony's back Then he'd ride hell-bent for election to the disgust of the little girls. They just wanted to ride her calmly down the lane. Take turns is what they wanted, but oh, no, he was Gene Autry, the leader of the cowboys. There was a deep gravel pit by the road. It was a great place to pretend, with a little valley and mountains to climb. Billy

Doris P. Burke

promised one day if the girls would make trails and dig hideouts, he'd play cowboy with them after he got through helping with the hay. The girls dug with their hands. They dug with a hoe, they even made a stream from some water standing at the bottom of the pit around the spindly trees that stood there. By suppertime, they stood back and viewed their cowboy hideout. It was a great accomplishment, they figured. After supper, they encouraged Billy to come see. "Wait till I get Molly," he said. "You girls go stand and watch."

They waited down in the pit, admiring their trails and dugouts, wanting their brother to hurry so he could admire them too. They heard him coming, riding fast and hard. They watched with mouths open as he rode the trails they had dug, pushing the dirt so it collapsed right before their eyes. Up and down and around he went, until everything was torn up, leaving no sign of trails or caves. He left, giving a smirk over his shoulder. They looked at each other. It wasn't Gene Autry who came riding through, it was the outlaw Billy the Kid for sure. They had a hard time getting over his wild ride and said they wouldn't play with him for a while after that. But of course, they did. And being good old cowpokes like they were, one night he talked them into smoking stogies. He built a small fire in the bottom of the gravel pit, just a tiny one so their mother and dad couldn't see it, and there they were sitting around the campfire with their cornsilk cigarette stogies lit. Then Doris burned her nose and she cried and the other two cowpokes were mad and told her she wasn't a good old cowpoke like they were as they coughed and spit out pieces of dried cornsilk. Their mother smelled the smoke on their clothes and noticed Doris' scorched nose and for a long time they were barred from the gravel pit. The stream dried up, the spindly trees never grew one inch and the trails were washed away with the rain. But for a while it was a cowboy haven in the minds of one boy and two little girls. The summer of 1936 was certainly the summer of mishaps. Still playing cowboy, Billy was learning to rope. In order to learn, he had June ride by on Molly and he would try to throw a lasso around her neck. His rope was heavy binder twine and he got lucky one day and caught June right around the neck. She went sprawling off the pony and was about choked to death before he got the rope undone. Their mother was mad — Oh boy! Was she mad! - when she saw the rope burns on June's neck. This was the end of the lassoing.

The next day, Billy and June were swinging on a long rope in the barn like Tarzan. He said, "Go." She wasn't ready and she fell, spraining her ankle. Everybody was mad, then, because it was movie night and nobody could go if she couldn't get her shoe on. They

The Family

watched with angry eyes as she pushed and shoved, trying desperately to get the swollen foot into the stubborn shoe. When she couldn't, all eyes turned toward the culprit who caused the accident. "I said go," his excuse was. "I can't help it if she can't hear good." This ended the Tarzan era. He was told never to do that again with his sister. They didn't have to tell June, she knew she'd never trust him again to tell her "go" when he knew darn well she wasn't ready. He was scolded a lot that summer, but his imagination always got the best of him. He seemed to stay awake nights, thinking of new games or a feat of danger and always wanted to include his two sisters in his folly. A couple of days later, after June's foot was better, he came up with another suggestion, "Let's ride King and Queen through the orchard, pretend we're trying to outrun the outlaws!" June and Doris did think that sounded like fun, being real rootin', tootin' cowboys riding through the woods escaping the bad guys. They mounted the big workhorses, Billy on King, both girls on Queen. He led the way, telling them to follow. He rode like a bat out of hell. They followed right behind, trying to cut their way through the tall trees. June yelled over her shoulder to Doris, "Duck down!" She didn't duck and a limb hit her hard and off the horse she went, her arm hitting a rock. The other two stopped, got off the horses and picked her up. She was crying hard and holding her arm. Billy glanced at her arm and tried to be reassuring. "It's just bent a little, but you'd better go up to the house and show mom."

It hurt bad. Doris held it with her other hand while she hurried as fast as she could to show her mother. By the time she got to the house, it was beginning to swell and she sobbed the more she looked at it. Her mother didn't have to be told it was broken, she could tell. Their dad wasn't there, but Keith was and he could drive but didn't have his driver's license. Nevertheless, they had to get to the doctor. It was a long ride into town, it seemed to Doris, as she listened to her mother fret about leaving Billy and June home alone. Here she was with her arm about broken in two and her mother was worried about those awful kids who sent her up to the house alone when they knew she was hurt bad. Oh, they were going to get it, she hoped! The doctor's office was up some steps and her mother helped her. She felt sorta sick to her stomach and especially so when Doctor Congdon said it was a very bad break. It had to be x-rayed, so they had to walk back down the steps and around the corner to Doctor O'Brien's office, where the only x-ray machine was. Her mother fretted some more about poor Keith having to sit in the car and wait so long. Doris didn't care if he had to wait all day and

Doris P. Burke

those awful kids, she knew, were hiding out in the orchard while she was here really hurting from this broken arm. Oh, they were gonna get it! The bad break was confirmed by the x-ray and the doctor put a cast on that was heavy and she hated it. Her mother helped her in the car where poor Keith was and they headed for home. Her big brother did smile sympathetically at her. He was nicer than Billy, she decided.

 Upon reaching home, her mother told her to lie on the davenport and take a nap. She did feel awful tired from her terrible experience, but she wanted to hear her mother give the kids the dickens. Keith was sent out to find them and they soon appeared and stood over her and stared at the cast. She didn't like either one of them. She closed her eyes. The littlest cowboy went to sleep and dreamed the outlaws got her.

The Family

Chapter Thirty-Five

Margie was learning to drive. She was old enough to get her driver's license. She had practiced going down the lane and back, steering the old Model T around the curves slowly and precisely and pushing on the stiff brake pedal with all her might. She was doing well. Keith, of course, could drive fast, leaving a cloud of dust as he tore down the lane, the old Model T jumpin' and rattlin'. He was good at it. He was a boy, a natural-born driver of tractors and automobiles. She had to work at it. Her dad encouraged her to drive the lane as often as possible. He wanted his eldest daughter to be a good driver, a safe drive. Keith felt superior. She was a girl and what did girls know about a fine-tuned motor? He didn't encourage her. In fact, he enjoyed seeing her struggle to conquer the art of driving that he was so good at. He even snickered a little, seeing her thin body behind the wheel, trying to reach the gas pedal with her short, thin leg. On a summer afternoon, her mother asked her to drive the lane to call the boys and her dad for supper. They were working in the fields back of the orchard. She felt confident and asked Doris to ride with her. Doris wasn't so anxious to ride with her big sister, but it was a ride and she was all for that.

Margie twisted the crank at the front of the car and with a bang and a backfire, it started. They climbed in and were off. Away from the garage, down by the tool shed, around the corner to the lane and they chugged along, with Margie smiling and steering a lot and Doris holding on. It was a nice afternoon, a good day to be driving. They reached the field and waved to the boys and their dad, yelling "Supper!" loud and clear. This done, Margie got the car turned around and merrily they rolled along beside the apple orchard. Doris noticing the apple blossoms had turned into tiny green nubs on the trees they passed. She also noticed her sister seemed to be driving fast. She wondered if she was trying to drive fast like Keith did. She hoped not. At the turn that led back toward the barn, they were still moving right along. Doris felt fearful now. Her sister had to turn quick because there was a fence right in front of them. She didn't turn and they crashed into the fence with force. The car sputtered to a stop and they heard bang! bang! bang! bang! As each tire went flat as a pancake. They climbed out, Margie very upset and Doris so upset she was crying and knowing she should never have ridden with her sister on this wild ride. She sobbed out, "Dad is really gonna give it to you!"

Margie, a little pale, stood staring at the flat tires and the front, which was stuck into the fence. She wanted very much to slap her little sister just for being there and especially for saying what she did. She didn't and they waited until they saw their dad and the boys coming in, with the team of horses pulling the wagon. They could see Billy and Keith pointing their fingers and talking. Their dad was snapping the reins, trying to hurry the horses. Doris was disgusted their dad didn't yell at Margie. She wanted him to, but he just seemed glad they weren't hurt. She was disappointed because she had been scared and she wanted her dad to punish her sister for driving so recklessly and about scaring her to death. He didn't. He and the boys fixed the tires after supper, backed the car away from the fence, fixed the fence and he told Margie to get in and drive again. Doris thought from then on that Margie was her dad's favorite because he didn't scold her for being a bad driver. She knew she would never ride with her sister again if she could help it. Unless of course, she was going someplace where she really wanted to go and that would be after her sister learned to turn the gosh-darn steering wheel!

Chapter Thirty-Six Lula called a couple of times that summer. It was always in the middle of the night, the telephone ringing shrilly, disturbing everyone's sleep. The kids would hear their dad's muffled voice talking and the sound of him moving around and then the door would open and shut. The car would be started up and he'd be gone. The next morning there she'd be, doting on them, with a freshly pressed apron on and a box of cookies ready to be gobbled up by the always hungry bunch. She'd stand at the stove, wanting to take over the cooking, but their mother would stand her ground, advising their grandma to sit and rest herself. They tried to hear about their grandpa, but she only whispered to their mother, who often replied, "My gracious, Mother, how do you put up with that?" Once in a while in the evening, she would sit in the rocking chair, mending the socks their mother allowed her to do, and she'd sputter out talk of a neighbor or a neighbor's daughter. "A terrible, brazen girl," she'd say. "Sits with her leg flung over a chair, with a cigarette stuck in her mouth and her nursing tit in her baby's mouth. Shameful hussy, don't think she's got a man!" She would shake her head in disgust and glance at the kids, as if to tell them they hadn't better turn out like this gosh-awful girl, with a baby from whomever. They enjoyed their grandma coming for a visit, but they often wondered why and where was the grandpa she whispered about?

She did smile when she talked of Ralph, telling the boys what

The Family

a great pitcher he was. She referred to Aunt Rosie as "the woman he married." Once they heard her whisper to their mother, "Painted face, lazy woman." Their grandma, they decided, was a funny little person, who baked delicious sugar cookies, said comical things, liked them very much and especially liked her two sons, whom she talked about whenever anyone would listen. They also decided whatever their grandpa did was a secret she didn't want them to know about. Sometimes she stayed for a week, sometimes longer. It was always the same: Their grandpa would pull in the driveway and before he got out of the car, she was packing her satchel and was ready before he got to the door. He'd say, "Are you ready to come home, Mama?" She'd say, "I'm ready, Dad." She would thank their mother for having her, wave to them, and happily follow their grandpa to the car and they'd chug away. The little girls thought he might be a traveling salesman. Billy punched them in the arm when they mentioned that. If he knew something about their grandpa they didn't know, he didn't tell them. And so, the secret of Grandma's husband went on for a few more years, never to be spoken of until they found out for themselves. Uncle Lou and Aunt Myrtle came from Flint often that summer and other summers. They had one daughter, Betty Jane. She was about June's age and the girls were always glad to see her when she arrived. Her enthusiasm for being on the farm was something and besides that, she liked to be with the lively bunch, who would think of so many things to keep her busy. Uncle Lou and Aunt Myrtle had adopted her.

    Aunt Myrtle was a tall, fleshy woman with a loud voice, ear-piercing laugh and she seemed to enjoy irritating her husband. The kids wanted to like her, but were always taken aback watching her eat. She was a human garbage can! Their mother cooked chicken often when they came because she said Louie liked chicken and she tried hard to please her brother, realizing his wife didn't. Aunt Myrtle ate everything from the chicken she could get ahold of. She chewed the bones, snapping them in two and sucking out the marrow inside. If it was stewed chicken, she ate the slippery skin like it was a delicacy. The noodles made in the broth were drawn into her mouth like a vacuum, making a noise so disgusting it made the kids want to cover their ears. And when they thought she was finally through eating, she ran her tongue up and down the fork up and down the knife and wiped her plate with her fingers. She then licked them one by one until she was sure she had every one of them clean. The kids left the table as quick as they could say, "Excuse me!" Uncle Lou was different, not a bit like their mother, who was warm and friendly. He never smiled. Had a permanent frown and

Doris P. Burke

when the kids said, "Hello," he grunted. He talked very little, shook his head in disagreement a lot. When their mother asked, "How are you Louie?", He would answer with a sharp, "All right!" Their mother liked her brother, her dad liked her brother, so the kids decided they liked their uncle, but never did understand him. Uncle Lou fished while he was there. He walked down to the lake, rented a boat and spent hours floating around. He usually bought back a nice stringer of perch for their mother to fry.

    They played pinochle at night, the four of them. Played sometimes into the wee hours of the morning. The kids could hear them bidding, Myrtle trying to get the bid and Lou outbidding her, knowing full well he and Lloyd could never make what he bid. They would hear Aunt Myrtle's loud laugh and she'd say, "It's yours, Louie." The kids would smile, knowing their Uncle Lou was glowering at her. He was letting her know he didn't give a damn if he didn't make his bid, just as long as she didn't get it. He seemed to be seeking revenge against her and it came out even in his card playing. After they left for home, their mother was always mad at Myrtle and would sputter, "I don't know why Louie married that woman." They heard their dad answer one day. When he didn't know they were listening, he said, very matter of factly, "You know, Onalee, love can go anywhere, even up a pig's behind."

The Family

Chapter Thirty-Seven

After a long hot summer on the farm and not doing anything other than spending their time there, the kids really looked forward to Lapeer Days. The boys would meet friends on Main Street and see the sights and ride the rides. The little girls would stick with their mother and dad until they could beg their sister Margie to take them on the Ferris wheel. And after that they wanted to climb on the pretty horses, which were all elaborately adorned and would move up and down to give you a merry-go-round ride to remember. They enjoyed every noisy activity they heard and saw on Main Street. The stood at the edge of the sidewalk, waiting for the parade to come wending its way, bringing decorated floats with colorful crepe paper wrapped every which way to cover the wagon underneath. The bands marched in step, playing old favorite songs that brought cheers from the crowds of people watching. The horses trotted, sniffing and snorting and leaving piles of poop. It was a great parade. In the evening there would be a dance right on Main Street, with fiddlers fiddling and moving their feet, people whirling and shaking to the musical beat. There was a free barbecue with long lines of kids and their folks wanting a taste of that roasted meat. There were games no one won at, but it was fun to try and they did so want to win one of those Kewpie dolls with their big eyes and painted faces.

Lapeer Days was the last event of the summer. It was like a celebration, saying goodbye to those hot days and warm nights and saying hello to the brisk weather ahead. A new school year was to be welcomed with enthusiasm and expectation and the joyous feeling of being young and alive. When the kids started back to school in the fall, Margie was a sophomore in high school, Keith was a freshman. Billy was in the seventh grade at Clover School, June in the fifth grade and Doris in the second. They were a busy bunch of kids, each doing their thing and their mother trying to keep them in clothes so they could do their thing. The Depression was still a harsh reality, but the fruit cellar was filled with canned goods from the garden. Even pork and beef were canned to get through the long winter. The potato bin was nearly full, as well as the apple bin. There were tall crocks filled with cucumbers, the dill and vinegar mixture fermenting to make the juicy dill pickles the kids liked so well. It was a proud mother who could stand back and see the fruit

Doris P. Burke

of her labor and know she had food enough to feed her family. Onalee and Lloyd knew of the struggle some families were having and they were thankful to have the resources to provide for their own and this came with much work and preparation. Christmas was looked forward to, but that year the kids didn't expect much, but the idea of Christmas was exciting. The sorta-crooked pine tree the boys cut in the woods was put up and strung with popcorn. They had electric lights finally and their mother managed to purchase a string of colorful lights from the money she received from selling cream to the creamery. The tree was set up in front of the living room window. It was a nice added attraction for the kids and they enjoyed coming in to see the lights shining and the homemade ornaments hanging from the tree limbs.

    The anticipation of Christmas was there a good long time before the 25th of December. No matter what they got, it would be something they didn't have and that was good. They didn't ask for anything, never wrote a letter to old Santa and really had no great expectations. They knew there would be something in the stockings they hung up: probably some hard candy to suck on and some nuts. They especially looked forward to the orange that was always there. It would be a fun Christmas, no matter what they got, and Christmas dinner would be special. Their mother would use her best dishes on her best tablecloth. There would be roast chicken with dressing, lots of mashed potatoes. Keith didn't like his potatoes pounded, he said, so their mother saved some for him, before she pounded them. She always fixed something special, usually red and green cut Jello squares. It looked pretty and was gobbled up in a hurry. There was a cake with gooey white frosting and most of the time she baked mincemeat pie just for their dad because most of the kids didn't like it. The juicy dill pickles were there and sometimes cranberry sauce. There would be a bowl of mixed nuts with the shells on that the boys would eye, wanting to get a hammer and get at them. That Christmas of 1936 was full of surprises. The boys got ice skates and mittens. Margie got some nice dishes for her "hopeless chest," as Keith called it, and June and Doris were really surprised to see a dollhouse, all handmade with tiny people made out of toothpicks. They also found a blackboard with Merry Christmas written on it. Doris mentioned to June later that the writing looked like their mother's. Her sister poked her a good one with her elbow, saying, "Santa writes like that."

The Family

Chapter Thirty-Eight

January of 1937 was like most of the winters before that — snowy, blowing and cold. On these especially crisp, sub-zero days, when their mother wouldn't allow them to go out into the elements, the kids either read, played card games or snooped. One day, Keith and Billy were helping in the barn, Margie was learning to cook from her mother, and June had her nose in a movie magazine. It was a weekend, homework was done and Doris was at a loss for what to do. She had already found her mother's hiding place for the bananas, which was in her folks' closet. She also found a bottle of Mogan David wine there, almost full, tucked in behind her mother's flannel nightgowns. She even took the top off to smell it and tipped it up to taste. It was sweet and good. It reminded her of the hard cider she found in the basement when she was five. Uncle Byron had brought it over and she liked it so much she drank a lot. Her head had felt weird and she sorta staggered up the steps to tell her mother, "I am so busy." Her mother, after hearing her repeat how busy she was and noticing the glaze in her eyes asked, "What are you so busy doing?" Of course, her mother had smelled the cider when she got close enough and she sputtered, "Have you been drinking that cider in the basement?" Doris nodded yes and very sleepily answered, "It made me so busy."

She was put to bed and when she woke up, she had a very bad headache. Her dad laughed and told her mother their youngest daughter had a hangover. Her mother didn't laugh. She still remembered the bad headache and she didn't drink any of the sweet Mogan David wine, because it might be like that cider. She covered it back up with the nightgowns and went upstairs. She hadn't ever peeked in Billy's closet, where her mother kept things high up on a shelf. She found a chair, climbed up and reached her hand around, trying to find something interesting. She got hold of a book and carefully pulled it down. The title was Medical Help and Pregnancy. She tried to sound out preg-nan-cy. Well, what was that? A strange word! She flipped through the pages. She noticed some pictures of tonsils. She knew what they were, hers hurt sometimes and her mother always put that god-awful-smelling rag around her throat. The book also showed people's insides, which were ugly. She remembered how her insides had gurgled when she had colory morbis. Part two in the book was, "A Mother's Help in Pregnancy." Well, this is

Doris P. Burke

what she wanted to find out, what did that word mean? She sat down on the chair and turned the pages slowly. She stopped turning when she saw a picture of a fat-bellied woman with something inside of her. She couldn't believe her eyes. She put her hands over her eyes and peeked through. Was that a baby poked in there, almost in a circle? It scared her and she slammed the book shut. What was that baby doing crammed in there and how would it get out? She climbed back on the chair and threw the book on the shelf. She didn't want to touch it again.

She had to find her sister June and tell her what she had found out. She found her still lying in bed reading Modern Screen Magazine. She stood in front of her sister and whispered, "I know somethin' you don't know!" She tried to be quiet, she didn't want her mother to know she'd been snooping. "Babies are in women's bellies!" She gasped it out, wanting to throw up thinking about it. June yawned, laid her magazine down, glared at her sister and answered, "I know it, I've seen the book." Doris really hated the smug look on her face and she shouted, "You big snoop. I might tell Mom on you!" She was really mad that her sister had known about babies and hadn't told her. This led to a good, hair-pulling, scratching fight. Doris ran down the steps and hid in a coat closet in the dining room. This is where they tried to fight quietly and her sister found her in there. In the dark with the door closed, they bit, pulled hair, then cried because it hurt. Their mother heard them finally and dragged them out and stood them in front of the buffet mirror and told them to watch their bawling faces. That did it: Their faces all screwed up and wet made them stop sobbing because they looked so terrible. Their mother made them sit in the kitchen and watch her peel potatoes. They made faces at each other, but that was the end of their fight for that day. Doris knew as soon as she liked her sister again — which may be never, but if she did like her again — she'd ask how that baby would get out of that fat woman's belly.

The Family

Chapter Thirty-Nine

Every morning in the small, brick schoolhouse after the Pledge of Allegiance was said, the song books came out. Miss Cheney seemed to think a good, rousing songfest got the kids enthused, livened up and ready to learn. She would sit at the piano waiting for the kids to pick the songs they wanted to sing and she'd accompany them with her piano music. "The Battle Hymn" was a favorite and the voices shook the building with the chorus. "Old Kentucky Home" was pretty and many thought "Carry Me Back to Old Virginia" sad, but a nice melody. All the kids thought they might get through one morning without the hand raised by Billy. In fact, they all hoped they wouldn't have to sing that blamed song again, but it was always the same. He waited until the teacher was about to start the classes and his hand would appear in the air and all the kids shook their heads and turned to page 26. He would have a smile on his face as everyone sang his silly song, "Solomon Levi". They frowned at him, they glared at him. It didn't matter. Some wanted to tear that page out the songbooks, particularly his sisters, who thought he was just picking that song to irritate everybody, which it did.

Every Friday was spelling-bee day. Teams were picked with Billy the team leader of one because he was the champion speller and someone else the other team leader. He got caught one day with one of his shenanigans. He was embarrassed by the teacher, who knew him better than he ever thought she did. Spelling was as easy for him as it was to ride Molly, with him jumping off and on her like a stunt man; as easy as it was to shoot marbles and collecting them in bags from disgruntled boys, who hated to lose their precious agates. Spelling came to him as easy as falling off a log. He always picked June as his first choice to be on his team. She could spell, too, but had never won. After the teams were picked that day the bee began. After an innumerable number of words had been spelled, Billy and June were the last ones standing. The teacher gave him a fairly difficult word. He held his head down and spelled it wrong. Miss Cheney sighed and said firmly, "Spell that word again, Billy, and spell it right." His face got red. He looked straight down at his shoes and spelled the word right. June was disgusted. She knew how to spell the word but she didn't know the next one and he was champion again. The teacher had caught him at his little

Doris P. Burke

game. She knew he didn't want to stand up there with all eyes on him anymore, he was going to let his sister win. The incident was never mentioned at home by June and Doris, but they knew what they had always known: what many tricks had lurked in the head of their brother Billy.

The Family

Chapter Forty

Doris didn't like the boy who sat across from her in the schoolroom. He stared at her a lot when he should have been doing his work and besides that, he tried to peek at her papers. One morning, he opened his mouth and said, "You look funny, you've got holes in your cheeks." Well, this really pained her. She didn't know why she had holes in her cheeks. Her dad told her she had been kissed by angels and her dimples were nice. She didn't quite believe that story, being as none of her sisters or brothers had been kissed. Why should she be the only one? The staring boy waited for her to answer. She didn't. She turned her back on him and kept on with her work. The new boy in school, who sat right behind her, spoke to the boy in a loud whisper, "Those are dimples and she's pretty." She sneaked a peek at him. He had curly dark hair and a round face that had a big old smile looking right straight at her. Her face flushed all up and she turned around quick. She knew his name was Gene and he lived at the lake with the people who ran the small grocery story. She had heard he was adopted or something. He was cute, he was nice and she immediately liked him.

After that, he told all the kids she was going to be his girlfriend. He was always there at recess time to ask her to come and sit by him. She felt funny about him wanting to be by her all the time. She didn't know why he liked her so much — her, with her dark skin and thick hair that her mother stuck a big bow in that made her look like she was all head — but he did and it made the other girls mad. They would push his arm or ask him to come play one of their games. He would if she did. His favorite thing was to get her to sit with him in the back of the school away from all the kids. Then, he would sing a song to her. The same song every time! She smiled as she listened to him raise his voice and sing the melody to "Red River Valley". She thought he had a very nice singing voice and she really liked music, so it was fun. He was her boyfriend all that winter. Her brother Billy teased her for having a singing boyfriend, but she didn't care, he was a very nice boy. In the spring that year, when the air was getting warm and the clouds were starting to fluff like cotton candy, Gene came to her house. She was standing under the clothesline unhooking some towels when he appeared. He had a different look on his face and she wondered why because he always smiled when he saw her. He sat down on the grass and

Doris P. Burke

she sat down beside him. He was going to run away, he told her, back to Flint to find his mother. He hated the people he lived with; they were mean to him. She felt sad for him and she wanted to cry when he said they had hit him with a belt. She couldn't ever imagine anyone doing that! She thought he was brave when he said he'd be all right. He would walk to Flint if no one came along to give him a ride. His face became sorrowful-looking when he told her he had to leave right away. He stood up and reached in his pocket and brought out a crinkled, wrapped candy bar and handed it to her. Then a big old smile came over his round face when he told her to always remember his song, "Red River Valley," and the boy who loved her so true. He gave her a quick kiss on the cheek and that made her face flush up.

She followed him to the road and watched as he hurried along, sometimes stopping and waving. She stood at the mailbox a long time after she couldn't see him anymore. She knew she would always remember him; after all, he was her first boyfriend and he had thought she was pretty and she knew she wasn't. He had been the nicest boy she had ever know in all her eight years, besides, of course, her dad and big brother Keith and maybe her brother Billy, but they didn't count. This had been her boyfriend and he walked down the road right out of her life. She would miss him and his pretty song. She looked at the candy bar she had clutched in her hand and a lump came to her throat. She turned and walked slowly back to the clothesline; she thought she might save the candy wrapper just to remember him by.

The Family

Chapter Forty-One

Movie magazines were not only entertaining for June and Doris, they were an obsession. The piles of magazines Aunt Rosie sent out to them after she had read them were read and reread by the girls. They wanted to know about these people who lived in the glamorous world of Hollywood. They stared at the pictures of Carole Lombard, Greta Garbo, Bette Davis and Joan Crawford, envying their slinky gowns and swooped-up hairdos, and the men: Clark Gable, Jimmy Cagney, Pat O'Brien and Humphrey Bogart, dressed in black tuxedos for an elaborate party. They were both in love with Errol Flynn, who was handsome and daring. These people all lived in that make-believe world of gangsters and monsters, like Frankenstein and vampires like Dracula, who could scare the living daylights out of anybody. It was an unbelievable place and they learned of Hollywood in these magazines. They became experts on knowledge of the lives and loves of all the actors and actresses. They called them by their first names when they discussed them with each other. It was as if they had become a part of the glamour, and they knew these people intimately. They were almost as knowledgeable as Hedda Hopper and Louella Parsons. And on a bright summer day in 1937, they were absolutely sure they met one of their favorite stars. Molly had been obstinate and they were taking her for a walk down the road. They had to lead her because she bucked every time they tried to get on her back. They figured a good walk down the road to the white gate and back and she would be more apt to limber up and be friendly.

It was a swell day to just fiddle around and stay away from their mother, who would have them weeding the garden or something. The road was quiet as usual. There was never much traffic. The mailman came late in the afternoon. Other than that, an occasional car in the evening went down the hill to the lake. They wandered along, peering over at the golf course, seeing men with golf bags over their shoulders coming down to the greens across from their house. June tugged on Molly's bridle and she finally stomped along with them, acting as if she was misused. They heard a car coming behind them and they moved to the side of the road. They stopped, pulling Molly up close to them so the car could go by. The car went along beside them on the narrow road, then slowed down. It stopped and backed up. It was a black, shiny car with a tire on the back, the kind they had never seen before, except for Uncle Ralph's and his was yel-

Doris P. Burke

low. A woman was driving and a man lounged in the front next to her. She was attractive and well dressed. They both smiled and the man spoke in a sort of rough way, "Can you ride the pony?" he asked. They nodded yes, suddenly very aware of their wild, uncombed hair and the dirt spots on their clothes. "Let's see you," he said, still smiling. June whispered to Doris, "You ride her." Well, good old Molly came through. She let Doris leap on her back and they galloped down the hill to the gate and back to the car. Doris could tell from the look on her sister's face, she was about to burst. She reined up Molly beside the shiny car and the man said in his deep voice, "That's really good, honey!"

The man and woman waved and said goodbye and continued down the hill. The girls watched as the car disappeared around the bend in the road. They stared at each other a minute, June finally finding her voice to say, "Who did that look like to you?" Doris, trying not to scream with excitement, answered, "It was Humphrey Bogart and his wife!" They were positive it was. Both of them saw and thought the same thing. They pulled Molly around and headed back as fast as they could, pulling her along to the house. They had to tell their mother whom they had seen right here on Golf Road! Their mother shook her head when they told her, both of them out of breath and panting from hurrying and the excitement. "You girls and your imaginations," she said and went on with her preparations for supper. They told Billy when he came in from the field. He scoffed and snickered and said hatefully, "You didn't see Humphrey Bogart!" Nobody believed them, but they didn't care. They knew they did and he even talked to them. After all, they weren't blind and they knew what his wife looked like from pictures in the movie magazines. They were absolutely, positively sure they had met Bogey and his wife. From then on, they felt Bogey was a good friend of theirs. He had smiled at them, talked to them and that's what friends do. It was a very exciting day for two little girls.

The Family

Chapter Forty-Two

It was the summer for aunts, uncles and cousins to come to the farm. Even Grandma and Grandpa La Preze, their mother's folks, came with Aunt Stella, their mother's sister and her husband, Uncle Elgy. Uncle Bob, their mother's brother, and his wife, Aunt Charlotte, showed up wanting to take Margie home with them to help with the fruit market they owned in Owosso. Uncle Bob was a big man, lots bigger than Uncle Lou. He was also a preacher, said he got the call when he was in the Great War. This always seemed to amaze Lloyd, who said somewhat snidely, "He was a rounder before he got himself converted." Grandma and Grandpa La Preze even stayed awhile. The little girls couldn't quite take their eyes off Grandma's shoe that was built up to give her balance with the other shoe. The one side of her body was shorter than the other is what their mother told them. Anyway, the shoe fascinated them because it resembled good old "clop, clop." Their Grandpa was nice, they thought. He was a small man like Uncle Lou, with white, white hair. Their grandma was a tiny, frail woman and it was hard for her to get around. She sat most of the time and peeled potatoes or shelled peas, insisting on helping their mother prepare meals. Doris thought she was a little bossy and she resented her grandma when she would call for her mother and her grandma would say in a disapproving voice, "You come to your mother, you're much younger than she is."

Uncle Lou and Aunt Myrtle drove on out from Flint to be there while Grandma and Grandpa were visiting. Aunt Myrtle liked to gather eggs and really liked to gobble them down at breakfast time. She would barely have them in the frying pan, then she'd have them scooped up on her plate, all runny and sliding around, raw but warm. The chickens seemed to know her. The girls would watch their aunt head for the chicken coop. Then they would hear a heck of a racket and see feathers flying and wings flapping. They giggled and whispered to each other about the poor things. They must have known if she got hold of one of them, she would eat everything but the feathers. They had never seen their mother smile as much as she did that summer. She certainly enjoyed having her mother and father there, even if it was a short visit. She was pleasant to Aunt Myrtle and still catered to her brother Louie, cooking him food he liked, which pleased Aunt Myrtle because she liked anything that was put on the table. Good old Cousin Walt and Caroline came that summer too, bringing their sons, Fred

Doris P. Burke

and Bernard and Basil, the twins. All three were over six foot tall. The girls knew when they saw them pull in the driveway they were going to be hugged until they would lose their breath. What grinning, happy, carefree boys they were. The kids could tell their dad was tickled to see Walt and their mother was too. He always kidded their mother until she blushed or until Caroline said, "Hush up, Walter. Onalee doesn't want to listen to your teasing." Walt would tell the story of the time he dressed up as a woman and he and Lloyd went looking for the culprits who were after Onalee. Then they would laugh until the tears ran down their faces. They had a great time reminiscing and it was fun for the kids to hear the stories.

    The twins would head for the barn with Billy, ready to participate in walking the beams or swinging from the hay ropes or anything to have fun. They were about the same age as Billy and Fred was right between Margie and Keith in age. So when the Walt Judd family arrived, a good time was had by all, except June and Doris, who were always trying to get their breath after being hugged so much. It was one of those summers when the kids just sat back and watched the relatives come and go. They decided their mother wasn't anything like her brothers or sister. Their Aunt Stella worried about her hair and her looks most of the time, and hardly ever said a word to them. Their Uncle Bob was pleasant, but different, with a kinda holy attitude, being as he was a preacher. And good old silent Uncle Lou, well, they could see why he didn't smile. He didn't have anything to smile about, living with a woman who ate like a pig, resembled a cow and cackled like the chickens she chewed up. They all liked Walt and his family; the cousin with the big grin and the outlandish stories and the wife who chuckled and said, "Well, Walter," all the time; and the tall sons who had the same grin as their dad and said, "Let me give you a big bear hug," all the time. Yep, they guessed Walt was their favorite relation and they always looked forward to the next visit from the cousins in Oxford.

The Family

Chapter Forty-Three

To make a shopping trip to the big city of Flint, you had to get ready. It was a once-a-year adventure and it was looked forward to by June and Doris with wide-eyed expectation. The day before they were to leave, their dad took the old car out by the well house and washed it all over to get the dust off. You had to be presentable to go to the big city. The girls had clean hair and shiny faces. Their mother always wore her best dress and a hat with a touch of a veil. Their dad was quite handsome with his dark tan and with his light-colored shirt on. The boys never wanted to go. They were more content to stay home and do their own thing. Margie was usually babysitting or staying with Uncle Bob, so it was just the little girls and their mother and dad making the long trip to shop in downtown Flint. It seemed many miles to the girls as they bounced along in the backseat, going past Uncle Byron's place and on past the Hodge's and the Tharot's. Davison was just a little burg and pretty soon they were through that place. Then they impatiently watched for the water towers, which gave them the indication the big city would soon be in sight. First, the little one appeared, then the big water tower came into view.

They stared out the window, waiting for their dad to steer the old car on the street where all the people and stores were. The Capital Theater was impressive, with flashing lights on the marquee showing favorite movie stars' names and the film playing there. The Palace and Rialto also were stately, with their array of pillars and bright lights sending a message out to come to the movies. The girls glanced at each other, both thinking, "By golly, it isn't Hollywood, but it's pretty darn nice." Their dad found a parking place and they began their walk down the main street. It was filled with people coming and going, pushing into the stores or stopping to stare at the conglomeration of window displays. They strolled along with the other people, waiting for their mother to lead the way to the store. She would spend lots of time checking prices. They had forgotten how she liked to putter and they hoped she wouldn't take too long. Maybe they could see a movie. There was Woolworth's Five and Dime Store and Neisner's and Kresge's. She picked Kresge's. The store had a lunch counter and the girls could smell coffee, dill pickles and relish. The aroma floated through the store and they had the urge to sit at the counter and watch what the people

Doris P. Burke

ordered and to maybe have one of those tall sandwiches made with toast and filled with chunks of bacon and tomatoes, with toothpicks holding them together. They were big and pretty. They followed their mother for a while. Getting tired of that, they found their dad and he suggested they do what they had been waiting to do. They sat at the long lunch counter and he ordered their food for them. They liked being with their dad, he made them smile with his jokes and he teased them about not being able to get their mouths around their big sandwiches. He was fun and a very nice dad. He winked at them and asked, "Do you think your mother will have time to take in a movie?"

They nodded yes, hoping she would quit looking and do something important. They found her with shopping bag filling up with all sorts of things. They peeked into the bag to see if she had bought candy. It did look like there might be some circus peanuts and orange slices at the bottom. They followed her to two more stores. They never saw anybody shop like their mother. She picked up just about everything and checked it over and then put it down and walked on to something else. She was a picky-wicky shopper and they wished she'd hurry up. At last she told their dad she had bought enough. They breathed a sigh of relief and they thought their dad looked relieved too. After the packages were deposited in the car, they found themselves in front of the Rialto Theater. It was fun to sit in the dark theater eating popcorn and watching the big screen in front of them. It was almost dark when they got back home. The girls were sleepy but very content. They couldn't wait to tell Billy of the movie they had seen and of the great big sandwich with the toothpicks holding it together. They hated to admit it, but they had sorta missed him and wished he could have a nice day like they had. But, of course, they wouldn't ever tell him. He might think he was important and they wouldn't want him to think that.

The Family

Chapter Forty-Four

In the fall of 1938, Margie was a senior in high school, a real grown up, the big sister of them all. She had boys interested in her. Even with Keith wondering why they would be interested in his straight-up-and-down sister, they still were. Their dad said he thought boys were coming right out of the woodwork. Some tall and gangly ones came walking down the road to visit, others drove in to stay and help fix old cars that seemed to always be under repair in the garage. They pretended to be helping, but most were giving little flirty glances at Margie. She didn't take to many of them. The one neighbor boy kept asking her out, really wanted to come calling on the pretty Judd girl. Nope, she didn't like him; he'd be the last one she ever went out with, she told her mother. He was persistent, had his eye focused on this little girl. His best friend Ray dated Margie's best friend Louise, so a blind date was set up. What a shock it was when she found herself sitting in the back seat with the neighbor boy she couldn't stand the sight of! She kinda took a liking to him after that and from then on they were dating. He did like to drive fast and roared up Golf Road in his shiny Model A, hurrying to see his new girlfriend. One night, he hurried too fast, coming in the driveway like a bat out of hell. He turned quickly and tipped his shiny little car right over, with he and Ray trying to scramble out from underneath.

Needless to say, Margie and Louise, who were waiting for their Prince Charmings, did not look too kindly on this exhibition of driving and neither did Margie's mother. They weren't banned from the premises — he still arrived regularly — but he entered the driveway quite a bit slower. His name was Jim. He was a fun-filled Irish guy who wanted to capture the heart of Margie. Now a constant visitor, he often brought his cousin Pat, who was near June and Billy's age. Pat became a regular visitor. If he didn't come with Jim, he rode his bike over, which he had put a motor on. You could hear him coming from the end of Golf Road. And so, Margie had a boyfriend and Keith was noticing girls a lot. Everybody was growing up and had new and old friends hanging around. June had girlfriends coming up from the lake and from everywhere to talk and whisper secrets. Billy had his bunch of boys who came to work on the old cars or just to tell what so-and-so said or did and just to laugh and act up. Doris felt quite left out. Billy and June had better

Doris P. Burke

things to do than to play with their little mutt of a sister, who was only eight. She missed the companionship and sorta resented the new friends they had made and she pouted sometimes, watching them enjoy themselves. She did have friends at school but they weren't allowed to wander too far from home to come visit and play. It made her mad when her sisters and brother stopped talking when she came around them and it especially made her mad when they frowned at her. From then on, she made sure she was right there when the car went out of the driveway, pushing her way into the back seat and then daring them to try to get her out. They knew darn well she would head for their mother and complain about "those kids!"

If no one volunteered to take her to the movies on Saturday night, she told her mother and whoever was taking the car that night had to take her and pick her up after the movie. It was hard to get rid of her. She made sure of that. She didn't give a hoot about the frowns and the exasperated sighs she heard. She was right there in the car the night they all rode to the lake. Keith was driving and didn't make the turn and they ended up in the ditch. It upset her and she cried loud, saying her favorite words, "Dad's really gonna give it to you!" They were all scrambling around, trying to get out of the leaning car and they all said their favorite words, "Shut up you, little crybaby!" She certainly didn't care what they called her. She just wanted some justice. She wanted her dad to yell at these reckless people. She thought her big brother could drive. He was as bad as Margie. Well, she'd tell her mother exactly how they acted. It was she, dad and her mother against these crazy, devilish kids. She was really put out when her dad said he was just glad no one was hurt. Maybe it would be just she and her mother against the rest of them.

The Family

Chapter Forty-Five

The rumbles of war for the United States were heard in 1939. With Germany invading Poland, Denmark, Luxembourg, the Netherlands, Belgium, Norway, France, Yugoslavia and Greece and having these countries fall to the Germans, the United States shifted its policy from neutrality to preparedness. It began to expand its armed forces and build defense plants. President Roosevelt called upon the U.S. to be "The Great Arsenal of Democracy" and to supply war materials to the Allies through sale, loan or lease through something called the Lend-Lease Bill. Hoping to avoid the war in Europe, the Americans waited without giving direct help, wanting the Allies to win the war without intervention from the United States. Life on the farm went on. Margie graduated from high school to the delight of her mother and dad. Their firstborn had a diploma to say she had completed her four years of high school in good standing. She wore her cap and gown and pictures were taken. The whole family was proud of her. She was the first of four to graduate. Doris would be eleven in April. She felt like she was growing up, but she was still the baby and treated as such. She sometimes wished she could be the big sister to a younger sister or brother. It was so tiring to be patted on the head or given that look of "You're too young to know a blessed thing."

She thought the rest of the kids had that superior, "I'm all grown up, you're still a little weasel" attitude toward her. Yes, it would be nice to have somebody around younger than herself. She had gotten a Dydee doll for Christmas when she was nine. The doll had pleased her so much. It had diapers and a bottle and the more water she poured in its mouth, the more it wet out of its behind. She thought it was very much like a baby and she pretended it was her baby sister. Riding into town with her mother and dad in March before her birthday, she was surprised to hear her mother ask, "What would you like for your birthday?" Well, this was unusual. Her birthday wasn't until the 20th of April and she was asking now? She really didn't know what to ask for. It took her by surprise. She needed time to look through the Sears catalog. There were lotsa things in there. But, being as her mother was asking, maybe she'd tell her a bathing suit would be nice. She had her mouth open to say this when her mother said, "Wouldn't you like a baby for your birthday?" Well, there it was. Her mother even thought she was still a

Doris P. Burke

little mutt, she wanted to give her another doll for her birthday. She wouldn't say anything about the bathing suit. If she wanted to get her a new doll that was OK. Her mother didn't notice she didn't play with dolls much anymore. Her mother was too busy to notice, with her cooking and cleaning and tending to those stupid chickens and with Keith graduating this year. If she got a doll, she'd put it up on her dresser and look at it.

The surprise came on the 31st of March in 1940 when she was out in the barn hangin' around with Billy and Pat, the motor bicycle person. She was running through the haymow, took a leap into the hay shoot that was supposed to be closed and wasn't and landed on the cement floor of the horse barn. They found her trying to get her breath. Billy stood her up and assured her nothing was broken, while she gasped for air. She hurt all over, but for once he was right. Nothing seemed to be broken. It was that night, after supper, when her mother complained of a backache and her dad obliged by rubbing it for her. Doris wanted to tell her mother of falling on the cement and about breaking her back, but she didn't. She went to bed. She awoke in the morning to a funny sound. She wanted to sleep some more but couldn't because of that stupid noise. She and June slept together and she noticed June was awake. She grumbled to her sister, "I wish that cat would shut up meowing!" She always hated her sister's know-it-all-tone of voice, but this time it was an odd tone of voice as she said, "That's no cat, that's a baby!" That was a shocker. Who knew their mother was having a baby? So maybe she had gotten a little plumper, but she didn't look like that horrible picture in that preg-nan-cy book. She figured her sister was telling a lie, but the noise did sound like a baby squalling. They both hurried down the stairs to the living room. There was Doctor Best and Grandma Judd and the other kids. Grandma was unwrapping this howling bundle to show everybody. A baby boy! Right here in the living room and he was their baby brother. Grandma was as proud of the baby then as if it were hers, telling how he rolled right over and how strong he was. Their dad looked exhausted, apparently from going to get Grandma and the doctor and having to be up all night. Doris was afraid to peek in the bedroom at her mother. What she must look like, having this monster of a baby, who was shaking his arms and legs and squealing like a baby pig?

A few days after her mother felt better and after Doris could look at her, her mother asked, "Did you like the baby I got you for your birthday?" Doris nodded yes. After all, he was here still squalling and Grandma was still here, smiling and so proud of him. What

The Family

else could she say? He was cute and round. If he would just shut up! Brother Richard Lee was born April 1st, April Fools Day. It surely was the best prank their mother ever pulled on them. Better than the cotton she always put in the biggest of the cream puffs she often made on April Fools Day because she knew her son Keith always took the biggest and it tickled her to see him pulling the soft mess from his mouth. Yep, it was a good one! The kids took to the new baby like a duck to water. They liked him. He was cuddly and sweet. They all spoiled him. He was "the new baby." The friends who came to see the new arrival would smile at Doris and say, "Cut your nose right off, didn't it?" Well, whatever that meant, she didn't answer. If it meant she was jealous of the baby because she wasn't the baby anymore, she wasn't. She was finally a big sister. It was going to be fun to boss somebody younger than her. She felt quite grown up now and on her eleventh birthday, when kids at school asked her what she got, she proudly said, "I got a new baby brother." That stunned them. She was the only one in school who got a real live baby boy doll for a birthday present. Now, she figured, if he could just get growing a little so he knew something an quit that bawlin', she'd be happy.

Doris P. Burke

Chapter Forty-Six

Uncle Art and Aunt Myrtle, Lloyd's sister and brother-in-law from Detroit, were seldom seen or heard from over the years. Once in a while, Grandma Judd would bring over a box of clothes that Aunt Myrtle had brought and left at her place to be given to Lloyd's girls. The kids hardly knew the two girl cousins, who were always so well-dressed and pretty. They really forgot most of the time they had cousins in the big city. They had heard their dad speak of his sister in a fond way, but they didn't go to visit them. In 1940, after Keith graduated from high school, he had an offer to work in Detroit. Uncle Art very generously suggested Keith stay with them. This was appreciated by Lloyd and Onalee. And so it was arranged that he would stay with them all week and come home weekends. He worked there almost a year and then Aunt Myrtle was taken sick. No one seemed to know what her trouble was. Keith reported to his mother when he was home that she was always filling a hot water bottle to use. It was a short sickness and tragically and unexpectedly she died. If there ever was a diagnosis for her death, no one ever knew what it was. This was in the spring of 1942 and as it was before, after Lady had died so suddenly, Lula and Bill grieved the same for their youngest daughter. Bill wondered why his lady babies had been taken from them. He grieved by taking swigs from his ever-present whiskey bottle and blaming the son-of-a-bitchin' injustice of it all.

The funeral was sad, the kids feeling so sorry for their cousins who wouldn't have a mother. Lloyd and Ralph wondered what had happened to their two sisters who had been strong and healthy as children. After Aunt Myrtle's death and after time had passed, in June there would be a wedding. Margie was marrying her Irish farmer. There would be a wedding right there on the Judd farm with family and friends. Uncle Bob would come to marry them and also be there to wish his favorite niece happiness in her marriage. And that's the way it happened. Margie came down the stairway a bit pale and stood by her intended and said the vows to make her a farmer's wife. The kids watched, smiling at their sister's apparent nerves, but they all liked Jim and it would be a good marriage, they thought. Doris watched, with her good pink dress on and her hair combed neatly, and wondered why anyone would want to get married. Marriage brought cookin', washin', cleanin' and babies. She

The Family

knew that Margie would soon be walkin' around looking like the fat lady in the carnival pictures she had seen. Well, she hoped she got one who didn't beller all the time like the little one they had. She swung him on the swing on the porch and the more she swung, the more he bellered. She wondered if he'd ever grow up to know anything.

Doris P. Burke

Chapter Forty-Seven

In December of 1941, life for the family became apprehensive almost immediately after the bombing of Pearl Harbor on December 7th. War was declared on the same day that President Roosevelt told the nation it was "a date which would live in infamy." On December 11th, Germany and Italy declared war on the United States and Congress in turn declared war on those two countries. With a war in Asia, the Pacific, Africa and Europe, immediate changes had to be made on the home front. Plants in the United States and Canada converted from civilian to war production with amazing speed. New plants were built rapidly by private industry and the government. Firms that had made vacuum cleaners before the war began to make machine guns. Automobile factories turned out airplanes, engines and tanks. It was "the man behind the man behind the gun" who built the tools for victory on the home front. By building weapons, producing food and clothes, paying taxes and buying war bonds, the United States came together in unison to put an all-out effort to win this war against their opposition. It was a shock to the family and to all families, especially those with sons who would be of age to enter the fighting. Keith was still working in Detroit. Billy was a junior in high school. The prospect of them entering the armed forces was quite inevitable.

Life did go on, there on the farm, even with the newspaper headlines telling of casualties and defeats and the radio blaring out a bleak outlook. Billy still had school to attend and football games to play. He didn't complain about his battered and bruised body, he liked to play. He brought his practicing home. He had to be good at his tacklin' and pushin' and shovin' baloney. So, his sisters were to help him be good. Did this mean they had to have bruises and stiff, aching bodies too? He thought so. His best friend, Earl West, played football with him at good old Lapeer High. He was a neighbor from way over on Bassett Road. No one ever quite knew when Billy's best friend became June's boyfriend, but it happened. He began making appearances on the farm often. Their dad got a big kick out of seeing Earl come on his old white plow horse. He'd stand in the yard and say to June, "By golly, here comes the Lone Ranger!" And then shortly, they would hear a motor puttsin' its way down the road and their mother would say, "Good heavens, here comes that Burke boy again!" She never knew how many would

The Family

be there for Sunday dinner, but she always put extra plates on the table and they were always invited to eat and they usually did. It was never the carefree life again, though. The war was raging on and the food and gas rationing started. Gas wasn't rationed to the farmers. It was essential to keep producing farm products. Keith joined the Navy in December of 1942. It was a sad time for the family and for the neighbor girl, Ruth, he had been dating. Billy waited until January of 1943, his senior year in school, and then he and five other seniors joined the Army. They left together, being assured of getting a diploma from high school. The farm became a lonely place there on Golf Road with the boys gone and most of the neighbor boys enlisting or already serving. It became a life of fear and uneasiness for those left at home.

Margie's husband, Jim, had been deferred from serving. He was a farmer. They had one daughter by then. He was helpful, exchanging work with Lloyd on the farm, which was loaded with work to do. It was good to keep busy and the thought was you were helping the war effort in a small way. Patriotism was there in the fields, on all the farms and on the faces of the mothers and fathers with boys fighting this hellish war.

Doris P. Burke

Chapter Forty-Eight

In 1943, Ralph was back in Lapeer for good. He bought his granddad's farm and he was home to stay. The last five years hadn't been a picnic for him. By 1938, he knew his baseball stint was over. He was 37 years old then, a "has been". He'd played with some of the best, had his day in the sun, now it was over. He was drinking too much and dwelling on the fact that Father Time had caught up to him. He'd been heaving balls at Hazelton, Illinois. Now they were letting him go. Nobody wanted him. His wife, Rosie, didn't even want him, she told him. He was a mean son-of-a-bitch, drinking to all hours of the night and then coming home to yell and holler about the injustice of time. She wanted out. There were other women. She knew that. She was tired of the fights he got into and of finding him in jail. And so the last time they called from the hoosegow, she told them to keep him. She started her divorce. The man she had once known was no more. He had become a belligerent individual who blamed the world for his troubles. He was in jail for two weeks. He had a long time to think about things. By the time he walked out into the sunshine a free man, he knew he wouldn't be back in jail again. He had some friends and some money. Rosie hadn't taken it all with the divorce. It made him mad to think about her walking out on him, but what the hell, who needed her? He had to get back on his feet, had to get into something new and different, but all he knew was baseball.

He had been a star, he'd played with the New York Giants. He'd miss the roar of the crowd. He smiled one day thinking of his Granddad Judd and his uncles and of what they used to say. He whispered out loud, "For a while Granddad, I guess I was the greatest, the strongest and the best." Now he was back in Lapeer. He brought a new wife with him and settled in for the quiet life. He bought some equipment and was gonna do some excavating. He figured he could make a living at that. Aunt Ann was hard to say, the kids thought, so everyone just called her Ann. She was a small woman, always dressed in taffeta or velvet, always dressed up. She adored Ralph. It showed with every movement she took. He was her Prince Charming, her knight in shining armor, her everything. He found what he needed, a cheering section. It wasn't quite the same as the roar of the crowd when he made a strikeout, but it would do. Lula was glad to have Ralph near her in Lapeer, even if

The Family

he had brought a new wife with him who was all dressed up and no place to go. She figured the new wife was a shorter version of his other one. She did manage to let her know in little ways that her son would always be her son. Bill had decided he didn't like farming a whole lot. He set Lula up in business in Columbiaville. With a nice little restaurant, she could start cooking again. She was the best cook in five counties, he knew that. It was a good location, too, adjoining the liveliest, noisiest bar around. It was convenient to the grocery store in the village. They could get supplies there. It was a perfect setup. She could cook and wait on people. He would greet them and take their money. It didn't hurt either that the bar was right there. He liked to hear people having a good time and if he needed a drink, it would only be a skip and a jump away.

Doris P. Burke

Chapter Forty-Nine

The farming was there. The hay had to be baled and the wheat and oats had to be shocked. Help was needed to drive the tractor and bounce around on the hay baler, pushing wire through and tying them. Doris was healthy, a sturdy 14-year-old. She was no substitute for a strong, athletic boy, but there weren't any. Her dad said she could help, the work had to be done. She wore her brother's old overall pants, one of her dad's blue denim shirts and there she was, driving the tractor or riding the hay baler in the 90-degree weather, thinking, "why me?" She wanted to do her hair up in curlers, go to parties and talk about boys. This war should be nonexistent. Now she would look like an idiot when she started back to school in the fall, with a brown face and dried out hair. A letter was written to her brothers, a few years after the war, summing up those fretful years: "A brother is a strange sort of creature. He's a person who swings through trees and from ropes, and you watch and wonder if your mother was scared by an ape when she carried him. "A brother is one who insists you play football with him because he has to practice a lot and he's got to be good. So he tackles you and knocks the wind out of you and then calls you a weakling while you're gasping for air.

"He is the one who never lets you become vain because he is always telling you how ugly you are. And when a stranger asked what your name was, you almost said, `My name is ignorant,' because you had sorta forgotten your mother and dad had given you a perfectly good name. A brother never uses that perfectly good name, so it is unfamiliar. "A brother also watches every boy you think you might like and maybe he doesn't so he manages to tell them how dumb you are in his own tactless way. "Brothers will pound on you, pull your hair, poke you with any sharp object and then dare you to tell your folks. They would almost beat you to a pulp, but kick hell out of anyone else who misuses you. "My brothers were the gung-ho guys who went off to war and I was mad because they made our mother cry. I even cried a little too, but didn't know why because I knew then my bruises would heal. "I watched my mother fight the war with them, spending every evening with a map in front of her, listening to Walter Winchell and his ships at sea giving tragic news. "Brothers made me resent the war and their absence. And as I drove that chugging tractor across those sun-drenched fields

The Family

with sweat running into my eyes, my thoughts were of my brothers. "I had become very close to my dad and I'd sputter to myself, "Me and Dad never did like those boys, it was always Mom who liked them!" "And then someone would ask me if I had brothers, I would stand a little taller and proudly say, "My brothers are fighting the war." "And when I'd see the boy at school who delivered the telegrams that said, "Killed in action," I'd think to myself, "If he brings one of those telegrams to our house, I'll kill him."

"Yes, brothers were a pain in the neck and a worry during the war, and I was so glad when they came marching home and our mother smiled again. "Brothers will agree with you some of the time, but most of the time will disagree with you on most subjects just to show you they are really smarter than you. "I was always proud of them, but didn't want them to know it because I remembered those hot days on the tractor and the worry. "Brothers are strange sorts of creatures, but we would have missed so much without them."

Doris P. Burke

Chapter Fifty

The free world celebrated May 8, 1945 as V-E Day, a victory in Europe. After five years, eight months and seven days, the European phase of World War II had ended. And on September 2, 1945, V-J Day was proclaimed. Victory over Japan! Three years, eight months and 22 days after Japan bombed Pearl Harbor, World War II ended. Boys who had left the safe environment of family to become entrapped in the vicious, unthinkable sights and sounds of war were now coming home men. It was a boozin', cigarette smokin', swearin' tough bunch of American men who gave their all and were now being greeted by the "Rosie the Riveters" and the wives and girlfriends who were damn glad to have them home. It had been a romantic time, in spite of the war or maybe because of it. Passions had run at an all-time high. Songs like "I'll Be Seeing You," and "You Belong to Me" had been listened to and hummed while tears streamed down the faces of those left behind. Movies had been made of intense, emotional goodbyes and eager, passionate homecomings. It was to be a never-to-be-forgotten time of bloody battlefields, of maimed bodies, of blue stars in the windows for those serving and gold stars for those who wouldn't be coming home. Even some laughs came when the Europeans said the Yanks were overpaid, oversexed and over here. They should have added, "and we're overjoyed!"

There was heartbreak and sorrow and joy and happiness and those who lived it and were a part of it knew for certain it was patriotism at its finest, in all of its courageous splendor.

The Family

Chapter Fifty-One

The war was over, Keith came home to wife Ruth. He had been married when he was home on leave. They had a little girl. June had lived with her folks during the war waiting for her husband Earl, whom she had married when he was home on leave. They had a little boy. Margie had had another daughter. Doris was sixteen when the war ended and she wondered if babies were part of the war effort, being as they were showing up everywhere. Dick, the baby brother who was tickled with all the new nieces and nephews, was five. Doris was happy for her mother, who smiled now and especially when she looked at her sons. And her dad had a big grin on his face as he watched the grandchildren playing. It was great to have the family together again. Billy appeared older, his hair grown long instead of the short cut he had always worn. Keith, dark and handsome, held his daughter who resembled him so much. The war years had separated them all and now there would be a new generation of children. The youthful days for the five of them were gone, they would each go on to live their lives away from one another. After the war, with the world recuperating from the disruption, life went on for all the families. Grandma Lula worked at the State Home in Lapeer as a cook and, as always, was highly praised by the management. Grandpa Bill obliged her by driving her to work every day and picking her up at night.

She worked until the diabetes she had caused her to lose her right leg. It was sad to see this short little woman, who had spent her whole life doing for people, now confined to a wheel chair. She tried to please Bill but her efforts weren't enough sometimes. She made one more call to Lloyd and he went again in the middle of the night to pick up his mother. She stayed for two weeks while Bill finished his drinking binge. Doris drove her home for the last time, pulling in the yard to see Bill hanging his clothes on the clothesline. Her grandma's words startled her as they watched him fumble with the clothes pins. She spoke with sympathy in her voice, "Look at your poor Grandpa, Doris. He has to hang his own underwear on the line." He walked slowly over to the car, never acknowledging his granddaughter, and asked, "Are you ready to come home, Mama?" And she said, "I'm ready, Dad." She went into a coma shortly after that right there at home with Lloyd and Onalee and some of the grandchildren around her. Bill paced and muttered,

Doris P. Burke

"The only thing that matters to me is dying right there in that bed." Some of them thought and even whispered, "The only thing that mattered to him was in his hip pocket resembling a whisky flask."

Ralph lost his wife Ann shortly after Lula died. He married another woman who pampered him, listened to his stories of baseball years and provided him with the booze that had become such a big part of his life. He missed the mother who had always been there to tell him he was perfect and to agree with him that he had chosen the right path to follow all those years. He died in 1956, leaving nothing behind. No children, no money, just memories of a boy who had followed a dream. Bill lived alone at the old homestead until a fire burned the house, leaving him with no alternative but to live with Lloyd and Onalee. He picked up beer bottles and pop bottles along his stroll to the small store near their home. This helped buy the booze that kept him going. He died in 1959. It was not an agonizing death. He just closed his eyes and went to sleep. He had caused trouble and misery to his wife, who never gave up hope her Bill would find himself and she truly knew the meaning of "for better or for worse." Onalee died in 1967 of cancer. She did get to see 25 grandchildren born and she loved them all. She was missed by the family and they were absolutely sure she was in heaven taking care of those who needed her. Cousin Walt died in 1976. Lloyd, Margie and Doris went to see him a few days before he passed on. With a grin on his face, he told again the story of when he dressed as a woman. He looked at Lloyd and they both laughed, the memory still lingering in their minds. Lloyd died in 1979. He was 79 years old. He had outlived his wife, his brother, his two sisters, his two brothers-in-law, Onalee's sister and her husband and most of his cousins and their wives. He and Onalee had not given to their children extravagant things, but had given of themselves the care and devotion it takes to make a family. It surrounded them, enveloped them and made the children love life.

Lloyd was a humble, quiet man with great courage and deep feelings. He was always happy where the path of life had led him. Not to fame and fortune, but to being a devoted husband and father. He was THE GREATEST, THE STRONGEST, AND THE BEST!

The End

The Family

Update on "Those Kids"

Margie and Jim have five children — four girls and one boy. They have 21 grandchildren and are now counting on many great-grandchildren. Keith and Ruth have six children — four boys and two girls. They have 12 grandchildren and three great-grandchildren. Billy and Jo have two children — a boy and a girl — and one grandson. June and Earl have five children — two boys and three girls. They have 13 grandchildren and are starting to count quite a few great-grandchildren. Doris married Pat, the guy with the motor on his bicycle who used to putt over to see her brother Billy. They have two daughters who have given them four very nice granddaughters. They are now counting many gas engines. Dick and his wife, Janet, have five children — four boys and one girl. They also have four grandchildren. Margie and Doris still live in Lapeer. Keith lived in Lapeer also before his death in 1996. June lives in nearby Clio and Billy and Dick reside in Florida. The brothers and sisters keep in touch with one another. Keith went on many years teasing Margie whenever he could and she retaliated with insulting birthday cards and remarks whenever she could. The closeness stayed with them. She was with him when he died, as he wanted her to be. June and Doris take trips together without ever pulling hair or scratching each other.

Dick calls his big sisters often, still trying to find out if everybody was nice to him when he was little. Of course, they tell him they weren't. Doris has a hobby of making dolls and one year very generously sent brother Billy an especially good-looking cowboy with holster, hat and boots — all handmade. She called the doll Gene, after Gene Autry, the cowboy Billy wanted to be like when he was a kid. While talking on the phone with him after it was received, she asked, "Do you like it?" He replied, "Sure, got it hanging by the neck on the porch." HER ARTISTRY! HANGING BY THE NECK! Well, you know who she wanted to see hanging by the neck! This proved to her what she had always said, "A brother IS a strange sort of creature!"